D0047665

ROMANTIC TIMES PRAISES BOBBI SMITH, WINNER OF THE STORYTELLER OF THE YEAR AWARD!

BRIDES OF DURANGO: TESSA

"Another wonderful read by consummate storyteller Bobbi Smith, *Tessa* is the second in the *Brides of Durango* series. Filled with adventure and romance, more than one couple winds up happily-ever-after in this gem."

BRIDES OF DURANGO: ELISE

"There's plenty of action, danger and heated romance as the pages fly by in Ms. Smith's exciting first book in this new series. This is exactly what fans expect from Bobbi Smith."

WESTON'S LADY

"Bobbi Smith has penned another winner."

HALF-BREED'S LADY

"A fast-paced frying-pan-into-the-fire adventure that runs the gamut of emotions, from laughter to tears. A must-read for Ms. Smith's fans, and a definite keeper."

OUTLAW'S LADY

"Bobbi Smith is an author of many talents; one of them being able to weave more than one story. . . . Ms. Smith creates characters that one will remember for some time to come."

THE LADY & THE TEXAN

"An action-packed read with roller coaster adventures that keep you turning the pages. *The Lady & the Texan* is just plain enjoyable."

RENEGADE'S LADY

"A wonderfully delicious 'Perils of Pauline' style romance. With dashes of humor, passion, adventure and romance, Ms. Smith creates another winner that only she could write!"

DO THE RIGHT THING

"Why didn't you tell me ahead of time that you were having doubts about marrying me?"

"I thought I was doing the right thing. Marrying you was what Papa wanted."

"What *Papa* wanted?" he sneered. "Funny, I thought it was what *we* wanted. I thought you loved me the way I loved you. I thought you wanted me as much as I wanted you."

Cole crossed the distance between them, his gaze darkening with the power of his intent. He remembered all too well how much he'd desired her. Hell, he was reminded of it every time he looked at her—even now!

Jenny stood frozen before him, mesmerized by the force of the emotions she saw raging in his eyes. She gasped in surprise as he took her by the shoulders and dragged her hard against him, crushing her to his chest.

Other *Leisure* and *Love Spell* books by Bobbi Smith:
WESTON'S LADY
HALF-BREED'S LADY
OUTLAW'S LADY
FORBIDDEN FIRES
RAPTURE'S RAGE
THE LADY & THE TEXAN
RENEGADE'S LADY
THE LADY'S HAND
LADY DECEPTION

The *Brides of Durango* series by Bobbi Smith:
ELISE
TESSA

BRIDES OF DURANGO: JENNY

BOBBI SMITH

LEISURE BOOKS NEW YORK CITY

A LEISURE BOOK®

October 2000

Published by

Dorchester Publishing Co., Inc.
276 Fifth Avenue
New York, NY 10001

ISBN 0-8439-4776-4

Printed in the United States of America.

This book is dedicated to Jill Brager of Romantic Times Magazine. *You're the best, sweetie! Thanks for all your support!*

ACKNOWLEDGMENTS

I'd like to thank Sarah Burnes, Judy Clain, Lucy Lockley and Martha Radginski of the St. Charles Missouri City-County Library District for their help with research.

JENNY

Chapter One

Jenny was standing in the vestibule of the church, wearing her full-skirted, lace and satin, pearl-studded bridal gown and veil, and waiting for the music to start so she could walk down the aisle on her father's arm and marry Cole.

The church was crowded.

It seemed to Jenny that everyone in Durango was in attendance. The wedding of rich rancher Paul Sullivan's beautiful daughter and rancher Cole Randall, one of the most eligible bachelors in the area, was quite a social occasion. Those who had been invited had shown up in force to witness the nuptials.

And now it was almost time.

Today was her wedding day.

Today she was to marry Cole.

A terrible sense of unease plagued her. She was

realizing, far too late, the seriousness of her situation. If the letter hadn't arrived four days before, she wouldn't have been in this desperate state, but the letter had arrived, and now she had a decision to make. She could delay no longer.

She had to decide what to do with the rest of her life.

She could go through with the wedding and marry Cole, or she could follow her lifelong dream and go back East to the exclusive girls' academy in Philadelphia that had finally notified her that she'd been accepted.

Jenny had applied to the academy over a year before and had waited endlessly for word that she'd been accepted. She had always wanted to further her education. She wanted to travel and see more of the world. After months of waiting with no response, Jenny had interpreted the academy's silence as rejection. Nearly a year passed before she'd completely given up hope of ever being able to live out her dream.

When Cole proposed, Jenny had accepted.

It had seemed the right thing to do at the time. She'd known him for what seemed like her whole life—ever since she was eight years old and he'd rescued her from being run down by an out-of-control buckboard.

She cared about Cole.

She liked Cole.

She knew he was a good man.

And so, the wedding had been planned.

Then, just those few days ago, the notification of her acceptance to the academy had come. The news had thrilled Jenny. Her father, however, had dismissed the prospect of her going away to school without a second thought.

"I thought you'd put all that nonsense out of your head," her father had said disparagingly. "You're marrying Cole."

Jenny had tried to explain to him again that she wanted to further her education, to become more than just an ornament on some man's arm.

Her father, however, had refused to listen to her arguments. He'd insisted that she would never find a better man to marry than Cole.

Jenny knew he might be right, but she wanted to be sure before she resigned herself to the role of wife for the rest of her life. She had to be certain that her true happiness was there in Durango—with Cole.

The remaining few days had passed far too quickly as Jenny agonized over her future. Now she was confronted with the reality of either marrying Cole or finally accepting the truth that she couldn't go through with the wedding. She realized to her horror that she should have said something sooner, but there could be no turning back the clock. She couldn't change what was past. She could only take charge of her future.

Jenny was glad that her father had already adjusted her veil. It was a protective shield against the real world, hiding from her father the desperation she was certain was showing in her eyes.

The realization of what she had to do was vivid in her heart and soul. There could be no delaying or avoiding it any longer. She drew a ragged breath as a shudder wracked her. Now was the time.

"Are you nervous, sweetheart?" Paul Sullivan asked.

He'd noticed that Jenny was trembling and wanted to reassure her. He was delighted that her wedding day had finally arrived. Cole was perfect for her. She couldn't have picked a better husband, and once they'd married, the joining of their two ranches—the Lazy S and Cole's Branding Iron—would make them one of the biggest ranches in the state. He smiled at the thought, proud of his daughter and the fine match she was making.

Jenny only nodded.

"Don't be," Paul said in a calming voice. "The wedding will be over in no time. You'll see."

Jenny knew true panic as she realized he was right—it would be over in no time if she didn't speak up.

Thoughts of Cole haunted her. She didn't want to hurt him. She cared about him. Cole was tall and handsome, with dark good looks. He was smart, too, having worked tirelessly to build the Branding Iron into a very successful ranch, well known for its fine horses and cattle. Determined and confident, Cole was the kind of man men admired and women adored. He was the kind of man who always got what he wanted, too. And her father was right—she probably couldn't find a better husband than Cole.

The trouble was she didn't want a husband—not now. She was too young and had too much living to do!

The wedding music started.

Jenny swallowed tightly as her father offered her his arm. She took it, wondering how to handle the situation.

Did she really dare call the wedding off?

The church was full of people.

Did she really dare to leave Cole standing at the altar and walk away while there was still time?

Cole—

Was she marrying him because she truly loved him or because it would please her father?

Again she agonized.

The few kisses they'd shared had been pleasant enough, but there had always been someone nearby to chaperone them. There had never been a time when she'd been able to relax and truly enjoy his embrace. They had never had more than a few moments alone together once they'd become engaged. Cole had always been the perfect gentleman, respecting her and protecting her.

Jenny knew that was the way of things. Her reputation had to be protected, but to what end? Was she marrying a man who could truly stir her passion? She didn't know. She'd read some of those dime novel romances, however, and knew how a woman was supposed to feel about the man she was to marry. Right now, she didn't feel that way about Cole.

How Jenny wished her mother were still alive! Her mother could have talked to her about all her confusing feelings for Cole and maybe helped her to understand herself a little better. But her mother had been dead for over ten years. Jenny had tried to talk to Frances, their housekeeper at the ranch, but the older woman hadn't taken her seriously. Frances had said that she was just having pre-wedding jitters and that everything would be fine once she and Cole were married. Frances thought the world of Cole. Jenny had considered confiding in her widowed Aunt Evelyn, who had come from Philadelphia to attend the wedding, but they didn't really know each other well enough to talk of such deeply intimate things. So here she was—alone in her dilemma—very alone.

Jenny had never wanted to hurt Cole, but for her, marriage was a very serious commitment. It would be for the rest of her life.

Her life—

Jenny realized painfully that she hadn't really even begun to live her life yet and she was about to pledge herself to be Cole's wife—to have and to hold until death did them part. She cast a quick, sidelong, nervous glance at her father. He was standing erect beside her, his head held high, his expression one of pride and immense satisfaction as he gazed down at her.

"Ready, darling?" he asked with real affection, his hand closing over hers where it rested on his forearm.

Jenny allowed him to draw her down the aisle, though with each step a greater and greater sense of desperation gripped her. She argued with herself, frantically questioning her motives in balking at the last minute.

And finally she could deny it no longer.

She knew without a doubt that she had to stop the wedding before she said her vows and became Cole's wife. Once they were married, it would be too late. She would become Jenny Randall and never, ever have the chance to be Jenny Sullivan, to find out what kind of woman she really was.

Jenny swallowed tightly as she looked up to find Cole watching her from where he stood before the altar. Cole looked intense and very serious. She knew he wanted this wedding. He had told her he loved her and wanted to marry her. Pain at the knowledge that she was going to hurt him ate at her, but she had made her decision: she could not go through the rest of her life living only to please others. She had to stand up here and now and fight for herself and what she wanted.

Her father stopped before the minister.

Paul very carefully lifted Jenny's veil. He smiled down at her and kissed her cheek, then stepped back, giving her into Cole's keeping.

This was the moment.

Jenny girded herself for what was to come.

She remembered Cole's vow of love when he'd proposed to her. She wondered if he loved her enough to forgive her for what she was going to do right now.

Reverend Ford smiled at them and asked in a quiet voice, "Are we ready to begin?"

"No—" Jenny said in an agonized whisper.

"Jenny?" Cole said her name quickly, frowning as he took a step toward her.

Jenny looked up at Cole and saw all his worry and concern for her in his expression. It hurt her to do this, but she knew she couldn't go through with the wedding.

"I'm sorry, Cole."

"For what?"

"I can't marry you."

"What?" He was shocked.

"I'm so sorry," she said quickly, nervously, as she backed away from the altar, "but I can't do this. I can't get married. Not now. Not yet. I'm sorry."

Without another word, Jenny turned and fled back down the aisle, leaving Cole speechless at the altar.

Those gathered for the celebration watched in disbelief as Jenny disappeared out the front doors of the church. Then a rumble of talk swelled through the crowd as the reality of what had just happened sank in.

Jenny Sullivan had just walked out on Cole Randall!

She'd left him standing at the altar!

Cole started after Jenny. He was confused and angry and worried about her. Something was wrong, terribly wrong, and he needed to get to the bottom of it. This was Jenny, the woman he'd loved for as long as he could remember. He couldn't imagine what could have happened to cause her to panic this way, but he was determined to find out and put her fears to rest. He loved her and he wanted to spend the rest of his life with her.

A strong hand clamped down on Cole's arm, stopping him when he would have given chase.

"Let me talk to her, Cole," Paul ground out.

He brushed past the younger man and went after his fleeing daughter.

Cole remained where he was in the middle of the aisle.

Jenny ran straight for the hotel where they were staying in town. Rushing past gawking strangers, she entered the lobby and hurried up the staircase to seek the safe haven of her room. She locked the door behind her with a trembling hand, then sat down on the edge of the bed. Her peace lasted only a moment, though, as the force of her father's knock on the door jarred her senses.

"Jenny! What's wrong? Open this door! Let me in! You've got a whole church full of people waiting for you! We have to get back over there!"

Getting nervously to her feet, Jenny stared at the closed portal, stalling the inevitable confrontation.

"Jenny? Are you ill, child? Please—let me in." His

tone sounded more worried than angry now.

With a confidence that was shaky at best, she told herself that if she was brave enough to walk out of the wedding, she was brave enough to face her father's anger. Jenny went to open the door. She stood before him, a woman who knew her own mind.

"Darling—" Paul charged inside, the look on his face one of concern and fear. "What happened? Are you all right? Are you sick? What is it?"

"I'm fine, Papa." She was amazed that her voice sounded so calm when there was nothing calm about the way she was feeling.

"You're fine?" he repeated, confused. "If you're fine, then we have to go back. Cole's waiting for you—"

He said it so matter-of-factly that Jenny almost smiled a bitter smile. He had no idea of what was behind her actions—none whatsoever.

"No, Papa." She remained firm in her conviction. "I'm not going back to the church. It's like I told Cole, I can't marry him. Not today. Not now—"

"What?" Paul roared at her in disbelief. He was a man used to having his orders obeyed without question. "Now, you listen to me, young lady." He stepped farther into the room, his stance aggressive. "You can't just walk out on your own wedding!"

She lifted her gaze to his, refusing to back down. "I just did, Papa. I don't want to—"

"It doesn't matter what you want!" He was all but shouting. "Everything is—"

"Paul! Listen to yourself!" his sister Evelyn admonished as she came hurrying into the hotel room behind him and shut the door. Evelyn had slipped out the side door of the church when Jenny had fled and she'd come after them. She knew her brother could be dictatorial, and she'd realized her niece was going to need all the moral support she could get. "Of course it matters what Jenny wants."

Had Paul been less angry, he might have been proud of the strength of will his daughter was showing in standing up to him. Certainly, he was the type of man who always went after what he wanted in life, and right now his daughter was doing the same thing. But Paul was too furious to recognize the familial resemblance. He glanced between the two women, confused and outraged over what was happening.

"What's going on?" He turned his gaze back to his daughter and waited. "I want an explanation now."

"I can't go through with the wedding, Papa. I tried. I really did, and I do care about Cole, but—"

"How could you care about him and leave him at the altar like this?" he roared.

"Don't you see? That's why I had to do it! It wouldn't be fair to marry him, feeling the way I feel. I'm not ready to be some man's wife. There's so much more I want to do—to experience. I want to go to school back East. I want to—"

"So that's what's behind all this," he snarled. "I should have torn the damned letter up. I never should have let you see it!"

"Paul! Shame on you," Evelyn scolded; then she looked at her niece. "Are you absolutely certain about this, Jenny?" Her tone was gentle, understanding.

Jenny nodded, glancing thankfully toward her aunt.

Evelyn quietly took charge, addressing her brother. "You need to go back to church and let Cole and Reverend Ford know that there will be no wedding taking place today."

Paul stiffened, his cold-eyed gaze narrowing as he studied his defiant daughter. "You're sure about this?"

"Yes." Jenny stood her ground, still a bit frightened by the magnitude of what she'd done, and yet certain that she'd made the right decision.

Without another word, Paul quit the room.

Chapter Two

Cole stared at Paul in disbelief as they stood in the small room at the back of the church. "I have to talk to Jenny myself."

"I don't know if that's a good idea," Paul cautioned.

"I love her. I just can't let her walk away from me like this," Cole declared.

Cole didn't bother to wait for a response from the man who was to be his father-in-law. He didn't care what he or anyone else thought. He wanted Jenny, and he was going after her.

Leaving the room, Cole was determined to convince Jenny of his devotion. The wedding guests had gone, but Cole was certain the minister would still marry them if he could get Jenny to come back to the church with him.

Cole strode purposefully through the streets, ignoring the curious stares he was getting. He could just imagine the talk around town right now, but he didn't care. All that mattered was Jenny. He had to go to her and find out what was wrong. If it was something he'd done that had upset her, he'd do everything in his power to make things right. He loved her and wanted her happiness. When he reached the hotel, he made his way upstairs. He was a determined man going after the prize he sought.

"Jenny?" he called after knocking on the door. The answering silence puzzled him, and he wondered if she was even in the room. "Jenny, it's me, Cole."

"Go away," she answered softly.

"I love you, Jenny, and I want to talk to you. Whatever is bothering you, we can work out."

"No—"

"How do you know until we've had a chance to talk? Trust me, Jenny. Talk to me."

Inside the room, Jenny steeled herself for what was to come. Her Aunt Evelyn had left her alone so she could have a few minutes of privacy, and now Jenny regretted that she'd gone. She could have used someone there to be a buffer between her and Cole. Knowing there was no escaping this confrontation, she unconsciously squared her shoulders and opened the door.

Cole stood before her, his manly presence seeming to fill the entire doorway. Jenny stepped aside to admit him, and he entered the room without saying a word. She closed the door and turned around to face him.

She expected incriminations and anger.

He surprised her.

"I love you, Jenny," Cole told her quietly. "I don't know what's troubling you, but I know that together, if we try, we can work it out."

"Cole, I'm sorry about what happened, but—"

"If the big wedding wasn't what you wanted, I don't care. I never wanted a big wedding. That never mattered to me. I was doing it for you. If you want to, we can sneak off and elope right now. You're what's important to me. I want you, Jenny."

"No, Cole, you don't understand," she interrupted.

"Understand what?" He frowned, his tone becoming cautious and guarded.

"That I don't want this—I don't want any of this—"

The blunt harshness of her words was like a slap in the face to Cole.

He loved her.

They were to be married.

This was their wedding day.

"You don't want me?"

"No," she blurted out, really wanting only to stop him from saying anything more. She was confused by all her conflicting feelings and wanted to try to explain everything to him. "I mean, I'm not ready to—"

"I know what you mean, Jenny," Cole said, cutting her off harshly.

His gaze turned cold as he glared down at her. His jaw tightened as he struggled for control over his emotions. He didn't trust himself to say another word. He turned and stalked from the room, shutting the door silently behind him.

Jenny was trembling as she stared at the closed door. Cole was gone, and his silent closing of the door had been more powerful than if he'd slammed it. Tears welled up in her eyes. She had never wanted to hurt Cole—

Her thoughts were interrupted by a knock at the door.

"Jenny? Are you all right?" Aunt Evelyn asked softly. "I just saw Cole leaving and he looked very angry."

She all but threw herself into the older woman's arms. "I'm sorry, Aunt Evelyn! I didn't mean to make such a mess of things!"

"There, there, honey, it'll be all right." Evelyn held her trembling, crying niece for a long moment, gently trying to reassure her. "For all that this has been so difficult for you, Jenny, I must tell you that I'm very proud of you."

Jenny drew back to look at her, her eyes wide in surprise. "You are?"

"Very much so," Evelyn said. "There aren't many women around who would have been courageous enough to do what you just did."

"I don't feel very courageous."

"But think about it. You realized in time that you

weren't ready to get married. You saved both yourself and Cole a lot of heartache by being brave enough to admit it."

"I don't think he saw it that way. He was furious when he left."

"He didn't try to harm you, did he?" Evelyn asked. She would not stand idly by and let anyone hurt her niece.

"Oh, no, Cole would never do anything like that. I'm so sorry I hurt him, Aunt Evelyn. I never meant to—"

"I know that, sweetheart, but now that you've talked to Cole, the worst is over. What will you do next?"

Jenny lifted her hope-filled gaze to her aunt's. "I'm going to go back East to school."

Evelyn nodded. "Then we shall leave town on the next train heading east. There's no reason why you should stay here and suffer the gossip that's bound to come. You pack. I'll find your father and tell him what our plans are."

Cole was drunk. There was no denying it, and, frankly, he didn't care. After leaving Jenny, he'd headed straight to the High Time Saloon, and he'd been sitting there drinking at the back table ever since.

"Hey, big guy, you ready for some fun now?" Suzie asked as she sashayed up to his table.

She had been watching Cole all night, waiting for

the right moment to approach him. She'd heard the talk at the bar about what had happened with Jenny and knew he could use some soothing—and she was more than willing to do it. Cole Randall was one hell of a man—sexy, rich, and handsome as all get out. She thought Jenny Sullivan was a stupid fool to have passed up the chance to marry a man like Cole. She would have married him in a minute—not that a girl like her would ever have a chance to marry a man like him.

"No." Cole's answer was sharp as he looked up from where he'd been seriously contemplating the whiskey in his glass. There was only one woman he wanted, and she wasn't Suzie.

"Well, you just yell if you change your mind," Suzie said seductively as she moved sinuously away. She was certain she could have shown Cole a good time. She could have helped him forget, if only for a little while, but she couldn't force him to come upstairs with her. "I'll be waiting."

Cole gave a disgusted grunt and took another healthy swallow of the potent liquor. This was supposed to have been his wedding night! He'd been waiting for tonight, excited by the prospect of finally getting to make love to Jenny. It felt as if he had loved her forever, and yet he'd held his passion for her in check. He'd controlled his desire, allowing himself only a few chaste, stolen kisses, when all he'd really wanted to do was make mad, passionate love to her. He'd been eagerly anticipating this night—the night he would finally make her his. Now the only consolation he had was in this whiskey bottle. All he wanted to do was drink himself to oblivion.

Damn her!

Cole didn't understand how Jenny could have done this to him—to them. He had thought they'd loved each other—cared about each other. Certainly, he loved her. He'd wanted to spend the rest of his life taking care of her, having children together, building a Randall empire on the western slope of the Rockies, but she'd walked away from him with only an "I'm sorry."

He snarled a vile oath and lifted the glass to his lips.

"You've had about enough there, don't you think, cowboy?" Fernada said as she came to sit down at his table. She all but ran the High Time and was beloved by those who knew her. She was a gentle, caring spirit who took care of her girls and her customers.

Cole slid his gaze toward Fernada, but even as drunk as he was, the fury he felt was still etched in his expression. "I don't know if there's enough liquor in this place to satisfy me tonight, Fernada."

She had heard what had happened at his wedding and knew he could use some real kindness right now. "Getting falling-down drunk isn't going to help anything, but talking about what's bothering you might."

He gave her a lopsided grin. "I already tried talking."

"You did?"

Cole nodded. "I went to the hotel to talk to Jenny, but it was no use."

"What do you mean?" Fernada frowned.

"She doesn't want to marry me."

She shook her head in confusion. "You're a man in a million, Cole Randall. A woman would have to be crazy not to want to marry you."

" 'Crazy Jenny'—I like the sound of that." His words were sarcastic and slightly slurred.

"What did she say when you went to see her? Maybe she was just having wedding jitters. Maybe she'll have second thoughts and come around."

"I don't think so. I told her I thought we could work it out, but she said no."

"Maybe Jenny just needs some time to think about it."

"We've been engaged for months now. She's had plenty of time to think about it." His growing anger was clearly evident in his tone.

"Well, if you want my advice, I think you should go see her again and try once more. Maybe if you took her some flowers or candy? You should try to sweet-talk her, you know—court her a little bit—woo her."

Cole looked up, and, for the first time that night, his expression was slightly hopeful. Someone was offering him a plan of action. "You think that might make a difference?"

"You still love her and want to marry her, don't you?" Fernada asked insightfully.

He paused, the pain of Jenny's earlier rejection still sharp. "Yes," he answered slowly.

"Then you need to go to her and try one more time. Don't give up if you really love her. True love is worth fighting for."

Cole drew a deep breath and looked a bit unsure as he set his glass back down on the table. "But she said she didn't want me."

"I don't believe that for a minute. Think about it. What were her exact words? Did she really say, 'I don't want you, Cole'?"

In his mind, he carefully went over the conversation, and he realized Fernada was right.

"No, she said, 'I don't want this,' " he repeated slowly.

"So she didn't say, 'I don't love you, Cole'?"

"No."

"All right, then all you have to do is figure out what 'this' meant. Go to her and ask her. If she's the woman you love, the woman you want to spend the rest of your life with, then try again. Convince her that she can't live without you."

He finally managed to smile for the first time since he'd come into the saloon. "Thanks, Fernada." He shoved the glass of whiskey aside and stood up.

"Good luck, Cole."

He nodded and started toward the hotel. It might be the wee hours of the morning, but he didn't care.

He loved Jenny, and he was going to find her and tell her that. He was going to convince her to marry him, and then he was going to spend the rest of his life loving her, just as he'd planned that morning when he'd gotten ready for the wedding.

That morning seemed very long ago now. He'd been excited, eagerly anticipating the night to come, never suspecting for a moment that it would end like this. But that didn't matter now. Cole knew Fernada was right—anything worth having was worth fighting for.

Cole started down the street toward the hotel where Jenny was staying; then he remembered a house a few blocks over that had a flower garden in the front yard. Since it was late and very dark, he didn't think the owner would miss a few flowers. As quietly as he could, he raided the garden, picking only the fullest, sweetest-smelling blossoms. Jenny deserved the best. Bouquet in hand, Cole headed for the hotel.

There was no one at the front desk when Cole entered. Not that it mattered—nothing was going to stop him now. He was a determined man. He was going to Jenny, and he was going to convince her to marry him. He crossed the lobby and took the stairs two at a time like an eager schoolboy. Cole stopped before her hotel room door, clutching the flowers in one hand, and knocked.

He waited.

No response.

He knocked again, believing her to be asleep. His anticipation grew.

When he heard no one moving around inside the room, he knocked one more time and called out, "Jenny. It's Cole. I need to talk to you again. It's important."

He waited.

No response.

Cole frowned. He was a bit angry and a bit worried, and he wasn't sure which emotion was more prominent. He'd known that persuading her to talk with him again might not be easy, but he hadn't fancied having to break down the door to get the chance. The way he was feeling right now, breaking down the door wasn't out of the realm of possibility, but he really didn't want to face her if he was angry. He wanted the opportunity to woo her—to sweep her off her feet—to convince her that he could make her happy forever.

"Jenny?" he repeated as he knocked, a little harder than last.

Still nothing.

"Damn it, Jenny—"

His patience about at an end, Cole was set to pound on the door one last, loud time when he heard a door open across the hall behind him.

"Hey, cowboy! Just in case you're so damned slow that you ain't figured it out yet, she ain't there!" the grouchy, sleepy man snarled at him.

"What?" Cole glanced over his shoulder in irritation.

"They checked out hours ago. They're long gone."

"She left?" He was stunned.

"What are you, deaf along with dumb?" the man snapped. "She's gone. Now get the hell outta here so I can get some sleep." He turned back inside his room and slammed his door.

Cole stood there, flowers in hand, staring at the man's closed door.

Jenny was gone?

She'd checked out hours ago?

He tried the doorknob to her room and found the door unlocked. He stepped inside and stared around himself. The room was dark and deserted. There was no sign of Jenny anywhere. She truly had gone.

Cole stalked out of the room and started back down the hall to the stairs. He wanted to find the clerk so he could ask him where Jenny had gone. He was startled to find the clerk on his way up.

"Sir, were you the one making all that noise?"

"What's it to you?"

"It's the middle of the night. You have to be quiet," the clerk told Cole, growing a bit nervous when he noticed his black scowl. It was his job to keep things peaceful in the hotel at night, but this cowboy looked more than a little like a troublemaker.

"I'll quiet down when I find Miss Sullivan. Where is she?" Cole demanded, his stance and tone threatening.

"Oh, they're gone, sir," the clerk said a bit nervously, realizing that wasn't the news the cowboy wanted to hear. "The Sullivans and Mrs. Anderson checked out quite a while ago."

"Where did Miss Sullivan go?"

"I heard them talking about taking the late train out of town."

Cole brushed past the clerk on the stairs and stormed from the hotel, a man on a mission. He made his way to the railroad station and woke up the clerk there, who'd been dozing behind the counter. The answers Cole got from him were the ones he'd feared.

Jenny and her aunt had boarded the late train to Denver.

Jenny was gone.

Cole turned his back on the man and walked away, disappearing into the night. He stopped in the middle of the dark, deserted street and stood in silence as he faced the reality of what had happened.

There would be no chance to win Jenny back.

What he'd thought was going to be the most wonderful day of his life had turned into a living nightmare—hell on Earth.

Jenny had never really loved him.

It was over.

Cole's heart hardened against the pain that stabbed at him. He realized with awful clarity just how vulnerable loving someone had made him. He vowed then and there never to allow himself to care so deeply for any woman again.

Cole glanced down at the flowers he held, still clutched in his hand.

Without emotion, he dropped them into the dirt.

He walked away into the darkness, a solitary man.

Chapter Three

Two Years Later

Cole sat across the desk from Andrew Marsden, staring at the lawyer, his expression dark. "Are you serious?"

"Very." Marsden nodded solemnly. "Paul Sullivan spelled it out in detail for me last year when we updated his will."

Cole swore under his breath. The last two days had been hell for him. It had been terrible enough when he'd learned that Paul had been killed in a riding accident. The funeral had been held yesterday, with the burial in the small family graveyard out at the ranch. Now he'd been summoned to the lawyer's office in town and informed that he'd been appointed the executor of Paul's estate. The news came as a complete shock. Cole's gaze was piercing in its intensity as he asked, "Why did he want me?"

"He trusted you," the lawyer said simply.

Cole fell silent. It was true that he and Paul had remained close friends even though Paul had never become his father-in-law. They had worked together to build up their herds after the bad winter the year before, but he'd never expected anything like this.

"Surely Paul had family—some relative who could do this."

"There's only Jenny and his widowed sister, Evelyn. I believe you met her when . . ." Marsden stopped awkwardly, not wanting to bring up the subject of Cole's almost-marriage to Paul's daughter. Their planned nuptials had been the talk of the town at the time. Then, when the wedding had been called off at the last minute, the news had been fodder for the town gossips for weeks.

"Yes, I met her," Cole said tersely.

"Paul loved his daughter and sister, but he told me at the time we were going over the will that if anyone could keep the Lazy S going, it was you. He knew what a smart businessman you were. He respected what you'd done with the Branding Iron, how you've turned it into a show place." Andrew paused and smiled sadly. "I still remember him bragging about how you'd made it through the blizzard that winter with the fewest losses of all the ranchers in the area."

"I was lucky."

"No, you were smart, and Paul knew it. He thought

the world of you." Andrew spoke with intensity, wanting Cole to realize how important Paul's choice had been to him.

Cole was touched by the sentiment. Paul had been a good neighbor and a good friend. "What do I have to do?"

"According to what Paul directed in the will, you're to run the Lazy S until Jenny turns twenty-five, until she marries, or until the ranch is sold, whichever comes first."

"Does Jenny know about any of this?"

"No. He did not tell her about the change in the will."

Cole's expression darkened even more at that news. He could just imagine how Jenny was going to react. They hadn't seen each other since their wedding day. She'd gone East and stayed there, and that had been fine with him. Now, however, thanks to Paul, they were going to be forced to deal with each other again.

"Or until it's sold, you say?" he repeated.

"That's right."

Cole nodded, hoping he'd get lucky and she'd sell the place. Hell, he was tempted to buy it himself. "Have you heard anything more from her?"

"No, I haven't heard anything new. You know Louis Hayden, the foreman at the Lazy S, don't you?"

"Yes."

"Well, Louie's the one who wired Jenny about Paul's death the day they found him. He received a message back from her saying that she was on her way home. From what I understand, she could possibly be here tomorrow, depending on connections. I don't think Louie's heard anything more from her since that first telegram, but you might want to check with him and see. In fact, it would be good if you could just step in and take over at the ranch right now. I'm sure the men are concerned about what's going to happen next. You could set their minds at ease."

"I'll head back out there today. Did Paul have enough cash set aside to meet payroll?" If he was going to reassure the ranch hands, he wanted to be certain of his facts.

"From what I understand, he has some money in the bank to cover expenses."

"Good."

"As soon as Jenny gets back in town, we'll set up a meeting for the official reading of the will."

"Thanks, Andrew."

Cole stood to go. They shook hands, and he left the office. His mood was black as he contemplated what to do next. He had told the lawyer that he was going to ride out to the Lazy S, and he would, eventually, but first, right now, he needed a good stiff drink. It didn't matter that it was only ten o'clock in the morning. He strode toward the High Time Saloon.

The High Time was relatively quiet, and Cole was glad. He walked straight up to the bar.

"Whiskey," he told Dan, the bartender.

"I heard the news about Paul Sullivan," Dan said

as he set a tumbler before Cole and poured him a healthy serving of liquor. "That's a damned shame. He was a good man."

"Yes, he was," Cole agreed. He lifted the glass and took a deep drink. The liquor burned all the way down, but he was glad for its power.

"Anybody know how it happened?"

"Riding accident," Cole answered. "His horse came back without him, so some of the hands went out to search for him. They found him up in a high pasture. It looked like he'd been thrown."

"I'm sorry." Dan was sincere. "I know you two were friends."

"We were." Cole took another swallow.

"What's going to happen out at the ranch?"

"It's going to depend on what Jenny wants to do." His tone was flat, emotionless.

"So she'll be coming back to Durango?" Dan was curious.

"For a while at least." He didn't want to see Jenny or to have anything to do with her, but he had no choice if he wanted to help his friend.

Jenny—

It had been two years since he'd suffered the humiliation of her walking out on him as he stood waiting at the altar. She hadn't been back home in all that time, and he hadn't missed her.

Cole drained his glass as painful memories of that day threatened to surface. He fought them down, determined to handle Jenny's return just as he'd handled all the other hard times that came his way. She meant nothing to him anymore. She hadn't since that night when he'd discovered she'd left town without a word. When she finally showed up again, he would make her an offer for the ranch and send her packing back East just as fast as he could.

"You want another drink?" Dan asked, interrupting his thoughts.

"No," Cole answered, but truth be told, he did. In fact, he would like to stay right there in the bar and drink for the rest of the day—and night. But he wouldn't. He denied himself. Paul had entrusted the future of the Lazy S to him. Cole knew how much the ranch had meant to his friend, and he would not let him down.

Cole paid his bill and rode for the Lazy S.

Cole stood over Paul's grave, staring down at the headstone that marked his friend's passing.

"Frances told me you were here," Louie Hayden said as he came up behind him. "Is everything all right?"

Cole cast a quick glance his way, a bit startled to find the ranch foreman there. He had been so deeply lost in thought that he hadn't heard him approach, and that was unusual for him.

"I met with Andrew Marsden this morning."

"What did he want?" Louie was curious about what had transpired. He'd heard the lawyer mention at

Paul's funeral that he needed to speak with Cole in private.

"Paul had made some changes in his will."

"He did?"

"Yes. He named me the executor."

"That only makes sense." Louie nodded and smiled in sad understanding. "You were one of the few people Paul trusted—one of the few he knew he could always count on."

"He was a good friend."

"And you were a good friend to him," the older man told him.

They fell silent, remembering the man they were both going to miss.

"That means you're in charge now, right?"

"That's what Marsden told me—until Jenny turns twenty-five or marries or decides to sell the place, whichever comes first."

"What do you plan to do?" Louie asked. "Things haven't been good around here, you know, ever since the blizzard. I didn't think it could get much worse after Paul lost so much of his fortune that winter and had to struggle so hard just to keep things going, but then we had that rustling— 'Course you know about that. All the area ranches have been hit at one time or another, and now, on top of it all, Paul's dead."

"It has been rough here, but I want to keep the Lazy S going," Cole answered firmly, though he knew Louie was right. Things hadn't been good there for quite a while. "This ranch was Paul's life."

"You're right. The man worked night and day trying to make this place a success."

"He was proud of it. There's no doubt about that, but in the long run, a lot is going to depend on Jenny." Cole's tone turned cold as he spoke. "If she wants to sell, I'll buy the place."

"That'd be the best thing that could happen." Louie was hopeful. Everyone respected and admired Cole's business sense. He'd turned the Branding Iron into one of the best spreads in the area. If anyone could make the Lazy S a paying proposition again, it was Cole.

"We'll have to wait and see what happens when she gets here. Have you heard anything more from her?"

"No. Last I heard, she said she'd be arriving in Durango on tomorrow afternoon's train. It's going to be hard for her, coming home this way, but there was no easy way to give her the bad news with her living so far away," Louie said. He and his wife, Frances, who was cook and housekeeper on the Lazy S, both loved Jenny. They'd worked on the ranch for years and had watched her grow up. Louie could just imagine how distraught she'd been when she'd gotten the wire he'd sent notifying her of her father's death. "I planned on going into town to meet her, unless you want to do it, being executor and all."

"No, that's all right. You go on ahead," Cole told him. "I've got to ride back to the Branding Iron tonight to check on things there, but I'll make it a point to come back over here tomorrow so I can speak with Jenny."

"Does she know you're in charge?"

"According to Marsden, Paul did not tell her what he'd done in the will, so I'll have to tell her when I see her."

"What if she doesn't want to sell? What if she decides she wants to try to run the ranch herself?"

"Since she hasn't bothered to come back once since she went East, I don't think that will be a problem. There's nothing left to hold her here now that her father's dead."

"What should I tell the men? They've been a little uneasy about what might happen. They're wanting to know if they're going to have jobs come the first of the month."

"Tell them they're still on the payroll until they hear different from me," Cole said with authority, taking charge just as Paul had intended.

"Why don't you come with me and tell them yourself? They'll be glad to hear the news that you're in charge." Cole was a man they could all believe in and trust. As much as Cole might resent the burden of taking over, Louie knew that Paul had done the right thing.

"All right. I'll be along in a minute and meet you there."

Louie walked off, and Cole was left alone with his thoughts once again. He remained at the graveside, mourning his friend's passing, wishing things could have been different, but promising to deal with everything the best he could—even Jenny. It was what Paul had wanted him to do, so he would do it.

Cole looked down one last time at the grave, then turned and walked away. He strode toward the house, ready to talk to the men and take care of ranch business.

Chapter Four

"We're almost there. Are you going to be all right?" Evelyn asked Jenny as the Denver & Rio Grande train slowed and headed into the Durango station.

Jenny looked at her aunt, her expression strained. "I'm going to try . . ."

Jenny fell silent. She was home. At last, she was home. In her heart, though, her home and her father were synonymous. She couldn't imagine returning to the Lazy S and her father not being there. She didn't know if she could bear it.

Her father was gone—dead—and she'd never had the chance to tell him she loved him. She'd never had the chance to say good-bye.

Anger suddenly flared within Jenny.

How dare he go and die on her!

Jenny embraced the emotion. The heat of her outrage was far better than the bottomless sense of emptiness and loneliness that had filled her ever since she'd received Louie's telegram. If she was angry, she could handle what was to come. If she was angry, she could cope with the loss that could never be restored.

How dare he have a riding accident! He was an excellent horseman.

The thought that he'd been killed while out riding was just too hard to accept. When she'd first received the wire from Louie, she hadn't believed it, but now, as they drew ever closer to Durango and to the ranch, there could be no hiding from it any longer. She had to face the reality of her situation—she had to face the truth, whether she wanted to or not.

Her father was dead.

"I'll be with you every moment, darling," Evelyn promised. She was devoted to her niece and thankful that they'd had these last few years to grow closer. She knew Jenny would need all her love and support to get through the heartbreak and devastation of her unexpected loss.

Jenny gave her aunt a grateful look and then turned to look out the window as the train finally came to a full stop. The trip home had seemed to last an eternity. There had been moments crossing the plains when she'd wondered if they'd ever get there, but now it was over. They had arrived in Durango.

The sight of the familiar surroundings suddenly left Jenny aching for the past—for the warmth of her father's embrace—for the security of a loving home—for her lost innocence.

She was home—

At long last, she was home—

Jenny swallowed tightly and struggled for control.

"We're here," she said in a pained voice.

Evelyn said nothing but reached out and took her niece's hand, giving it a gentle squeeze.

Jenny stared intently out the window, searching the crowd gathered at the station for some sign of her father. Logically, she knew he wouldn't be there. Logically, she knew she would never see him again. But there were moments in life when the heart and soul ignored logic. For just an instant longer, she allowed herself to pretend that he might be there.

And then she saw Louie.

Louie was the one who had come for her.

Louie was there waiting for her—not her father.

Her father would not be coming for her—not today, and not ever again.

The pain in Jenny's heart as she finally accepted the brutal truth was devastating. She longed for the anger that had sustained her moments earlier, but could find no trace of it. There was only deep, abiding sorrow in her soul.

Evelyn knew what Jenny was feeling. She, too, had been brokenhearted at the news of her brother's death. "Do you see anyone from the ranch?"

"Yes—Louie's here." Her words were choked.

"Are you ready?"

Jenny only nodded, not trusting herself to say anything more. She stood and started from the rail car. Evelyn gathered her few belongings and followed.

The conductor was waiting to help them descend from the car, and Jenny allowed him to assist her. He handed her down, and Jenny stepped out onto the platform.

She was home. She was in Durango.

She was unprepared for the rush of memories that returned as she looked around the station. The last time she was there had been on the night of her "wedding," when she'd left town quickly and quietly on the late train. Images of all that had happened that day surged in her thoughts—visions of Cole—first, the way he'd looked standing so tall and proud before the minister in church waiting to marry her, and then later, the way he'd looked so dark and dangerous when he'd stalked from her hotel room and never looked back. She remembered her father's confusion over her refusal to go through with the wedding, and his anger over her desire to go back East to school. Ultimately, though, she remembered how he had supported her decision to leave. She'd known that he'd disapproved of what she wanted to do, but he hadn't stood in her way. He had loved her enough to let her go.

Jenny glanced nervously around the crowded station, dreading the possibility that Cole might have come with Louie to meet her train. She wasn't ready to see Cole Randall, and she truly hoped that she would never have to. Only when she saw that the ranch foreman was making his way through the crowd alone did relief sweep through her.

"Louie—" She went to greet the older man and was swept into a warm bear hug.

"Jenny, girl, it's good you're home," he said, his voice tight with heartfelt emotion.

Jenny clung to his strength and support. Louie and Frances had always been there for her. They were like family to her, and she hugged him tight. "I've missed you."

"We've been missing you, too. I wanted you to come back home, but not . . ." Louie stopped himself from saying *like this*.

"I know, I know." Her words were tortured as she drew away, wiping at the tears that could no longer be denied.

"Hello, Louie," Evelyn said as she came to join them.

"It's good to see you again, ma'am."

" 'Evelyn' will do just fine," she said with a gentle smile.

"Yes, ma'am," he told her. "I've got the buckboard tied up right out front. You go ahead out while I get your bags. I'll meet you there."

Jenny and Evelyn made their way to the front of the station to wait for him.

"Is there anything I can do to help you?" Evelyn asked Jenny as they stood by the buckboard.

"I wish there was something that would help, but I know there isn't. It's just so hard—with Papa not being here, and I keep remembering . . ."

"Remembering what, dear?"

"My last day in town. I know how badly I disappointed Papa. He did so want me to marry Cole."

"Do you think you'll see Cole again? Is he still in the area?"

"From the few times Papa mentioned him when he came East to visit, I think Cole's doing fine on the Branding Iron. I doubt if I'll see him again, though, and I really don't want to." She had not had any contact with him since that fateful day so long ago and didn't relish the thought of a reunion with him.

Her aunt nodded. "I understand. Things are difficult enough as it is."

Louie rejoined them then and loaded their luggage in the back of the buckboard. He helped them in and then climbed up, too, and took the reins. They moved off through the streets of town, heading for the Lazy S—heading for home.

The trip to the ranch was long, but Jenny didn't notice. She was too enthralled by the beauty of her surroundings, and she found herself wondering how she could have stayed away so long.

"I didn't realize how much I missed home," Jenny said, her heart swelling with the absolute magnificence of the mountains.

"I wondered why you didn't come back sooner," Louie remarked. "And so did your father."

She cringed inwardly at his words. "I guess I needed to see more of the world, so I could better appreciate what I had. I'm just sorry it took this to make me realize it."

"Don't feel guilty. We can never know what's going to happen in life. Your father wanted only your happiness. You meant the world to him," Evelyn offered. "He loved you, and you loved him."

"Louie . . ." Jenny was suddenly very serious.

The foreman glanced at her, hearing the change in her voice and wondering at it.

"What happened that day? How did Papa die? I know you said it was a riding accident, but he was such a good rider. . . . It just doesn't make sense that he'd be thrown and—"

"No, it doesn't make much sense, horseman that he was, but when his mount came back to the house without him, me and the boys went out looking for him right away. We figured we'd find him walking back and probably cussing and spitting mad. We thought we'd get a good laugh out of it. We were all set to give him a bad time. . . ." He paused as he remembered that terrible day.

"Where did you find him?"

"It took us a while, but we finally found him near the creek in the high pasture."

Jenny shivered at the thought of her beloved father dying that way—all alone with no one to help him. "It's good that you were able to find him at all."

"We buried him with your mother," he offered, not really wanting to talk about it, but knowing that she needed to know all that had happened.

"Thank you, Louie. I don't know what I would have done without you."

They fell silent, each lost deep in thought.

Jenny was dreading returning to the empty house and seeing the last and final proof of her father's death—his grave.

Evelyn was wondering what her niece was going to do now that she was owner of the ranch. Jenny loved living in the East. No doubt she would sell the Lazy S as quickly as possible, so they could return to the lives they'd been leading before Paul's deadly accident.

Louie was worried about what was going to happen when Jenny discovered that Cole was running the ranch—with her father's blessing. Their past history was going to make any kind of relationship between them difficult, to say the least. He just hoped they could work things out, so the ranch didn't suffer. Lord knows, things had been rough enough on the Lazy S lately. They didn't need any more trouble.

It was late in the day as Cole Randall sat at the desk in Paul's study staring down at the ledger open before him. He glanced up at the mantel clock again, noting with irritation that only ten minutes had passed since the last time he'd checked. Louie was due back with Jenny at any time now—if she'd made it into town on the train today.

Cole was tense, not relishing the upcoming reunion. It was difficult enough knowing that he was going to have to deal with Jenny that very day, but over the last several hours as he'd started reviewing the ranch's finances, he'd come to realize just how bad things had gotten there. He'd known that times had been hard for Paul; he just hadn't known how hard.

"They're coming!"

The sound of Frances's call interrupted Cole's thoughts. He swore silently as he slammed the ledger shut. There would be time for dealing with the figures later. Right now he had something more serious to attend to.

Jenny was there—

Cole shoved himself away from the desk and stood up to make his way toward the front of the house.

As the buckboard topped the low rise and the two-story ranch house and outbuildings came into view in the valley below them, Jenny's heart was filled with joy. If only her father had been there waiting for her, the moment would have been perfect, but, tragically, he wasn't. She remained quiet as they crossed the remaining distance and drew to a stop before the house.

"You're here," Frances cried as she came hurrying out of the house and down the front porch steps, her arms flung wide.

Jenny climbed down from the buckboard and was immediately enveloped in Frances's loving embrace.

Jenny returned her hug warmly. "I've missed you, Frances."

"We've missed you, too, little girl," Frances said lovingly, hugging her all the more tightly to her heart. "You've been gone too long—much too long." When at last she freed Jenny from her embrace, she still grasped her hand tightly. "I think I may just hold on to you forever and never let you go again."

"I think I may just let you," Jenny replied, and was embraced one last quick time.

"Hello, Miss Evelyn," Frances greeted the other woman. "Louie and the boys can take care of your things. You both come on inside now with me, and we'll get you settled in." She kept a protective arm around Jenny's waist, drawing her toward the porch stairs.

Jenny stopped and glanced off toward the small grove of trees in the distance.

"No—I don't want to go inside yet." she said to Frances. "I have to go see my father—"

Frances understood. "Louie told you we buried him with your mother?"

"Yes," she said softly, sadness revealed in her eyes as she looked over at her aunt. "I'll be back in a little while. You go on inside."

Evelyn and Frances watched in silence as Jenny made her way toward the small family grave site.

Chapter Five

As Jenny drew near the burial plot, she could see the freshly turned earth and the marker that were the final proof of her father's passing. A sob tore from her throat as she stood over the grave, and she finally gave in to the devastating sorrow that she'd held at bay for so long.

There could be no hiding from the truth any longer.

Jenny dropped to her knees, her hands clutched before her. Her keening was heart-wrenching as she faced the truth and told her father good-bye.

"Cole?" Evelyn blurted out as she stepped inside the house and came face to face with him in the hallway. He was as tall and handsome as ever, and her surprise at finding him there was immense. She could just imagine how shocked Jenny was going to be when she found out that Cole was waiting for her.

"Hello, Evelyn," he said. Then looking past her down the hallway, he asked, "Didn't Jenny come with you?"

"Yes . . . yes, she's here," she answered, feeling as if she were babbling.

"Jenny went out to the grave," Frances explained as she followed Evelyn indoors. She knew that Cole had been waiting all afternoon for Jenny's arrival. "I'm sure she'll be in in a little while."

"It's good to see you again, Evelyn. I just wish it were under better circumstances. I'm sorry about Paul."

"Thank you," she answered, still confused by his presence but appreciating his sentiment.

"I'll be in the study if you should need me, Frances."

He retreated to Paul's study and went to look out the window. In the distance he could see the small cemetery and could make out Jenny kneeling beside her father's grave. He allowed himself to feel sorry for her, but only for a moment; then he banished any gentle feeling toward her. It was all well and good that she'd shown up now, but where had she been during the long, lonely months when Paul had been here alone missing her?

There was no room in Cole's heart for any tender emotion where Jenny was concerned. She would get precious little sympathy from him. She had chosen to leave the ranch and stay away all this time. Only her father's death had drawn her back. Cole fully expected her to sell out to him immediately, so she could return quickly to the life she obviously loved so much back East. He would be glad to see her go. Cole turned away in disgust from the window, not looking forward to the reunion to come.

Jenny slowly got to her feet and wiped the tears from her eyes.

It was true.

Her father was dead. She would never see him again—never hug him again—never have the chance to tell him she loved him again—

She drew a sobbing, ragged breath and struggled to pull herself together. It wouldn't be easy. She had loved her father dearly and would miss him always.

With a heavy heart, Jenny looked around her. She stared out across the valley and then let her gaze sweep across the beauty of the mountains. This was her home. She'd enjoyed her time in Philadelphia. She'd excelled in school and had traveled extensively, even taking a grand tour with a group from the academy, but now she realized that this was where she belonged. Her heart, her life, was here on the Lazy S.

In that moment, she made her decision. No matter what Aunt Evelyn wanted her to do, she wasn't going back.

Jenny gave a determined lift of her chin as she made her way toward the house.

She was home.

She was staying.

The house looked warm and welcoming, quiet and peaceful. There was no one around outside. Louie had already carried all their bags indoors and driven the buckboard off to the stable.

Jenny's heart ached as she climbed the porch steps and let herself in. She could hear the sound of voices coming from the back of the house and started down the hall. A sense of warmth and love surrounded her, embracing her.

Home . . . How could she have stayed away so long?

And then Cole stepped out of the study into the hallway, blocking her way.

Jenny gasped and took a step back, startled. "Cole!"

"Hello, Jenny."

His voice was deep and mellow, and a shiver of awareness ran down her spine. She blinked, staring up at him, momentarily speechless.

Of all the things Jenny had imagined happening to her upon her return home, finding Cole in her father's study had not been one of them. He was taller than she remembered, and his shoulders seemed broader. He was as handsome as ever with his dark hair and dark eyes, and there was an aura of power, maturity, and control about him now. His was a commanding presence, and he seemed to fill the entire hallway. She took an unconscious step backward.

"I'm sorry about your father," he said quietly. "He was a good man."

"Yes . . . yes, he was," she stammered, finally managing to pull herself together enough to speak. She couldn't imagine what he was doing in her house.

"How was your trip?" Cole asked.

He found himself staring down at Jenny and was irritated by the realization that she had matured into a stunning woman. Her hair was smoothed back into a bun at the nape of her neck in a style that on another woman would have been severe. On Jenny, though, it gave her a regal look, emphasizing the classic beauty of her features. She wore a sedate traveling gown, but even so clad, there was no disguising the feminine grace of her figure.

Something deep and elemental stirred within Cole, but he fiercely denied it.

He harshly reminded himself that this was Jenny—the woman who had left him standing at the altar—the woman who'd left him open to public ridicule.

Any momentary attraction he'd felt for her vanished as he hardened his heart. He would have to deal with her, true. He couldn't avoid it, but he would make sure that their dealings were strictly business. Then she would be gone.

"The trip was fine," she answered quickly, his unexpected appearance embarrassing and unsettling her. "Cole—what are you doing here?"

"Louie told me you would be arriving today, and I needed to speak with you."

"About what?" She couldn't imagine what they had to say to each other. It would have been better, less awkward, if they'd never seen each other again.

"If you'll come into the study with me and sit down for a moment, I'll explain." He motioned toward the doorway behind him.

Frances and Evelyn had heard them talking, and they appeared at the far end of the hallway just then.

"You're back?" Evelyn was surprised to find Jenny and Cole in conversation.

"Yes, but Cole needs to talk to me for a moment, so I'll be with him in the study."

The two women disappeared back into the kitchen as Jenny followed Cole into the room that had been her father's haven.

The study embraced her with nearly overpowering memories of her father. From the masculine scent of his leather-bound books to the sight of his massive desk and chair, nowhere else in the house was her father's presence more evident than in this room. The study had been his special place. It had been the place where he'd gone to work, the place where he'd gone to read, the place where he'd spent long hours teaching her how to play a serious game of chess. Tears burned in her eyes, and the ache of missing him grew in her heart.

Jenny moved farther into the room. She couldn't imagine what Cole was doing at her home or what business he could possibly have with her. She resented his being there.

Cole waited until Jenny had come all the way inside the room, then closed the study door behind her. He gestured toward a chair before the desk.

"Please, sit down."

Jenny was taken aback by the fact that Cole was telling her what to do in her own home. She sat down without comment, though, just wanting to get this conversation over with as quickly as possible. They had parted under terrible circumstances, and, though he had been nothing but polite since they'd come face to face, she could well imagine what his true feelings were toward her. It would be best if he would just say whatever he had to say and then leave.

"I trust you've been well?" Cole asked casually as he sat down at the desk and faced her.

"I was until the news about Papa came." Jenny's answer was terse. She certainly didn't want to make small talk with Cole, and she was greatly irritated that he'd taken it upon himself to sit at her father's desk as if he had the right.

Just who did he think he was?

"Your father's death was a horrible thing, and that's what I need to talk with you about."

Cole gave up trying to be cordial and got down to business. She was being so cold that he was more than ready to see her board the eastbound train and head back the way she'd come—the sooner, the better.

"It was important that I meet you here today because I needed to make you aware of some of the provisions in your father's will."

"Didn't he have a lawyer who handled all this?"

"Yes, Andrew Marsden, and yesterday Mr. Marsden sent word to me to meet him at his office. I made the trip into town and spoke with him at length."

"About what?" she asked cautiously.

"Marsden informed me that your father had made some changes in his will a little over a year ago—changes that no one else was ever made aware of."

"What kind of changes?" She suddenly had a terrible feeling about what was to come.

"Your father had directed Marsden to make me the executor of the estate."

"He what?"

"According to the terms your father set down, I am to be in control of everything until you turn twenty-five years old or get married or decide to sell the ranch, whichever comes first."

Jenny stared at him in disbelief. *Her father had named Cole the executor?*

"But you're not even family," she protested. Even as she said it, she was a bit embarrassed, for she realized that they could very well have been man and wife right now had she not walked out on their wedding.

"I pointed that out to Mr. Marsden, but he said your father was most explicit in the terms of the will. We can arrange a meeting with Mr. Marsden tomorrow if you'd like. He can go over the will with you then, so everything can be straightened out."

"Can you be removed as executor? Surely that was some kind of mistake on my father's part," she remarked, hoping it was possible.

She couldn't imagine what her father had been thinking when he'd chosen Cole to run things. She was perfectly capable of taking charge of the ranch. Hadn't she just proven that by going back East to school? She was an educated woman, a woman full grown, and she didn't need anyone to take care of her or oversee her interests.

Cole stared at her, and if it were possible, the look in his eyes turned even colder.

"I had nothing to do with this, Jenny. Your father specifically set things up this way. Marsden will explain that to you when we meet with him. I didn't know anything about being named executor until yesterday, and believe me, I am not thrilled with the arrangement either."

His words lashed at her, and she paled.

Cole hated her.

"I would much rather have your father alive and well and here with us right now, but that's not possible," Cole continued harshly. "It was his request that I do this. He's the one who wanted me to take charge of the estate and see that things are handled properly. I will respect that request."

"I see."

"If you're agreeable, handling the estate shouldn't

prove too difficult. We should be able to conclude most of the business in just a few days, I would think."

"What do you mean?"

"I'm more than willing to buy the Lazy S from you. Name your price. We can let Marsden handle all the paperwork, and then you can be on your way."

Jenny stiffened at his cold, calculating statement. She glared at him as she replied, "And just what makes you think that I'm prepared to sell?"

"You can't very well run the Lazy S from Philadelphia."

"And who said I was going back to Philadelphia?"

"Well, since you haven't bothered to come back here for the last two years . . ."

Cole's accusation hit a nerve with Jenny, and she lifted her gaze to his, her expression challenging and angry. "I have no intention of leaving again. I've come back home, and I plan to stay."

It was the first time she'd said it out loud, but now that she had, she knew it was the right thing to do. Aunt Evelyn was going to be shocked by her decision, but it was her decision to make. As much as she'd enjoyed her time in Philadelphia, this was where she was meant to be. This was where she belonged.

Cole stared at her in open irritation. He'd known that dealing with her wouldn't be easy, but he'd never imagined that she would decide to stay on at the ranch. He'd thought she would come home, take one look around, and leave again just as fast as she could.

Certainly, she'd shown no interest in being here before. But now, if she didn't sell out to him, he would be forced to work with her until she married or turned twenty-five, and that was years away. He wanted to swear in frustration.

"Let's meet with Mr. Marsden tomorrow afternoon. The sooner I speak with him, the better," Jenny told him. "And while I appreciate your offer for the Lazy S, the ranch is not for sale. I'm back, and I intend to take over and run things just like my father did."

Cole was tempted to tell her about her dire financial situation right then and there to discourage her, but he held back. Tomorrow would be time enough for her to find out what bad financial shape the ranch was in. If she heard it from him tonight, she might think he was lying or exaggerating just to anger her, but if it came straight from Marsden, she would have to face the truth. Then maybe she would change her mind and sell out to him and leave.

The last thing Cole wanted was to be forced to deal with Jenny on a regular basis until she was twenty-five—and if she stayed and tried to take over the everyday running of the ranch, that was exactly what would happen. Even though she had been raised on the ranch, she was a woman, and some of the ranch hands might have a problem with working for a female.

"I'll set things up with the lawyer for tomorrow afternoon, and I'll meet you at his office." Cole stood up, ready to leave, wanting to get away. He deliberately did not offer to accompany her into town. He was certain she could find her own way into Durango.

"That will work out just fine," she agreed, rising, too, to see him out. She could tell by his surly expression that he wasn't pleased with the way things were going. "I am sorry that this has been forced upon you."

"Believe me, so am I, but it's what your father wanted. I'm doing it for him," he said curtly as he walked toward the door. "I'll see you in town."

Jenny followed him from the study, but he strode down the hall and out of the house without looking back. She closed the front door and walked slowly back into the study. She was standing just inside the doorway when Evelyn found her.

"Is everything all right, dear?" Evelyn asked.

"I'm not sure—"

"What's wrong? Cole didn't try to cause any trouble, did he?" She had been worried about Jenny running into Cole again; finding him here at the house had been disturbing.

"Papa made Cole the executor of the estate," she explained.

"He did? But why?"

"I don't know. Whenever Papa came to visit, he rarely mentioned Cole, and when he did, it was only in passing. I know he always liked him, but I had no idea that he would do something like this to me."

"You're worried about dealing with him?"

"According to what Cole told me, he's in charge

of everything until I turn twenty-five, get married, or sell out. I have no intention of selling out, and I certainly don't plan to get married any time soon," she said with conviction.

"But I thought we were planning to return home to Philadelphia once you'd settled everything here." Evelyn was taken aback by her declaration. Living on the Lazy S was nice enough, she supposed, but she was accustomed to life in a big city.

Jenny turned to look at her aunt, her expression serious. "Aunt Evelyn, I am home."

"Oh, my." The older woman sank down on a chair, her own plans in chaos. She knew how headstrong her niece could be, and she could tell that Jenny had made up her mind. Still, she had to ask, "But what about Cole? Are you going to be able to work with him? He didn't seem all that friendly today, and four years is a long time to be forced to deal with one another."

"I can do anything when I set my mind to it," she declared. "I'm going to make Papa proud of me."

"He was always proud of you," Evelyn said with certainty.

Jenny knew there had been times when he hadn't been proud of her—like when she'd walked out on Cole. But that had been then, and this was now.

"Well, I'm going to make him prouder. I want the Lazy S to be the best ranch around." She went to look out the window. The land stretched before her in seemingly unending glory. "It's so beautiful here,

Aunt Evelyn. This is my home. This is where I want to stay. I hope you understand."

"Oh, I do, dear, and if you want me to, I'll stay here with you," she offered.

Jenny looked at her in surprise. She'd expected her aunt to be anxious to leave. "But what about your life in Philadelphia?"

Evelyn smiled gently at her as she went to stand beside her. "You're my family, Jenny. I love you and want to help you in any way I can."

Jenny hugged her. "We'll make Papa proud, you'll see. It may have taken me a while to realize that this is where I belong, but now that I'm back, I never intend to leave again. I'm home, Aunt Evelyn. I've come home."

Jenny turned to gaze out the window again at her beloved ranch, and her heart filled with love and fierce determination.

She was going to do this—for her father and for herself.

Chapter Six

So, Jenny planned to stay.

The ride to his ranch was a long one, and Cole was glad. He needed the time to calm down. He'd known that seeing Jenny again was not going to be easy, but he'd had no idea it was going to be this difficult. He'd thought that he would only have to meet with her two or three times, and then she'd be gone from his life forever. But it looked like that wasn't going to happen.

Cole could only hope the lawyer and banker could talk some sense into her tomorrow and make her see that it was pointless for her to stay around and try to run the Lazy S. The easiest thing for her to do would be to let him buy her out. He would pay her a fair price, and then she would be free to go on her way and do whatever she wanted to do. If only she would listen to reason.

Paul had once told him that his daughter was as stubborn and headstrong as he was, and Cole was finding out for a second time just how right his friend had been. He had wanted her out of sight and out of mind, but it was obvious that she wasn't going to cooperate with what he wanted.

As always, Jenny was going to do exactly what she wanted to do when she wanted to do it.

Cole's irritation grew as he thought about her. He hadn't thought it possible, but Jenny was even prettier now than she had been two years before. She'd been lovely then, but she was even more beautiful now. He had been in love with her for some time before he'd finally proposed. He'd waited until she was old enough to marry, and he'd been thrilled when she'd said yes. He had played the perfect gentleman—never letting on how much he desired her. There had been any number of occasions when he'd been tempted to do more than just give her a chaste kiss, but he'd controlled himself. He had always respected and honored her, for he had wanted their wedding night to be special for them.

Cole's mouth twisted bitterly at the thought of their wedding night.

It had been special all right—especially painful.

Cole vaguely recalled all those hours he'd spent drinking at the High Time. He had thought he would be making love to Jenny that night, not downing a large portion of a bottle of whiskey all by himself at a saloon.

He had thought Jenny loved him as much as he loved her.

He had thought they would have a wonderful life together.

He'd been wrong.

Cole had sworn he was never going to make a mistake like that again. It didn't matter how beautiful a woman was or how much he wanted her, he was never going to let himself care about anyone the way he'd cared for Jenny. He'd learned the lesson the hard way, and it was a lesson he would never forget.

When the main house at the Branding Iron came into view, Cole was glad. His fury had subsided some, but he still felt in need of a drink. Things were not going to get any easier for him until the future of the Lazy S had been resolved. He could only hope Marsden would convince Jenny that the smart thing for her to do was to sell out to him.

Cole let himself into the house and poured himself a whiskey. He savored the liquor as he thought about the days to come. As much as he tried not to think about it, he couldn't help wondering how he would manage if Jenny really did stay on.

His worries would not be dismissed as he retired that night. What sleep he managed to get was restless.

Morning found Cole up early. He took care of his own ranch business and then got ready to ride to Durango. His lack of sleep had not helped his mood, and he doubted that it was going to improve any until the meeting with the lawyer and Jenny was over.

Jenny dressed sedately as she prepared for her trip into town the following day.

"You look lovely, dear," Evelyn told her when she came downstairs. "Are you sure you don't want me or one of the hands to ride into town with you?"

"There's no need," Jenny said, knowing that her aunt must be exhausted from all the traveling they'd done.

"Are you sure?"

"It's an easy ride. I'll be fine," Jenny said.

In truth, she selfishly wanted some time alone just to think about all that had happened. She needed to plan how she was going to handle things. It was plain to see that a lot of work needed to be done around the ranch, and she was ready to get started once this meeting with the lawyer had been taken care of.

Evelyn waved from the front porch as Jenny drove off in the buckboard. The prospect of seeing Cole again did not improve Jenny's mood, but there was no way out of it.

The ride into town passed quickly, and Jenny girded herself for what was to come as she entered the lawyer's office. As she'd expected, Cole was already there when Andrew Marsden ushered her into his inner office. What surprised her was not only the presence of Judge Harold Lawson, but also the town's most prestigious banker, Lyle Stevens. A short time later, she understood all too clearly why the banker was also in attendance.

"But you can't be serious!" Jenny exclaimed.

Her expression was one of complete disbelief as she looked from Andrew Marsden to Lyle Stevens and then over at Judge Lawson, who was there to oversee the reading of the will. Lyle Stevens had just given her devastating news, and though she wanted to deny it, from the looks on their faces, she knew it was true.

"I'm sorry to have to be the one to tell you these things, Jenny," Lyle Stevens said.

"But my father was too good a businessman to have let this happen!"

"I'm afraid it's all true," Andrew Marsden said. He'd known this moment was coming and, as much as he regretted having to give her bad news, there was no way to avoid it.

"My father would never have let things get in this condition," she insisted.

"Miss Sullivan, it's true your father was very astute in his business dealings, but the trouble on the Lazy S all started with the blizzard we had winter before last," Lyle Stevens explained. "Ask Cole, here. He can tell you how bad things were. The Lazy S lost a large part of its herd. Cole had been working with your father for over a year now, trying to help him rebuild the stock."

Jenny was aghast at what she'd just learned. Why hadn't her father ever told her any of this? Why hadn't he let her know that the Lazy S was in dire financial straits? She was hurt that he hadn't confided in her. She could have quit school and come home to help him! Instead, from what they'd just explained to her, he had borrowed heavily from the bank to keep things going. It seemed that Cole, not she, had been there to help her father after the hard times had befallen him—hard times that she'd known nothing about!

"And then your father reported to me that several times a number of head disappeared."

"You mean there was rustling going on?" Jenny asked, even more shocked by this bad news. Why hadn't her father ever told her? She wondered if they had anything positive to tell her.

"It's been widespread. A number of ranches were hit, mine included," Cole put in.

"Do you have any idea who's behind it?"

"No. There was talk for a while of hiring a range detective, but the losses let up, so nothing was done," Cole explained.

Jenny looked back over at the banker, trying her best not to let her distress show.

"How much money is available?" she asked, trying to figure out how much time she had to turn things around.

Lyle Stevens went into detail with her. He showed her the books and explained all of the transactions that had taken place.

Cole listened closely, too, as they went over all the

facts and figures. As executor, the Lazy S would be his responsibility, and he needed to know all that was going on.

"So what you're telling me is that, basically, I have only enough money to keep the ranch going for four more months," Jenny said quietly.

She frowned as she considered the seriousness of her situation. Things did not look good. The possibility of taking Cole up on his offer to buy the ranch flitted through her thoughts, but she immediately dismissed it.

"If you're lucky and nothing unexpected happens, yes," Lyle answered honestly.

"Cole's offer for the ranch is a substantial one and quite fair. It would be enough to pay off your debts and see you comfortably settled with an inheritance in the bank to live on," Marsden put in, trying to encourage her to take that course of action. He knew what a hard job it would be to bring the ranch back to its former glory. Paul had been having a terrible time trying to recoup his losses. Marsden could just imagine how difficult it was going to be for Jenny.

Jenny looked up at the lawyer, her expression determined and a bit mutinous.

"I'm not going to sell the ranch," she declared with finality. "It meant too much to my father, and it means too much to me."

The lawyer and the banker exchanged concerned looks, while Judge Lawson counseled her.

"Miss Sullivan," Lawson began, "I understand that

this bad news about the state of your finances is upsetting to you right now, but it's important that you make your decisions based on sound logic and hard facts, not just emotion. I would hate for you to ultimately lose everything because you wouldn't listen to reason."

Jenny rose to her feet, glaring at him. "So would I, Judge Lawson, but I have no intention of selling out and running away from my responsibility."

Cole was startled by her fierce determination to stay. She'd thought nothing of packing up and running away from him on their wedding day. He'd expected her to do the same now—pack up and get out of town as soon as she'd heard the truth about the state of her finances.

"But restoring the ranch will be a monumental task," Marsden cautioned her. "Your father hadn't been certain that he could bring the Lazy S back. We've shown you what bad shape it's in. If your father had serious doubts, what makes you think that you can do it?"

She gave a stubborn lift of her chin as she leveled a serious gaze upon the lawyer. "The Lazy S is my father's legacy to me. I owe it to him to do everything I can to make sure the ranch is a success."

"While I admire your spirit, Miss Sullivan—" the judge began.

"I'm sure Cole will work with me and help me do whatever is necessary to make the ranch pay again," she interrupted, looking at Cole. "After all, he is the executor and has been entrusted with the job of making sure everything in my father's estate is handled properly until I'm twenty-five, isn't that right?" She deliberately didn't mention the "or married" part in her father's will.

Marsden, Stevens, and Judge Lawson all looked expectantly at Cole.

"Cole?" Marsden asked, waiting to see what he had to say about her decision.

Cole had been listening to the exchange in silence. He glanced up at Jenny, who stood proudly and defiantly next to him.

"Are you absolutely certain that you don't want to sell out and go back East?"

"Why does everybody keep asking me if I want to sell? I'm not going to run away from my responsibilities here."

"If things get tough, you're not going to just up and disappear?" Cole pressed. He felt a bit of shame over the satisfaction he got when he saw her flinch at his words.

"I'm not going anywhere," she declared.

After a moment, Cole gave a terse nod. "If this is what Jenny wants to do, then we'll do it."

"But, Cole—Paul was having one hell of a—Excuse me, Jenny—Paul was having a lot of trouble making ends meet. If he couldn't keep things running smoothly at the Lazy S, how is one woman going to—"

Cole silenced him with a sharp look. "I'll work

with Jenny to see that everything is handled properly, and that all debts are paid in a timely manner."

"You are the executor of the estate, Cole. As such, you're in charge. Whatever you say goes." Judge Lawson then looked at Jenny and directed his next comments to her. "You should report to Cole directly. He is the authority on Lazy S business."

"If that's the way my father wanted it, then that will be fine," she agreed with less than enthusiasm.

It bothered Jenny greatly that she was indebted to Cole for the help he'd given her father. She'd had no idea that Cole and her father had remained such good friends after the canceled wedding. There was no doubt that Cole had little use for her. Establishing and maintaining any kind of relationship with him would not be easy for her, and she was certain that he felt the same way. She would have to do her best to keep any contact with Cole to an absolute minimum.

"Good," Marsden stated.

"Things will remain as they are, then. If any problems arise, just notify me." Judge Lawson turned and spoke directly to Cole next. "And, Cole, you will be diligent in performing all the duties appointed to you?"

"I will," he told the judge.

"I will expect a report from you regularly."

"Yes, sir."

"I guess we're finished here for now, unless you have any more questions, Miss Sullivan?" Marsden announced.

"I think everything is settled," she said.

As Lawson and Marsden walked with Stevens into the outer office, Jenny and Cole were left alone.

Jenny felt victorious. She had stood her ground against these men, refusing to sell to Cole when it would have been the easy way out. She knew her father would have been proud of her. The Lazy S was too important to be cast aside. There was too much of her father in the ranch. She loved it, and she was going to bring it back to its former glory.

"Is there anything you need from me?" Jenny asked Cole.

"Not a thing," he answered coldly, and he meant it as he rose to leave. There had been a time when he had needed and wanted a lot from her, but not anymore.

For some reason, Cole's response bothered Jenny, but she wasn't about to let him know it. She nodded and started from the office.

"Fine. I'll be going. I'll let you know if I incur any major expenses. With Louie there to help me run things, everything should be all right."

Cole watched her as she turned her back on him and, without another word, walked away. Something about the proud way she carried herself impressed him, in spite of himself. He didn't want to be impressed by her. He didn't want to feel anything for her, but he did begrudgingly admire her determination to try to save the ranch.

His gaze shifted lower then, and he found himself

watching the sway of her hips as she left the office. When he realized what he was doing and the direction of his thoughts, he gave a silent curse and tore his gaze away.

She meant nothing to him!

She was pretty, but so were a lot of other women.

It was only when she'd finally gone from the outer office that he went to join the other men.

"As executor, Cole, you'll be in charge of what's going on out at the Lazy S. It's your responsibility now, and from the looks of things, Jenny's going to need all the help and guidance you can give her," Judge Lawson informed him. Then he asked, daring to broach the subject that no one had spoken of yet, "Working with Jenny is not going to prove too awkward for you, is it? If you find you can't deal with her, there may be some legal way to replace you." He had sensed an unspoken tension between them and wanted to make sure that they would be able to get along.

"No. There won't be a problem. I'm doing this for Paul. It was what he wanted," Cole assured him.

They shook hands all around, and Cole left.

Jenny had already gone when Cole emerged onto the street. For some reason, it disappointed him, though he wasn't sure why. He mounted up and started home to the Branding Iron. He had ignored his own duties for too long.

Even as Cole made the ride home, though, his thoughts lingered on Jenny. In spite of all his irritation over her decision, he reluctantly admitted to himself that she was an exceptionally brave woman. He didn't know another female who would be capable of taking over and running a spread the size of the Lazy S. Of course, he wasn't sure Jenny could do it, but the ranch obviously meant a lot to her and she was going to fight for it. She was proving to be every bit as stubborn as Paul had told him she was.

Cole decided that he would make a weekly visit to the ranch to check on things. He would also continue with the plans that he and Paul had made to rebuild the Lazy S's herd. He wasn't looking forward to the next few years of being in charge there, but with any luck at all, the time would pass quickly.

Chapter Seven

Jenny was deeply troubled as she made the trip back home. The news from the banker had not been good. She had to admit that even though she'd put on a good show for them in the office, she was more than a bit scared about what the future held for the Lazy S. There was only one thing she was sure of—no matter what path she chose to take, the next few years were not going to be easy.

The main buildings of the Lazy S came into view in the distance then, and Jenny reined in. She sat there quietly in the buckboard, surveying the scene below with new eyes. The day before, she had seen only what her heart had wanted her to see. She had not taken the time to look at things critically, but had pictured the love and warmth she'd known existed there. Now, though, she was staring at the bunkhouses, the stable, corrals, and the main house with a critical eye, and to her dismay, she found them wanting.

It was all too obvious that her father had not kept up the property as he should have. Things were starting to look a bit run-down. The revelation was startling to her and reminded her that her father had kept so much hidden from her about their financial troubles, even while he'd been sending money to her back East to pay for her expenses. Guilt followed, knowing the ranch had suffered for her way of life.

"I'm going to pay you back, Papa," she vowed out loud as she gazed down at the scene before her. "I promise."

Urging her team on again, Jenny drove the rest of the way down to the stable. She left the buckboard with the hands and went up to the house. She greeted Evelyn and Frances, giving only vague answers to their questions about what had happened at the meeting in town. She didn't want to worry them yet. Then she secluded herself in the study, determined to make a plan for the future.

As the hours passed and Jenny didn't emerge from the study, Evelyn began to worry. She sensed that something was terribly wrong, yet she wasn't sure how to approach Jenny and get her to talk about what had happened. Using dinner as an excuse to seek her out and engage her in conversation, Evelyn brought a tray of food to the study. It took her a few minutes to encourage her niece to open up and tell her the truth, but when she finally did, Evelyn was glad. The ranch's financial troubles were real, and Jenny was going to need all the help and support she could get.

"What are we going to do?" Evelyn's concern was real.

"You are so sweet," Jenny said with heartfelt emotion.

"I am? Why?" She was surprised by niece's statement. She wondered what her being "sweet" had to do with saving the Lazy S.

"You just said 'we,' " Jenny answered.

"Darling, you should know by now that I couldn't love you more if you were my own daughter. Anything I can do to help you, I'll do. I have some money put away in the bank, and you're more than welcome to use it."

"No. I refuse to take your life savings." Jenny quickly dismissed that idea. "That money is all you've got in the world. Getting the Lazy S back in good financial shape is something I have to accomplish on my own. I can't rely on anyone else."

"But how?"

"I don't know yet. I only know that it's not going to be easy. I have to figure out the best way to turn the Lazy S into a money-maker again."

"Did you ask Cole? Did he have any suggestions?"

"I didn't ask, and he didn't offer. I think Judge Lawson, Mr. Stevens, and Mr. Marsden were all a little angry with me for refusing to sell the ranch to Cole."

"That is the logical thing to do, you know," Evelyn pointed out.

"When it comes to the Lazy S, I'm not logical. I love this place, Aunt Evelyn. It's like it's a living, breathing part of me. I don't want to lose it."

"I knew you got homesick occasionally, but I always thought you enjoyed the life we led in Philadelphia."

"I did. I enjoyed my time with you very much. I just didn't realize how much I missed Colorado until I came back. Now that I'm here, I don't ever want to leave again."

"So how did things work out with Cole?"

"I'm sure he would have preferred that I sell him the ranch so we wouldn't have to spend any time together," she answered.

"Has he ever said anything about what happened between the two of you?"

"Not a word, and I'm glad. That's all in the past. It's over. I'm sure he doesn't harbor any fond feelings for me, and I really can't blame him. The one thing I'm glad about is that after talking with him and the judge and lawyer today, I believe Cole and I should be able to work together to take care of ranch business."

"Good. I'm glad it turned out that way. I know how worried you were about the possibility of just seeing Cole again, and then to find out that he was the executor— Well, I was very concerned for you."

"Everything will be fine once I think of a way for

the Lazy S to make some money. Papa never told me how bad things really were. I wish he had. I might have been able to do something to help him sooner." She quickly explained about how her father had lost so many head of cattle to the blizzard and rustlers and how he'd been working to build things back up.

"Are there any other ways to make money on a ranch besides running cattle?" Evelyn asked.

"That's why I've been sitting here going over the books. I need to make some money—a large amount, as quickly as possible."

"You could sell some of your cattle," her aunt offered, trying to be helpful.

"Yes, but I don't have enough head to make the kind of profit I need."

"What else could you do here? Take in boarders like the Widow Harrison did in Philadelphia?" Evelyn laughed as she thought of how remote their location was and how few people would happen to ride by the ranch and decide to stay.

"Or like Tessa does in Durango." Jenny thought of the young woman who ran a very successful boardinghouse in town. She frowned thoughtfully at her aunt's suggestion. "You know, you just may have something there."

"Have something where?"

"The boarder thing. Did I ever tell you how many of my friends back at school envied the fact that I grew up on a 'real Western ranch'?"

"They did? I was afraid they were going to make

fun of you for having come from Colorado—"

"Not at all. Any number of the girls wanted to know what it was like to live in the 'Wild West.' They were very excited about it." A slow, enigmatic smile curved Jenny's lips as an idea took shape in her mind.

"What are you thinking, Jenny? I know that look of yours, and it usually means trouble."

"Not this time. I think you're brilliant, Aunt Evelyn!" Jenny jumped up and ran around the desk to hug her aunt and plant a kiss on her cheek. "Thanks!"

"For what? What did I do?"

"It's not what you did, It's what you said! You gave me an idea!"

"I did?"

"Yes. About boarders."

"What about boarders?" Evelyn was totally confused.

"That's exactly what I'm going to do. I'm going to start taking in boarders—or maybe I should call them 'guests.' I'll charge them a considerable sum to stay here on a 'real ranch' and experience what it's like to live in the honest-to-gosh Wild West!"

Evelyn stared at her niece as if she had lost her mind. "Who would you take in? Who would want to come here?"

"Easterners!" Jenny was growing more excited with each passing minute as she considered the number of people who'd be interested. "It will work out perfectly. Of course, I'll have to come up with a plan on how to get the word out."

"But where will you put the boarders once they arrive?" Evelyn was confused. There were only three bedrooms in the main ranch house, and she and Jenny were using two of them.

"I can fix up that old bunkhouse that nobody's using right now. I can convert it into a cabin for our paying guests."

"Even if you did get someone to come, how long would they want to stay, and what would they do while they were here?"

"They could stay for as long as they wanted to. If they have the money, we've got room for them. We could take them out riding, and they could go on roundups. There might even be some who'd want to go hunting or fishing."

"Do you really think anyone would come?" Evelyn was still doubtful.

"I'm positive. I'm going to write to my friend Rose right away. I know she would want to come for a visit, and probably her cousin Melanie, too. Rose always talked about how much she wanted to see the West. If I could get enough money together, I could run ads in the newspapers back East. I'm sure that would get people excited about coming." Jenny's mind was racing as she considered all the possibilities.

"How long will it take to get things ready?"

"I don't know. I'd better talk to Frances and Louie

first and enlist their help. I'll need Frances to take care of all the extra cooking and cleaning, and Louie will have to be in charge of arranging the hunting and fishing trips."

"You know, it just might work."

"I know!" Jenny was truly excited. "First thing tomorrow morning, I'll take a closer look around that bunkhouse and see how much work needs to be done. I would think if everything goes all right, I could have the place ready for paying guests in less than a month."

"But it's going to take a lot of money to fix everything up the way you want it. Have you got enough set aside in the bank?"

"Yes, but I don't think the repairs will be that expensive, especially if I do them myself."

"You know how to do that kind of work? Why, that's manual labor!" Evelyn was amazed.

"Papa insisted I learn everything about running a ranch, and that included mending fences and fixing anything that was broken."

"Well, I'm not too old to learn how to use a hammer. I'll help you with whatever you want me to do," she volunteered.

"Thanks, Aunt Evelyn." She lifted her gaze to her aunt's. "I don't know what I would have done without you."

Evelyn hugged her. "You're a smart young woman, Jenny. If anybody can make this work, you will. Should you notify Cole of your plans?"

The thought of having to go to Cole to ask him for anything irked her, especially after the way they'd parted earlier that day. She had a feeling that he would probably try to argue with her and convince her that the idea wouldn't work. But she was going to show him. She was going to show all of them.

"Not right away. I'll start repairing the bunkhouse and try to get that in order before I tell him anything about it."

"That's going to be a big job. You'll need some building supplies, won't you?"

"Yes, and if Cole asks about the bills, I'll tell him. But until he does, I'm not offering any information."

"I'm sure he'll think it's a brilliant idea when he finds out," Evelyn said encouragingly.

Jenny didn't agree with her, but said nothing. There would be plenty of time later to argue the point.

"When do you want to get started?"

"First thing in the morning," she said with determination. "The sooner I get to work on the repairs, the sooner the Lazy S Guest Ranch is going to be ready to open for customers."

Tired as she was, Jenny stayed up late that night. She was too excited to think about sleeping. She wrote a long letter to her friend Rose, explaining everything and inviting her to come and visit. Rose was quite a force in her prestigious social set back in Philadelphia, and Jenny was sure that she could be instrumental in encouraging others to come to the Lazy S to enjoy a real Wild West adventure. Word of mouth was a powerful thing, and she had already learned how curious Easterners were about anything Western.

Jenny was up with the dawn. She rummaged through the old clothes in the back of her closet until she'd found just what she was looking for—a pair of boy's pants and a work shirt. Before she'd gone away to school, she'd worn them regularly whenever she worked with her father around the ranch.

Jenny tugged on the clothes and felt a sense of freedom at being so clad again. There was something very liberating about wearing pants, especially when she was riding astride. She wondered why more women didn't just defy convention and wear them. She thought of her friend Rose then and knew she would be scandalized at the thought of a female wearing men's pants. Jenny smiled, thinking of how much fun it would be to scandalize Rose when she came to the ranch.

After eating a quick breakfast, Jenny headed out to the bunkhouse to assess the repairs that needed to be done and to make a list of the supplies she'd need to complete them. The deteriorating building definitely needed a substantial amount of work, but she felt she was up to it. The roof was in poor shape, and a window needed to be replaced. After serious consideration, Jenny decided she could partition the building off, giving the women their own private quarters. The bunkhouse was big enough to accommodate both the men and the women with separate entrances.

Her decision made, Jenny wrote out the list of materials she needed. She sought out one of the hands and sent him into town to pick them up and to mail her letter off to Rose. With any luck, Jenny hoped that by the time she heard from her friend, the improvements to the bunkhouse would be completed.

"Jenny! What in heaven's name are you wearing?" Evelyn exclaimed as Jenny came back inside the house. It was the first time Evelyn had seen her that morning, and she was shocked by the sight of her niece wearing pants.

Jenny grinned at her. "I've got a lot of hard work to do today, so I dressed for it."

"But pants? That's scandalous!" Evelyn was still staring at her, aghast.

"In Philadelphia, yes, but here it's actually very practical, Aunt Evelyn. I used to wear them all the time."

"Thank God you never wore them at school!"

"I was tempted a few times, believe me," she laughed. "And after a few more weeks of living here with me, I bet I can convince you to start wearing them, too. They're really very comfortable."

Evelyn only looked stricken at the thought of being caught wearing men's pants. "But aren't you the least concerned that someone might see you—"

"No, Aunt Evelyn, I'm not," she said more gently as she kissed her aunt on the cheek. "I'm home now, and this is how I dress when I've got work to do. I don't have time to worry about what other people might say. I've got a ranch to run."

Evelyn watched her walk off down the hall, and in spite of herself, she found she was smiling. Jenny had certainly grown into a woman who knew her own mind.

Chapter Eight

Cole had no idea what was going on at the Lazy S, but he was bound and determined to find out. He'd thought he and Jenny had had an understanding about the way to handle things—that she would come to him and clear any expenditures with him before she bought anything. It had only been a week since he'd spoken with her, but judging from the sizable bill he'd just received, she had decided to take care of things on her own without bothering to consult him.

Cole couldn't imagine why Jenny thought she needed all the building supplies she'd purchased. Her house was in good shape, and so was the stable the last time he'd checked. He could think of no logical reason for the expenses she'd incurred.

His mood was positively surly. He really didn't

want to go to the Lazy S. He really didn't want to see her again.

As the ranch house came into view, to Cole's surprise he spotted two people working on the roof of one of the outbuildings. He continued on, trying to make out who the people were and what they were doing. He reined in abruptly when he realized one of the workers was Jenny.

There was no mistaking her.

Even though it had been two years since he'd last seen her so clad, there was no forgetting the way she looked wearing pants. And that was what she had on today—a tight-fitting pair of trousers just like she used to wear all the time before she'd gone back East to school.

Unbidden heat surged through Cole. Watching her brought it all back—the passion he had felt for her, the way he'd ached with wanting her—The way he'd denied himself waiting for their wedding night. He had loved her so . . .

Cole swore to himself as he pushed those memories aside.

What the hell was Jenny doing up on that roof? Was she trying to get herself killed?

He urged his horse to a gallop and charged forward, determined to get her down before she fell and hurt herself.

Jenny heard the sound of a rider coming and looked up.

"Looks like we've got some company," she told Tom Wilson, who was helping her. He was the youngest hand on the Lazy S, and Louis had delegated him to work with her on the roof repairs.

"Isn't that Cole Randall?"

"Yes, and I don't know why he's in such a hurry. I hope nothing's wrong."

They both stopped their work and moved closer to the roof's edge to wait for him to draw near.

"What are you doing up on the roof, woman?" Cole demanded harshly as he reined in before them. He ignored Tom, fixing his angry gaze directly on Jenny.

His unprovoked verbal assault irritated Jenny. She faced him defiantly, glaring down at him.

"I'm working," she answered sarcastically. "What did you think I was doing?"

Had he been in a more conciliatory mood, Cole would have thought she looked like an avenging angel, but he was too furious to harbor any gentler thoughts.

"That's what you've got hired help for! Get down from there right now!" It was an order.

Jenny bristled at his tone of command. He had no authority over her. He might be the executor of the will, but he wasn't her boss. She was her own boss. She was the one running the Lazy S, and she was doing what needed to be done to save the place. That was all that mattered to her.

"Tom's been helping me," she answered. "He was the only hand Louie could spare, and we both know there's no extra money to hire more help."

"Well, get down and I'll finish it for you," he dictated as he dismounted and started toward the ladder.

"There's no need for you to help. Tom and I can do it. In fact, we're almost done. This is our second day."

Cole stood near the foot of the ladder and looked the building over. It was in poor condition. It was very obvious no one had lived in it for quite a while.

"Why are you wasting your time and money fixing this place up? You don't need it for anything."

"Oh, yes, I do," she told him. Then she looked at her helper. "Tom, why don't you go get us another bucket of nails? I left them just inside the barn door."

"Yes, ma'am." The youth climbed down from the roof and hurried off, leaving her alone with Cole.

Cole decided to take a look at the work they'd been doing. He climbed the ladder to survey their handiwork.

Jenny wasn't sure why he was coming up to the roof, and she took an uneasy step backward to keep the distance between them.

"Does our work meet with your approval?" she asked when she noticed that he seemed to be inspecting what they'd done.

"Not too bad a job," was all he said, though he was impressed that she knew how to repair a roof. "If you're not hiring any new hands and don't need an extra bunkhouse, what are you planning to use this for?"

Jenny had been waiting for just that question. "It's going to be my guest house," she announced with pride. "I've decided to turn the Lazy S into a paying guest ranch."

"A what?"

"A guest ranch," she repeated with dignity. "There are any number of people back East who would willingly pay a lot of money to stay here for a few days."

"Are you crazy? This is a working cattle ranch."

"Exactly, and that's what people want to see. They read about ranches all the time, but few ever get to really experience what it's like in the 'Wild West.' They want to understand how a ranch really works. I can give them a taste of that right here on the Lazy S, and I can make money doing it."

"It won't work," he said disparagingly.

"Oh, yes, it will! You'll see. Besides"—she sobered and looked him straight in the eye—"what have I got to lose by trying? I had to come up with a new idea. After what the banker said about how low the cash reserve was, I had to think of a quick way to make some real money."

"Which brings me to the reason why I'm here today," he interrupted her. "The bill I got—"

"Was for the materials I need to transform this bunkhouse into more accommodating quarters for my paying guests," she said finishing his sentence for him. "I know it's a lot of money, but think of it as an investment. I've always heard that when you're in business, you have to spend money to make money."

Cole was staring at Jenny thoughtfully, seeing a side of her he'd never seen before. He'd always known she was an intelligent woman, but he'd never known that she had any business sense.

"And just what makes you think this wild idea of yours is going to make any money?"

"All the talk I heard while I was back in school! If it was any indication of the way people really feel about coming out West, once I start renting the rooms, we're going be full of travelers all year round."

"You really believe there are people who would pay money to stay here?"

"Oh, yes. In fact, I've already written to my friend Rose and invited her to come and visit for a week or so. She's quite the social butterfly in Philadelphia, and once she goes back home and starts to talk about her trip, she'll get the word out nicely for us. Then, once the guests start arriving, the sky's the limit to what we can do at thc Lazy S Guest Ranch."

"You really believe that?"

"Yes." She met his gaze straight on. She refused to let him know how afraid she was that he would block her efforts. She knew Cole could stop her if he chose to, and knowing how he really felt about her, she was afraid he would try to ensure her failure. "This is my home, Cole. I can't lose it. I won't lose it. I'm going to do everything in my power to keep it going—and to make it a success."

Cole fell silent for a moment, considering the constraints of her financial situation. The bill for supplies was a big one, but her sentiments were so real and so heartfelt that he found he couldn't refuse her. He had serious doubts about her idea, but he knew what he had to do: he would pay the bill out of his own pocket and not mention it to anyone. What Jenny didn't know couldn't hurt her.

"Cole?" she said after a long moment. "Are you going to go along with me on this? I really think I can make it work."

His expression was unreadable as he answered gruffly, "If this is what you really want to try, then I'll do what I can to help you."

"You will?" She stared at him in disbelief, relief and delight rushing through her.

"Yes."

"Thank you! You won't be sorry! You'll see!" she told him, smiling widely at him. She couldn't believe Cole was being so kind and supportive. She'd expected to have to fight him. She almost hugged him, but controlled the impulse.

"I hope not," he muttered under his breath, feeling a bit uncomfortable. Lord knows, he was sorry enough about other dealings he'd had with her.

Tom had returned and was standing at the bottom of the ladder, waiting to climb up and go back to work.

"Come on up, Tom. Despite your boss's objections, I'm going to help you finish the roof. With three of us working on it, we can get it done that much sooner," Cole offered climbing off the ladder to stand on the roof with Jenny.

Jenny was surprised by Cole's offer and glanced quickly at him. "You don't have to help. We can handle it."

For some reason, it irritated him that she didn't seem to want his help.

"Humor me. At least if I'm up here with you, I'll be able to catch you if you start to fall."

He said it so harshly that she took an unconscious step backward. "I'm not going to—"

Even as she started to say it, she stepped on an uneven shingle. Her foot twisted and slipped out from under her. With a gasp, she lost her balance and fell awkwardly. She started to slide toward the edge, certain that she was going to fall completely off the roof.

His worst fear realized, Cole reacted instinctively. In one quick move, he managed to grab Jenny. He hauled her up bodily against him, saving her from certain injury.

"Miss Jenny! Are you all right?" Tom shouted as he scrambled quickly the rest of the way up the ladder.

Jenny couldn't answer right away. Her heart was pounding in her throat as she clutched at Cole. One minute she'd been certain she was going to fall, and the next she'd been swept into the safe haven of Cole's arms.

As her terror slowly gave way, she became aware of more than just his strong arms around her. She realized she was pressed full-length against Cole, her breasts crushed against the hard width of his chest, her thighs tight against his. She was trembling, but this time it wasn't from fear. There was something elemental about being this close to him, and the unexpected power of her reaction to Cole left her confused and unsure.

"Jenny?" Cole said her name slowly, worriedly, as he looked down at her.

Fear had filled him when he'd seen her lose her balance and start to fall. His reaction had been immediate and instinctive, just like his physical reaction to her now. Everyplace she touched him, he ached and burned. He didn't want to release her. He wanted to keep her close. He wanted to hold her and never let her go.

Logic returned, but it still took a herculean effort for Cole to finally set her away from him.

A part of him wanted to hold her longer, to keep her near.

But he didn't.

He told himself to stop fantasizing about Jenny. There was nothing between them. She had made that clear two years ago, and it was going to stay that way now, because that was the way he wanted it to be.

"Thank you, Cole—" Jenny finally whispered, drawing a ragged breath as she steadied herself.

"You're all right?"

"I think so."

"That was close," Tom said nervously as he came

to stand with them. He looked up at Cole admiringly. "You saved her."

Cole shrugged, casting one last quick look at Jenny. "You sure you're all right?"

Jenny nodded, her gaze meeting and holding his. For an instant, she was lost in the depths of his intense dark eyes. Cole was such a strong man. And he was handsome, too—definitely more handsome than she'd remembered. She found herself wondering why some other woman hadn't snatched him up.

Jenny vaguely realized that she couldn't recall Cole ever holding her close like that before. Their time together two years ago had been very closely chaperoned. As she thought about it, Jenny realized that she and Cole had never really had much time alone during their engagement. She realized, too, that although they had known each other for years, she had never known him as a man. They had always been friends. The startling realization made her frown, and she tore her gaze away from his, lest he see the confusion in her eyes.

"We'd better get to work if we're going to finish today," she said, distracting herself.

Jenny did not want to reflect too deeply on what had just happened. In the back of her mind, though, she knew there was no denying that she'd been stunned by the sensual awareness that had rocketed through her when she'd been crushed against Cole's hard, lean body. She reached for the bucket of nails that Tom had brought with him, ready to go back to work.

"Yes, ma'am," Tom answered.

"I'm ready if you are," Cole told her, his business-like tone completely changing the mood that had momentarily existed between them. "Let's go to work."

Tom didn't know what had transpired between the two of them, and he didn't really care as long as Miss Jenny wasn't hurt. He grabbed his own hammer and started pounding. With Cole's help, he knew they could easily be finished that afternoon.

Just then Evelyn and Frances came hurrying out of the house.

"Jenny! Were you hurt? What happened?" Evelyn called to her niece as they ran to the bunkhouse. "Frances and I saw you fall, and we were worried about you!"

"I'm fine, thanks to Cole," Jenny answered, a little embarrassed by their attention as she cast a sidelong glance at Cole working beside her.

"That was quick thinking on your part, Cole," Evelyn said earnestly, smiling at him. "Thank you. Jenny could have been seriously injured if you hadn't been there to save her."

"I'm just glad I was able to help," he replied.

He didn't look at Jenny, though he was very much aware of her nearness. He was glad she hadn't been hurt, but if she'd had any sense at all, she wouldn't have been up there on the roof in the first place. Even now as they continued to work side by side, he would have felt much better if she'd been down with the other women where he could be sure she was safe.

"How much more do you have to do up there? Are you going to be much longer?" Frances asked.

"It'll probably take about another hour with the three of us working," Jenny answered.

"Well, that's perfect. I was getting ready to start fixing dinner, so, Cole, why don't you stay on and eat with us tonight?" Frances invited.

Cole knew the smart thing to do would be to finish the roof and get out of there. The farther away from Jenny he stayed, the better, but for some reason he found himself accepting Frances's invitation. He told himself it wasn't all that unusual for him to eat there at the Lazy S. He had often stayed for dinner when Paul was alive.

"I'd like that, Frances. Thanks."

Chapter Nine

Cole didn't know why he'd agreed to stay. He'd come to the Lazy S strictly to talk finances with Jenny, had ended up working on the roof, and was now obligated to spend even more time in her company over dinner.

And spending time with Jenny was something he didn't want to do.

Again, Cole wondered why Paul had put him in this position; he must have guessed how awkward it would be. Paul could just as easily have picked Andrew Marsden or Lyle Stevens to do the job, especially since he'd known how Cole felt about Jenny.

Thoughts of Paul brought Cole up short, and he immediately regretted the resentment he'd been feeling. Sadness filled him. It would have been easy to stand by and let the Lazy S go under. Then he could have bought it up cheap, and Jenny would leave. But

Cole took the job Paul had entrusted to him seriously. His friend had known the ranch was in trouble and needed his help. That was why Paul had chosen him, and Cole would do his best, no matter how difficult it was to be near Jenny.

Cole worked on the roof at a tireless pace. He focused on the job before him, trying to ignore the fact that Jenny was always near—the curve of her hip always visible from the corner of his eye. Ignoring her was proving to be next to impossible—especially after what had transpired earlier—but Cole had always prided himself on being a man of iron will and self-control. As physically attractive as he might find Jenny to be, she meant nothing to him. The woman he had thought he loved years ago, never really existed. He was there helping out because it was what Paul would have wanted him to do.

When the final repair had been made, Cole stood up, more than ready to call it a day.

"Do you need any help getting down?" he asked Jenny, holding out his hand to her as she carefully made her way toward the ladder carrying her tools.

"No, I'll be fine."

He found himself frowning when she dodged his outstretched hand. Cole couldn't decide whether he was glad she hadn't wanted his help or irritated because she'd so obviously avoided his touch.

After Jenny had descended the ladder, Cole let Tom go down ahead of him. When at last Cole climbed down, Jenny had already started off to the main house; that was fine with him. He stopped at the water pump to clean up before following her inside.

"Come on in, Cole. We'll be ready to eat as soon as I get these last few dishes on the table," Evelyn called to him from the dining room as he came in the front door.

The aroma from Frances's home cooking was mouthwatering. For all his misgivings about staying for dinner, Cole would never regret taking the opportunity to eat one of her meals. She was one of the best cooks around. He entered the dining room to find the two older women bustling around the table.

"Jenny went upstairs to freshen up. She'll be down in a few minutes. Sit down and relax. You've been working hard," Evelyn invited as she sat down at the table.

"Thanks." He took the seat across from her, with Frances on his left.

"Did you finish the roof?" Evelyn asked.

"It's all done. Of course, Jenny won't know for sure how good a job we did until the next rain," he said with a grin.

"I'm sure it'll be fine," Frances joined in. "It's going to be interesting to see how the interior turns out."

"It's a wonderful idea," Evelyn said, and then looked at Cole. "Did she tell you what she intends to do inside?"

"She only mentioned that she was turning it into a guest house of some sort," Cole answered.

"She's going to partition the house—one side will be for men and one for women. Each side will have its own private entrance. That will guarantee the guests' complete privacy."

"So Jenny's really serious about doing this?" he asked thoughtfully.

"Very," Evelyn confirmed. "And she's right about the very real interest people back East have in the Western way of life. The idea of a guest ranch is clever and different. If she lets the right people know what we have to offer here in the way of accommodations and good food and hospitality, I honestly think she can make some decent money at it."

Cole heard the enthusiasm in her voice. "I hope you're right. She's investing a lot of money in fixing up the place."

"If hard work is any sign of ultimate success, then I think we're going to be rich," Jenny said with a laugh as she came into the room to join them.

Cole glanced her way and was surprised by the sense of disappointment that filled him at the sight of her sedate day gown. He'd been expecting her to return still clad in her work pants. He grew irritated with himself for even noticing what she was wearing. It didn't matter if she looked like a sophisticated woman wearing a gown or if she looked like a woman who could take charge of any situation and run things single-handedly in her Western wear. What mattered was that he knew how fickle she could be. At the thought, his heart hardened against her.

"I can't remember the last time I was this tired . . . or this sore," she went on.

"But look at what you've accomplished already," Frances said. "Louie is going to be so impressed when he gets back from working the herd and sees what you've done."

"I want to get the place up and running as quickly as possible. The sooner we open up for paying guests, the faster we can get the Lazy S back on its feet financially."

"Shall we say grace?" Evelyn prompted, folding her hands before her and waiting for the others to do the same. "Bless us, Lord, for these gifts from Thy bounty, through Christ, our Lord. And thank you for a friend like Cole, who is so kind and generous with his help. Amen."

Cole echoed Evelyn's "Amen." He was surprised and touched by her words. He doubted that Jenny agreed with her, though. She probably wanted him to stay as far away as possible for as long as possible. When and if she ever really did need him, it would probably be only for cash.

"How soon do you think you'll have all the work on the bunkhouse completed, so you can start taking in these 'guests'?" Cole asked Jenny as he helped himself from the bowl of steaming potatoes that Frances passed to him.

"If everything goes as planned, I should have the work done in less than two weeks," Jenny answered. "There's enough extra furniture here in the main house to furnish the bunkhouse comfortably, although I will need to buy some new bedding—if that's all right?" She glanced at him, fearing he might deny her the needed funds.

"Get what you think you'll need," Cole told her as he made a mental note to watch for another bill.

She refused to thank him for giving her permission to spend her own money, but she did nod in his direction. It irked her to have to answer to anyone this way, but it especially bothered her to get permission from Cole. Still, he was being amazingly cooperative, and she appreciated that.

"Have you been thinking about the kind of activities you want to arrange for the guests?" Evelyn asked.

"Horseback riding would appeal to both men and women. I think the prospect of hunting and fishing trips will bring in the most men."

"Let's just hope they know which end of a gun to use," Cole put in with a grin.

"Just because they'll be Eastern gentlemen doesn't mean they won't know how to shoot," Jenny said in defense of the men she imagined would be frequenting her ranch. "There are any number of places I could take them where they might find suitable game."

As she considered the best locations on the ranch to hunt in, an image of the high pasture came to her, and with it came the memory of her father's accident.

Her excitement about her plans vanished as her mood suddenly darkened.

"Is something wrong?" Frances asked, seeing the sudden change in Jenny's expression.

"I was just thinking about Papa. It's still so hard for me to believe that he died that way—all alone, and in a riding accident. It doesn't make sense to me."

"We were all shocked when we found out what had happened. It was a terrible thing," Frances sympathized.

"One of these days I'm going to ride up there and take a look around," Jenny said.

"Is there any reason why you think his death wasn't an accident?" Cole asked.

"You would know more about that than I would." Her tone was a bit sharp as she gave vent to some of the resentment she felt at his closeness to her father during the time she'd been gone. "The two of you were close. Was there anything unusual going on? He was an excellent horseman. What could have happened to him to cause him to lose his seat and fall that way?"

Cole couldn't imagine why anyone would want to harm Paul. "Your father was very well liked in town. He didn't have any enemies that I ever knew about. There wasn't anyone who wished him harm. And as far as trouble in the area, the only thing that's been going on is the rustling, and everybody has been hit equally."

"What about Indians? Were there any raids or groups off the reservation?"

"No. Everything's been quiet. There's been no trouble that way at all."

They all fell silent for a moment as they each remembered Paul in his own way—as friend—as brother—as father.

Evelyn and Frances changed the topic then, wanting to lighten the conversation. The rest of the dinner passed easily.

"Thanks for the delicious meal," Cole said as he stood to leave.

"I'll be in touch."

They said good night, and he left the house as Frances began clearing the table.

When Evelyn was certain that Cole was out of earshot, she smiled sweetly at Jenny. "We're very fortunate that Cole's the one your father chose to be executor."

"You really think so?"

"Oh, yes. Not everyone would be as supportive of your trying something so new and outlandish as a guest ranch."

"I know. I was worried when I first talked to him. I was afraid he'd refuse to approve the money. I don't know what I would have done if that had happened."

"Well, it didn't. Cole's a good man. But, you know, you still seem uncomfortable around him," Evelyn said. "Is there something wrong? Has he said anything to you or done anything that has upset you?"

"Oh, no." For some reason, she found herself coming quickly to Cole's defense. "He's been a perfect gentleman—for all that I'm sure he resents every minute he has to spend with me."

"I thought Cole was being most helpful, especially today working on the roof with you like that. Somehow I have trouble picturing either Mr. Marsden or Mr. Stevens pitching in and helping out with manual labor if one of them had been appointed your executor."

"You're right." The mental image of the lawyer or banker on the rooftop made Jenny smile. She stood up and started from the dining room. "I'll be back in a minute."

She followed Cole from the house. She hoped to catch him before he rode away. She wanted to thank him again for his support of her daring endeavor.

Cole was already mounted up and about to leave when Jenny came outside.

"Cole?" she called quietly as she stood at the porch railing.

He was surprised by her appearance, and he wondered what she wanted. "Is something wrong? Did you need something else before I go?"

Cole sounded so terse that she almost changed her mind about thanking him. Instead, telling herself that it was important they keep a good working relationship, she forged ahead.

"No, I don't need anything else. I just wanted to tell you how much I appreciate your help today—and your support of my plan for the guest ranch."

Imitating some of the businessmen she'd seen in Philadelphia, she left the porch and approached Cole.

His gaze narrowed as he watched Jenny coming toward him. He wondered what she was up to. He was taken by surprise when she stopped beside him and reached up, offering him her hand in a very businesslike handshake.

"Thanks, Cole."

There was no way he could refuse to take her hand. He leaned forward, his big hand enveloping her smaller one in a firm, warm grasp. Cole tried not to notice how delicate she seemed or how smooth her skin was to his touch. He released her hand as quickly as he could and straightened in the saddle.

"You're welcome. Just have the rest of the bills sent to me and I'll see that they're paid."

She nodded, feeling a bit sorry that all they had to talk about was business and money. She remembered another time when they used to laugh and have fun together.

Cole rode off and Jenny remained standing where she was, watching until he'd passed out of sight and marveling that the simple touch of his hand had sent a shiver down her spine.

Chapter Ten

It was dark when Cole finally reached the Branding Iron. Though his house wasn't as spacious as the Sullivan place, it was his home and looked good to him.

Cole was surprised to see that his front parlor was lit up. Usually whenever he wasn't around for the evening meal, Fred, the hand who doubled as his cook, just stayed in the bunkhouse and left the house dark. Cole was curious, so instead of riding to the stable first, he went straight to the house to investigate.

"Cole—at last! You're back." Mira Jameson came hurrying out the front door to greet him.

"Mira? What are you doing here?"

Cole was surprised to find her there. He had last spoken to her in town a few weeks ago when he'd escorted her to a social, but he'd had no opportunity to see her since. Life—and Jenny—had interfered.

He supposed Mira was pretty enough with her blond hair and shapely figure, but he had no intention of regularly courting her or anyone else in town. He and Mira got along well. He enjoyed the time they spent together, but that was where it ended for Cole. He had no interest in a serious relationship with any woman.

"I've been missing you, Cole Randall, and thought I'd just come by for a visit. Aren't you glad to see me?"

Mira smiled seductively at him as she closed the distance between them. Without any invitation, she looped her arms around his neck and pulled him down for a hungry kiss. She wanted Cole—had wanted him for ages—and she intended to get him, one way or another. She'd been trying to seduce him for some time. She had managed to maneuver him into several passionate encounters, but she'd never been able to break his self-control. He was proving to be quite a challenge, and she was the type of woman who loved challenges.

Mira's plan was simple. All she wanted to do was make love to him once and then a few weeks later claim that she was carrying his child—whether she was pregnant or not. She was certain that Cole would marry her without question, and they would live happily ever after.

Mrs. Cole Randall—

The thought encouraged her. She deepened the

kiss, pressing herself even more tightly against him, loving the feel of his hard body against her. She had considered waiting naked for him in his bed, but she hadn't been certain that he would respond to so blatant and outrageous a seduction. He was a man who liked to be in control, so she knew she had to appeal to that part of him. She had to let him conquer her. With that in mind, she gave a throaty laugh and drew away from him.

"I am so glad you finally got here, Cole," Mira said. "I've been waiting for you since this afternoon."

"I had some business to take care of," he answered noncommittally. Mira's kiss was enjoyable enough, but he wasn't in the mood—especially after spending the afternoon with Jenny.

"Well, you're home now and that's all that matters. Fred fixed dinner earlier. I can warm something up for you, if you'd like?"

"No. I already ate."

He started indoors, and she fell in beside him, daring to take his arm as they walked. She pressed it to the side of her breast in a seemingly innocent move.

"The reason I came to see you is that I just heard that the Women's Solidarity is going to have a dance in a few weeks, and I couldn't wait to tell you. We had such fun at the last social that I'm really looking forward to this one."

Cole found himself putting her off, although he wasn't sure why. "I'll have to wait until it's closer to the time before I'll know if I can make it or not."

At his statement, Mira's suspicions were confirmed. Cole was always ready for a good time, but now he was being evasive. She'd heard talk that Cole had been named Paul Sullivan's executor and that Jenny had come back to town. It looked like Jenny Sullivan was going to interfere in her life again.

Hatred for the other woman filled Mira. She had despised Jenny for most of her life. Jenny had always been rich, while her own family had had to work hard for their money. It seemed to Mira that she had been in love with Cole forever, but Jenny was the woman Cole had proposed to. When Jenny had walked out on him at the wedding, Mira had been completely shocked. She didn't understand how any woman could not want Cole. She'd been trying to win his love ever since Jenny had gone, but he'd made it plain he wasn't going to get involved with anyone again. That was why she'd come up with her plan to trap him, and she was going to enjoy every minute of the trapping!

When Mira had learned that things were going badly on the Lazy S, it had given her great satisfaction. Jenny Sullivan deserved every miserable, rotten thing that happened to her, but now that her rival had come back, Mira was upset. The farther Jenny stayed from Durango—and Cole—the happier Mira would be.

Mira wondered suddenly if Cole had been over at the Sullivan place. She was tempted to ask, but didn't. She had her own ways of finding things out.

Damn that woman! Thoughts of Jenny's return enraged Mira and made her all the more determined to lure Cole to her bed. If she could manage it, she was going to arrange to spend the night at the Branding Iron tonight. Surely, if she was alone with him, she could arouse him enough to get him to make love to her.

Mira knew her father had started drinking earlier in the day and had passed out by late afternoon. He'd never miss her if she stayed away all night, and her brother was off whoring in town someplace, so she was free to do whatever she pleased—and it pleased her to be there with Cole.

Cole's mood had not been good on the ride home, and finding Mira waiting for him didn't improve it any. He needed some time alone. He stopped at the front door, hesitant to take her inside with him.

"Was there something else you needed, Mira?" He wasn't sure why she had stayed on so late waiting for him. The news of the upcoming social was not that exciting or important to make her so vigilant.

"Only to see you again," she said seductively.

She stopped and turned to look up at him. She gave him her most enticing look, wanting him to take her in his arms and kiss her. When he didn't respond immediately, she kept her disappointment hidden.

"As late as it is . . ."

Cole was not in the mood to be with anyone tonight, not after having held Jenny that afternoon, and he was certainly not going to get seriously involved with another female. He knew that was what Mira wanted—marriage.

"I know it's late. If I'd realized you were going to be gone so long, I wouldn't have stayed on. Now that it's dark, though, do you think I should head home alone or spend the night here with you?" She made the question sound innocent.

Cole hesitated. With no other woman to chaperone them, it would be awkward for her to stay, but he didn't know how he could just send her on her way.

"It's up to you. I can have one of the men ride with you, if you'd like. I wouldn't want to put your reputation at risk."

Mira was so frustrated with Cole, she was ready to curse out loud. Only a flash of distant lightning and the accompanying rumble of thunder saved her from being forced to leave.

"I guess I'd better stay. I'm sure my father will understand when I explain everything," she lied.

Cole wasn't so sure, and he wasn't about to set himself up for trouble. In a way, he regretted that he'd ever let anything come of his casual acquaintance with Mira. He knew she wanted much more from him than he ever planned to give.

"Let's go in. I'll see about fixing up the extra bedroom for you."

She didn't protest his offer but played along. She was delighted that she'd be staying the night. What was going to happen next was anyone's guess, but she was ready and eager for anything.

They sat in the parlor and talked for a while. Then Cole went to make sure the bedroom was ready for her. He was startled when, he turned and found her standing in the doorway watching him. There was a heavy-lidded, almost seductive look about her, but he ignored it.

"I didn't hear you come down the hall," he said as another streak of lightning rent the night sky and was quickly followed by a loud clap of thunder that shook the house.

"I just thought I'd come along and see if you needed any help," she offered.

"No, everything's ready."

"Thanks. And where's your room?" Mira was already planning how she was going to seek him out in the middle of the night. She could tell he was bound and determined to play the gentleman with her, but she was just as determined that he be anything but a gentleman. She wanted him to love her. She wanted him in her bed.

"My bedroom's right there across the hall," he told her, nodding toward the closed door.

"I'm glad you'll be close in case I get frightened in the storm," Mira said innocently.

"Well, this should blow over soon. I'll wake you in the morning before I leave."

"You have to go somewhere early?"

"I'm a rancher. I've got livestock to tend to. If I don't do it, it doesn't get done."

"That's what I love about you, Cole Randall. When

you set your sights on achieving something, you don't stop until you get it, and I know you've always wanted the Branding Iron to be the biggest and the best ranch around."

"That's what I'm aiming for," he agreed with a smile. "Well, good night, Mira. I hope you sleep well."

It irritated her that he was dismissing her so easily, but the night stretched long and dark before them. She would wait until the time was right, and then she would go to him. She was certain he wouldn't refuse her, especially if she came to him wearing only the sheet from her bed.

Cole was glad when she went inside the room and shut the door. His need to be alone had not lessened, and he drew a deep breath of relief as he walked back to the front of the house. The last thing he'd wanted was to find Mira waiting for him tonight. Dealing with Jenny all day had worn him out; putting up with Mira all night could prove nerve-wracking.

He stalked to the kitchen and opened a cabinet to pull out his whiskey bottle. He poured himself a single shot and downed it without flinching. Then, turning out the lights, he grabbed a slicker and headed down to the bunkhouse. He would spend the night with his men. There was an extra bunk there. In the morning, he'd make certain he had others with him when he went back up to the house. He had no designs on Mira, and he would have witnesses to the fact that nothing had happened between them.

* * *

Mira undressed slowly, then slipped into the bed that Cole had turned down for her. She'd decided to sleep in the nude just in case he came into the room for any reason. She hoped she got that lucky. The sheets felt cool against her skin, and she fantasized about how she and Cole could heat them up. It was a very arousing fantasy.

Outside, the storm raged on. Inside, Mira bided her time, waiting for the hours to pass, waiting for the right moment to go to the man she wanted more than anything in the world. It was after midnight when she finally decided the time was right. The storm had not abated. Rain still poured down in torrents. Rising from the bed, she wrapped the sheet around her and moved quietly toward the door. It opened silently, and she tiptoed across the hallway, ready for what was promised to be the most momentous few hours of her life. Mira figured that after tonight, it could only get better, because she would soon have Cole all to herself.

Mira reached for his doorknob and turned it. For a moment, she feared he might have locked the door, but it opened easily, soundlessly. She stepped into his bedroom, ready for him, wanting him. She moved a few steps farther into the room and then let the sheet drop away. She shivered in anticipation of what was to come. Her plan to ride over here to see Cole had been brilliant—he was going to be hers.

"Cole." She said his name softly.

She was surprised when he didn't respond. It was dark in the room; she couldn't see him and realized that he was probably sleeping soundly. With utmost care, she crept nearer to his bed, intending to slip in beside him and press herself up against him. She hoped he would be caught up in the excitement of the moment. No words would be necessary between them—only actions.

She knelt carefully on the side of Cole's bed and reached for the covers, wanting to curl up against the warmth of his body, wanting the heat of his passion to sear the night chill that was settling over her.

"What?" The word was torn from her as she discovered that Cole's bed was empty.

Mira jumped up, her hand at her throat as she backed away, snatching up the sheet and clutching it to her. Her shock turned to anger as lightning lit up the sky and she saw that his bed had not been slept in.

Mira wondered where he'd gone. The house was dark. She made her way down the hall and looked for him in the parlor. But he was not there. Cole had chosen not to stay in the house with her. When he'd spoken about protecting her reputation, he'd been serious—*Damn him!*

Mira swore out loud as thunder rent the night, and tears of frustration burned in her eyes. She'd wanted to make love to Cole. She'd wanted to lie in his bed, in his arms, and know the full beauty of his possession.

But it wasn't going to happen.

Not tonight.

Mira returned to Cole's room and lay down on his bed. It was soft and welcoming. The scent of him was on his pillow, and she clutched it to her breasts, aching for him, willing him to return, yet knowing that he wouldn't. She lingered there for hours, not leaving the bed's comfort until near dawn. She remade the bed, straightening the covers so he would never know that she'd tried to come to him in the night.

It was just at sunup when Mira heard Cole enter the kitchen accompanied by some of his men.

"Did you sleep well?" Cole asked when she joined them.

"Very well. Thank you for the hospitality," she answered.

Her gaze was hungry upon Cole, unmindful that Fred and another ranch hand were present. Even first thing in the morning, she thought him the most handsome man she'd ever seen. The dark shadow of a day's growth of beard on his jaw only added to the attraction she felt for him. If they had been alone at that moment, she would have gone into his arms and never let him go, but she was forced to control her emotions and her needs. Damn! She'd been thwarted in this plan, so she was going to have to come up with another. Nothing would stop her from becoming Mrs. Cole Randall.

Mira ate breakfast with the men, then was on her

way home. She was not pleased with the way her trip to the Branding Iron had turned out, but at least she had gotten to see Cole for a little while—and she'd gotten to sleep in his bed.

Mira wondered how many other women could say that.

She hoped there were none.

"Damn, Cole, that was one hot woman," Fred told him after Mira had gone. "Why in the hell did you spend the night in the bunkhouse with us when you could have had her all to yourself?"

Cole looked over at him and smiled slightly, though he wasn't amused. "That is exactly why I stayed in the bunkhouse."

The men laughed with him. Cole was trying to make light of the moment, but, in truth, he was asking himself the real reason why he hadn't spent the night in the house. Mira was a good-looking woman, and she had made no secret of her desire for him. She had been there for the taking, but he'd turned his back and walked away.

The truth was there for him to see. He'd spent the night thinking of Jenny and of how she'd looked wearing those pants, instead of thinking of Mira, ready and willing under his own roof.

Cole grew irritated.

Mira was gone.

It was a new day.

He needed to start concentrating on the work he had to do.

And he would, if he could keep himself from remembering his first sight of Jenny on that roof.

Chapter Eleven

"We will have so much fun! Haven't you always wanted to experience the real Wild West?" Rose Stanford said excitedly to the friends gathered around the dining room table in her palatial home. Her dark eyes were sparkling with delight. "This is your chance! Who's going with us? Melanie and I are planning to leave a week from Friday, so that gives all of you plenty of time to get your personal business organized so you can travel with us. We'll be away for a few weeks, so plan for a big adventure."

Rose's enthusiasm was contagious—as usual. Rose lived life with such vitality that any time she got excited about anything, others were automatically drawn along with her. Her excursion to the Lazy S Ranch was no exception.

"Aubrey and I will join you," Richard Donathan III announced immediately.

"Good! Anyone else? One hundred dollars a week per person is nothing, really, and that will cover all your expenses—except for traveling, of course," Rose told them, making up a figure that she knew her companions could easily afford.

The members of her social group were all from the best families in Philadelphia, and money was no object to them. She knew that if she'd quoted too low a price, they would have considered the trip beneath them. She hoped Jenny wouldn't be upset by the price she'd set, but judging from the tone of Jenny's letter, Rose sensed that her friend needed all the cash she could get, as quickly as possible. She was going to do her best to help her out.

"What exactly does one do on a guest ranch?" Aubrey Miles asked, now that he had been committed by Richard to participate.

"Anything you want," Rose told him, smiling to herself as she tried to envision Aubrey dressed in cowboy garb. High-fashion gentleman that he was, she had never seen him less than perfectly attired. It was going to be interesting to see how he adapted to a rougher, more physically challenging environment. "There will be horseback riding, trail hikes, hunting, and all kinds of outdoor activities, I'm sure. It should be quite wonderful. The Lazy S is a working cattle ranch, so we'll actually get to see real cowboys at work. From what Jenny tells me, the scenery is magnificent, so I'm taking my camera equipment along to take lots of photographs."

Several others expressed interest in making the trek, and they promised to make a definite commitment in the next day or two.

"For those of you who can't make it, I'll tell you all about the Lazy S as soon as we get back. This is going to be the best trip ever," Rose declared, and she meant it. If nothing else, she'd get to see Jenny again. She missed her friend desperately.

Rose had been interested in the West ever since she'd first met Jenny at school several years before. Jenny's tales of what went on at a real ranch had fascinated her, and she was thrilled now to have the opportunity to go out West and experience it firsthand. She'd taken lessons in photography and prided herself on taking pictures of unusual characters and settings. As popular as everything with a Western theme was right now, she hoped she might be able to sell some of her photos. If that happened, she might establish a career for herself as a photographer.

Her father, of course, thought it was ridiculous for her to even think of a career. Anthony Stanford, business tycoon, wanted his daughter's happiness, but he also believed in following convention. Women were to be cosseted and adored—first by their fathers and then by their husbands. They shouldn't have to concern themselves with anything as common as the workaday world. But for all his old-fashioned, almost dictatorial ways, Rose knew that all she had to do was smile at him and he would give in to her wishes. She knew she was most fortunate to have a rich father who adored her, so she took full advantage.

"How is Jenny doing?" Richard asked conversationally, although his interest in Jenny was far from casual.

"From the tone of her letter, I think she's handling everything as well as can be expected," Rose said. "I have to admit I was shocked when she wrote that she'd decided to stay on in Durango. I thought for sure that she'd come back here once she'd taken care of all her father's business concerns."

"It's definitely been too quiet around here without her. Maybe Richard can convince her to come back," Aubrey said with a good-natured laugh as he looked over at his friend.

"I'm certainly going to try," Richard declared.

Tall, sophisticated, and handsome, Richard was the oldest son of a very wealthy family. He was used to getting exactly what he wanted out of life. If he couldn't win it on his own, his parents purchased it for him.

That had all come to a frustrating halt, though, when he'd set his sights on Jenny Sullivan. He'd been attracted to her from the first time he saw her when she arrived in Philadelphia. He'd arranged an introduction and had escorted her to several dances, but as hard as he'd tried to woo her, she'd proven remarkably resistant to his amorous efforts.

Richard had never been so challenged by a woman

before. Females usually chased him, and the fact that Jenny was different had intrigued him even more. He'd made up his mind that Jenny was the woman for him. The only difficulty he'd had was convincing her of that fact. Still, Richard wasn't one to give up when he wanted something. Jenny Sullivan was going to be his—even if it meant he had to go to Colorado and bring her back.

"From what you told me about her letter, it sounded as though she wanted to stay on at the Lazy S permanently," Rose's cousin Melanie put in.

"For the time being, maybe. Once she's established it as a successful guest ranch, she'll have plenty of money to hire someone else to run it for her. Then she can do whatever she wants to do, and I'm sure we can convince her to come back here to us."

"This should be great fun," Aubrey remarked. "Just making the trip to Colorado will be interesting. I've never traveled that far west before."

"None of us have," Rose said. "That's why it's such a wonderful opportunity! Once we've experienced it, we can tell others and get people excited about going and really help Jenny to succeed."

"You're a mastermind, Rose," said Cherilyn Bates, another longtime girlfriend. "You've already got this all figured out."

"When I get excited about something, there's no stopping me!"

"We know! We know!" they all agreed with good humor.

"Who is going along to chaperon you and Melanie?" Cherilyn asked.

"I'm hoping my Aunt Tillie will agree to accompany us. She'd be the most fun, that's for sure."

"Why do you need a chaperon if you're traveling with Richard and me?" Aubrey asked, a wicked, humorous glint shining in his blue eyes.

"That's precisely why," Rose retorted, grinning at him. Everyone knew that Aubrey and Richard were notorious rakes. "No matter how daring and wild I may seem to be in my madcap adventures, a lady's reputation must be protected at all costs." She quoted the last as if she were teaching a course in etiquette.

The conversation drifted on to other things as they all left the dining room. Richard and Aubrey wandered into the study and helped themselves to snifters of brandy, wanting to enjoy an after-dinner drink.

"Why are you so intent on making this trip to Colorado?" Aubrey asked. He'd been surprised when his friend had agreed so quickly to go along.

Richard glanced at him. "Let's just say I have a great deal of interest in the West."

"Since when? I've never known you to care one way or another about anything west of the Mississippi."

He shrugged. "Maybe I'm expanding my horizons."

"And maybe your interest lies with one young lady who just recently moved back there."

Richard's expression turned calculating. "Jenny is

proving to be quite a challenge to me. I find that intriguing."

"This should be a most interesting trip," Aubrey mused. He knew his friend considered himself to be a ladies' man, and he also knew that when Jenny had not fallen easy prey to Richard's seductive charm, he'd grown frustrated. Richard was not a man accustomed to being denied anything he wanted. "I don't think I shall be bored at all."

"Indeed."

"You were worried about being bored?" Rose repeated, coming in on the end of their conversation as she joined them. "There's no way you'll be bored, Aubrey. There will be so many different things to do, I imagine we will be going from sunup to sundown with all the activities Jenny has planned."

"I'm not the most active outdoorsman," Aubrey explained.

"Maybe this will encourage you to take up some new interests."

"It also might encourage me never to leave home again," Aubrey said drolly. He enjoyed a quieter life than Richard. Richard was the one who was always looking for new challenges to keep things exciting.

"There will certainly be plenty to keep us busy," Richard said.

"Fine horseman and crack shot that you are, Aubrey, I'm sure you'll find plenty to do. Jenny mentioned that there might be hunting expeditions," Rose went on.

Richard nodded, but didn't say anything more. He was going to Colorado to hunt, all right, but it wasn't big game he was after. He was after a woman—a woman who had proven far too elusive until now. He would be ready to leave as soon as Rose got everything arranged.

Cole didn't know what it was that had drawn him to the high pasture at the Lazy S, but he found himself riding there late the following week. He had stayed away from the ranch on purpose since that day he'd worked on the roof with Jenny. He'd seen that any bills submitted to him for the ranch were paid in a timely fashion, but he had not contacted Jenny again. He didn't want, or need, the aggravation that dealing with her caused him. He didn't want, or need, the conflicting emotions she aroused in him.

Cole was scowling as he rode at a steady pace toward the scene of Paul's accident. His heart was hardened against Jenny. Despite the fact that he might still feel some kind of physical attraction to her, he'd had enough time these last days to think things through, and he knew for certain that he wanted nothing to do with her. Jenny had walked off and left him standing alone at the altar. She'd humiliated him before the entire town, and then she'd run away in the night like a coward, leaving him to face the talk and the speculation about what had gone wrong with their wedding.

His anger returned as he mentally relived those turbulent times. After she'd first gone, he'd tried to drown his fury in liquor and wild women. He'd done a damned good job of trying, too. After a while, though, Cole had realized that he had to sober up. He'd considered leaving Durango and starting over somewhere else, but he loved the area too much. This was his home. His family had been one of the pioneer ranching families there in the San Juan country. They had endured and succeeded. His father had worked hard to establish the Branding Iron, and after his parents' deaths, he'd continued to work at building up the ranch. When the town of Durango had been established and the railroad had come, the area had flourished. The Branding Iron had just been starting to turn around when he'd had the trouble with Jenny. Since it had looked as if Jenny was never going to be coming back to town, Cole hadn't contemplated leaving for very long. If Jenny wasn't around, there was no reason to go.

Cole had forced himself to face reality and had sobered up. He had a ranch to run.

Telling himself that the best revenge was success, he'd begun to work day and night to make the Branding Iron the most successful spread around. At the time, he hadn't known if Jenny would ever find out, but *he* would know, and that was all that mattered.

Cole was pleased that the endless hours of hard work had paid off. Few ranches could match the

Branding Iron. He was by far the most successful rancher in the area right now, and it felt damned good.

Cole was satisfied with the way things had been going in his life. He could have just about any woman he wanted, but he didn't want commitments. His failed wedding with Jenny had left him very cautious about taking any kind of vows with a woman. If a female was out for a good time, he'd oblige, but he wasn't going to get involved.

That was why he'd been so careful around Mira the other night. He was not about to get trapped in a tricky situation that could lead to an unwanted wedding. That was why he made it a point, too, not to spend too much time with any one woman. He didn't want to get anyone's hopes up, because he knew he wasn't the marrying kind.

Cole reined in as he reached the general area where Louie had told him they'd found Paul's body. He dismounted and, leaving his horse to graze, walked around, studying the ground, looking over the lay of the land.

All was peaceful.

All was quiet.

There was no sign that anything untoward had happened there, and that only made him wonder all the more if Jenny was right. What could have caused Paul to have such a deadly accident in such a peaceful spot?

The sound of a horse in the distance surprised Cole.

He reached for his sidearm, cautious, wary. He wondered fleetingly if Paul had run into anyone when he'd been riding there. The place certainly was deserted enough.

Chapter Twelve

Cole tensed as he'd waited to see who was riding up. He feared it might be trouble. He knew that it was trouble all right—just not the kind of trouble he'd been expecting.

He wondered what twist of fate had brought Jenny there at that particular moment. He'd wanted to spend this time alone, trying to piece together the truth of what had happened to Paul without anyone else around. Now he was going to have to talk to Jenny. In disgust, he slid his gun back into his holster.

Jenny had tied her hair back and was dressed in pants again, but even from this distance, there was no mistaking that she was all woman. His expression darkened as he waited for her to draw near. He didn't like the effect she had on him. He could deny it all he wanted but the fact remained that he was still attracted to her. Cole told himself that what he felt for her was a purely physical thing. Jenny was nothing to him but an obligation.

Cole prided himself on being in complete control of his emotions. He fought down the desire that stirred within him as he watched her ride closer. He waited for her to come to him, his expression guarded.

When Jenny caught sight of a man in the distance walking the very ground where her father had been found dead, she pulled her rifle from its sheath, knowing this might mean trouble. To the best of her knowledge, none of her men were supposed to be working up here. Whoever it was, he didn't belong there. She rode forward at a steady, cautious pace, ready to confront the trespasser.

When she drew close enough and recognized Cole, Jenny was surprised. She couldn't imagine what he was doing on Lazy S property. His unexpected presence unsettled her—just as finding him at the house on her first day back had troubled her. She felt uncertain and knew she had to be cautious as she rode on to confront him.

"What are you doing here?" Jenny demanded as she reined in before him.

"Are you planning to use that gun or put it away?" Cole challenged, ignoring her question as he eyed the rifle she was holding.

"I wasn't sure who you were at first, so I thought I'd be prepared for trouble," she quickly explained, sliding the rifle back into its sheath. "Feel safer now?"

"I was never worried."

He said it so casually that Jenny was a bit stung by his attitude. She'd always been a good marksman, and Cole knew it.

"So why are you here? I'm surprised to see you."

"I've been thinking over what you said at the house last week about the way your father died. I thought I'd ride over and take a look around."

"What are you hoping to find? Louie and the men looked around the day they found Papa, but Louie said that there was nothing unusual here."

Cole gazed out over the land. "I don't know that I'm looking for any one thing in particular. Just something that might explain the 'why' to us. Sometimes, though, no matter how hard we try to understand why something bad happened, we never get a straight answer." His voice turned cold as he spoke, but he never looked her way.

Jenny chose to ignore his unspoken question. "Well, according to what Louie told me, Papa was lying face down on the bank of the stream about ten yards up farther." She pointed, indicating the location.

Cole nodded and walked in that direction. Jenny dismounted and watched him as he moved carefully, studying the ground and surrounding landscape.

Jenny had ridden up to the pasture hoping to find some peace about her father's death. Instead, she'd found Cole—and there was absolutely nothing peaceful about being around Cole. She could sense his unspoken hostility toward her, and the worst part of it was that she knew his feelings were justified.

She'd always thought of herself as a gentle spirit, the kind of person who never deliberately hurt anyone, yet what she'd done to Cole had hurt him badly. The fact that he had managed to be civil to her surprised her.

Jenny wasn't quite sure what to think about Cole anymore. Theirs was a difficult and awkward situation, compounded by the knowledge that there was no end in sight. They were going to be forced to endure this unwanted but binding relationship for several years.

Cole kept his gaze focused on the ground as he slowly covered the area, but he could find no trace of anything untoward. It was simply a pasture used for grazing stock. There was nothing remotely significant about the area that might stir up the interest of a neighboring rancher or even of a roaming band of Indians from the reservation. The only thing he could imagine was that Paul might have accidentally come upon some rustlers, but it stood to reason that they probably would have shot him. And Paul had suffered no gunshot wound.

"In his letters to you, did your father ever mention that he was having trouble with anyone?" Cole finally asked, glancing back at Jenny.

"No, but then he never mentioned the rustling to me, either. The first I heard about it was from you."

"Did you ask Louie if he'd noticed anything unusual around the ranch?"

"Yes, and he said things had been real quiet."

Cole realized that there was nothing more for him to see or do there. He slowly made his way back toward where Jenny waited with the horses. He knew that he had nothing more to say to her, either, so there was absolutely no reason for him to linger. Yet Cole didn't hurry to mount up. It was the first time he and Jenny had really been alone together—completely alone.

Not that it mattered . . .

The moment was a quiet one. Only the screech of a soaring bird and the echo of the wind rent the stillness.

With each step Cole took, Jenny grew more and more aware of him. Her gaze went over him. She missed nothing—his confident, serious expression; the proud way he carried himself, his stride easy yet self-assured as he made his way to her. She noticed, too, the wide set of his powerful shoulders, his lean waist and long legs. He was an impressive man, there was no denying that, and she wondered why she hadn't been so physically aware of him before.

Jenny wanted to say something, to initiate a conversation with Cole, but she wasn't sure how to get started. She remembered times when they had talked easily together, and she regretted that it had been so long ago. A distant memory of laughing with Cole came to her, and a warmth filled her. There really had been occasions when they'd enjoyed each other's company, but she knew those days had been lost forever—destroyed when she'd walked away from him at thc altar.

Jenny wondered suddenly if there was any way to broach that subject with Cole and make amends. She wondered if they could at least be friends.

Jenny girded herself, prepared to try. The worst thing that could happen was nothing. They would continue on as they were—acting barely civil to one another, dealing with each other only when forced to.

"Cole?"

He looked at her questioningly.

"You've never forgiven me, have you?"

"Hell, no." He said the words with some force.

She was surprised by his honesty, though she knew she shouldn't be. If there was one thing Cole had always been with her, it was honest.

"I didn't mean to hurt you that day. I really didn't."

Cole turned on her, and the look on his face was anything but kind, conciliatory, or forgiving.

"All right, then, why in the hell did you wait until the last possible minute to break it off? Why didn't you tell me ahead of time that you were having doubts about marrying me?"

Guilt filled her, but she faced him, squarely. She wanted to clear the air between them.

"I thought I was doing the right thing. Marrying you was what Papa wanted."

"What *Papa* wanted?" he sneered. "Funny, I

thought it was what *we* wanted. I thought you loved me the way I loved you. I thought you wanted me as much as I wanted you."

Cole crossed the distance between them, his gaze darkening with the power of his intent. He remembered all too well how much he'd desired her. Hell, he was reminded of it every time he looked at her—even now!

Jenny stood frozen before him, mesmerized by the force of the emotion she saw raging in his eyes. She gasped in surprise as he took her by the shoulders and dragged her hard against him, crushing her to his chest. Cole had never been so physical with her before, and she held herself rigid, trying to resist him.

Cole bent to Jenny, and his mouth captured hers in a dominating kiss. It was a kiss meant to punish, not to pleasure. Anger was driving him, and a desire that could not be denied.

But then something happened.

Jenny felt the desire, too. It flamed to life deep within her, searing her consciousness with its recognition. So *this* was passion. . . .

She gave a soft whimper and surrendered to the feelings that were burning in her.

Jenny's unspoken surrender was more powerful to Cole than any aphrodisiac. The harshness of his lips moving over hers softened. He became coaxing rather than demanding. He deepened the exchange, delving into the sweetness of her mouth, tasting of her beauty, wanting to know the fullness of her love. Rendered mindless by the power of their kiss, Cole started to caress her, lifting one hand to seek the soft swell of her breast.

At his bold touch, Jenny gasped his name in delight. Ecstasy shimmered through her. Cole had never caressed her before, and she was startled by the feelings his touch aroused.

It was her gasp that jarred Cole and made him aware of just where he was and what he was doing.

As quickly as the encounter had started, it was over.

Cole abruptly released Jenny as if he'd been burned and stepped away from her. He was furious with himself for his lack of control. He kept his expression starkly indifferent as he looked down at her.

"I guess we were both wrong about why we were getting married," Cole said flatly. "And that *was* a long time ago."

"Yes . . . yes, it was," Jenny stammered.

She lifted a hand to her lips as she took a nervous step backward, still unsure of herself. She needed to put more distance between them; it was hard for her to have a straight thought with him standing so close.

Cole's kiss and touch had been overwhelming. The power of the emotions that had been awakened inside her shocked Jenny, and the boldness of his caress left her breathless. Cole had never kissed or caressed her that way before. She remembered his kisses from when they'd been engaged. They had always been nice and sweet and gentle—nothing like this one.

This kiss had been arousing and sensual and overpowering and had left her wanting more from him—much more.

Her head reeled with confusion. Was this really Cole? Her Cole?

"A lot has changed since then," Cole went on.

"Yes, it has," she answered a bit breathlessly. "And that's why I thought we should talk about what happened and straighten things out between us—"

"I thought you said it all that night in the hotel room," he said tersely.

"I tried to explain what I was feeling to you. It wouldn't have been fair to marry you feeling the way I did then. I wanted to explore the world. I wanted to learn more about life. I wasn't ready to become just some man's wife—"

"No, Jenny," Cole said with cold fury, watching as she paled a little. "You weren't going to become 'just some man's wife.' You were going to be *my* wife."

The tension between them built as she hurried on. "But getting married for the sake of getting married wasn't my dream. I wanted adventure. I wanted to further my education. I wanted to—"

"So what happened that night was all about what *you* wanted," he said bitterly.

"Marriage is a lifetime commitment," she continued, trying to justify her actions but feeling she was failing miserably. "I wasn't ready to take those vows." She was trying to explain to him what had seemed so logical to her at the time, but nothing was coming out right. "I cared too much about you to marry you feeling the way I did. You deserved someone who loved you, not someone who would ultimately resent you."

"That all sounds real good, but if you cared so much about me, you wouldn't have had to sneak off in the middle of the night."

"Well, I—"

"Did you know that I went back to the hotel to see you again? I wanted to talk to you one more time, to explain to you how much I loved you, but you'd already gone."

"Aunt Evelyn thought it would be best for us to leave as quickly as we could, what with all the gossip that would be going on around town."

"So you just took off and left me here to face all the talk alone." His tone was condemning.

Jenny swallowed tightly. "Yes. You're right. I did, and I'm sorry. If I had to do it over—"

He stopped her, not wanting to hear another word. "It doesn't matter."

"Cole, there's nothing I can say or do that will change what happened between us. But because of Papa's will, we are going to have to work together for the next few years. I'd like us to be able to get along."

Cole smiled easily at her as he took his horse's reins and swung up into the saddle in one easy, fluid motion. "You won't have any problems with me, Jenny. Ours is strictly a business relationship, and it's going to stay that way—just the way your father set it up."

"Good. I was hoping we could work things out amicably."

"Of course. Just keep me informed of what's going on at the ranch. I'll check in regularly with you when I have any news." With that, he wheeled his mount around, ready to ride off. "You'll be all right getting back home?"

"Yes."

He nodded and rode away without looking back.

Jenny stood unmoving and watched him until he had disappeared from sight. She'd gotten exactly what she'd wanted out of the conversation. She should have been pleased with the way things had gone, but instead she felt more uneasy than ever. Her emotions were in turmoil. Acknowledging the truth to herself, she admitted that she hadn't wanted him to leave. She'd wanted him to take her in his arms and kiss her again.

Gathering her own mount's reins, Jenny climbed into the saddle and started back. She barely noticed the miles she covered on the trip to the house. Her thoughts were of Cole's harsh words and his disturbing kiss and caress.

Jenny had never known that a single kiss and touch could evoke such passion. But Cole's had. There had been such pleasure in his embrace—such excitement. It had been wonderful.

Jenny frowned as she drew closer to home. She

tried to push the memory of what had happened between them from her mind and concentrate on the fact that he had agreed they should get along without any difficulties—that theirs would be a strictly business relationship. That was good. That was what she'd wanted.

Much later that night, though, when Jenny lay in bed thinking about her encounter with Cole, she wondered why she felt so bereft that he had agreed to what she'd wanted.

They would get along as friends.

Theirs was a business-only relationship.

Cole sat in his study at the Branding Iron, thinking of what had happened earlier in the day with Jenny. He was not proud that he'd lost control of himself and kissed her. In fact, he was angry with himself for having done it.

Cole supposed he'd kissed Jenny to prove to himself that he really didn't want her. He'd expected to feel nothing. The kisses they'd shared years before had been chaste and carefully controlled, never arousing or passionate. He hadn't thought he would have any reaction to her kiss today.

He'd been wrong.

Getting up from his desk, Cole poured himself a straight whiskey and stalked to the window, glass in hand, to stare out into the night. It was a dark, moonless night as black and unforgiving as his soul felt just then. He took a deep drink.

It disturbed him greatly to know that Jenny was still a weakness for him. Her unexpected response to his kiss had aroused him and left him more determined than ever to stay away from her. He would keep her at arm's length and make sure any contact between them was minimal.

Cole drained the glass and slammed it down on his desk. He made his way to his solitary bed, but sleep was long in coming. When it finally did claim him, it was restless and fitful, giving him no peace.

Chapter Thirteen

The Lazy S was as ready as it ever would be for its first guests. Jenny had worked nonstop to get the guest house finished in time for Rose's arrival, and she was thrilled with the way everything had turned out.

"We've thought of everything, haven't we?" Jenny asked Evelyn as they left to make the trip into town to meet their guests. Jenny was driving their carriage while Tom followed them with the buckboard. They were going to need all the room they could get for their arriving guests and their luggage.

"Yes, dear. It's all done. All we need is for Rose and Tillie and the others to show up, and you'll be officially in business," Evelyn told her with confidence. "I'm so glad Tillie's coming along. Of course, they did need a chaperon, and who better than my best friend, who just happens to be Rose's aunt? I'm glad Tillie is a hardy, adventurous soul."

"Everything has worked out well," Jenny said cautiously. "I guess that's why I keep expecting something to go wrong."

"Nothing's going to go wrong. They'll enjoy their stay, and the Lazy S will gain the reputation of being the place to go if you want to experience the real Wild West."

"I hope you're right. We've got a good cook. We have comfortable accommodations, and we have any number of activities to keep them busy. I think they'll have a good time."

"They will. You and I both know that Rose is coming simply because she wants to see you. She would follow you to the ends of the Earth if you asked her to, and Durango is hardly the ends of the Earth." Evelyn reached over and squeezed her hand reassuringly.

Jenny squeezed back.

"I'm really excited."

"Me, too."

They reached town and drove to the station to await the mid-morning train. According to Rose's telegram, their group of five would be arriving that day.

"I can't wait to see Rose again. It really hasn't been that long since we were together last, but it feels like ages," Jenny said as they went inside the station.

Tom stayed behind with their vehicles.

"Well, look at all that's happened to you in only a few short weeks," Aunt Evelyn said. "Who would have dreamed that you could have accomplished so much in such a short period of time? I'm proud of you, honey, and I'm sure your father is, too."

Jenny's smile was tinged with sadness. "I hope so."

"It will be nice to see Richard again, don't you think?" Evelyn asked, leading the conversation a bit.

She personally thought that Richard would make the ideal husband for Jenny. She had encouraged her niece's interest in him when they'd been in Philadelphia. He was handsome, well-mannered, and quite rich. In Evelyn's mind, that made him perfect husband material. Although, she had to admit, Cole fit that description, too.

"I like Richard," Jenny agreed easily.

Richard had a reputation of being quite a ladies' man. She had seen him in action through the years and knew he could be a charmer. She had gone to social events with him, and he had kissed her a few times. She had known from the start not to take him seriously, and so they had gotten along nicely.

As she thought of Richard's kisses, the memory of Cole's exciting embrace returned—full and flaming. Jenny knew there was no comparison between the two.

"I like Richard, and Aubrey, too," Evelyn agreed. "I'm glad they both decided to come along with Rose. Melanie is always a delight to be around, of course, so we should have quite a nice time while they're here."

"How could they not have a good time with all the

plans you've made? You've arranged something for everybody. There's not going to be a dull moment the whole time they're here."

"Good. That's what we wanted."

From a distance, the sound of the train's whistle came to them.

"They're almost here!" Jenny said, allowing herself to be truly excited now.

They hurried out to meet the train as it pulled in.

The train had barely stopped when Rose came flying out of the passenger car and ran straight into Jenny's arms.

"I missed you!" Rose cried as she hugged her friend close.

"I missed you, too!" Jenny hugged her back.

When at last they broke apart, they were smiling at each other in open delight, like two very young girls.

"Just look at you! You really are a cowgirl!" Rose said, staring at Jenny. She was accustomed to seeing her friend in the latest fashions. It was a revelation to find her wearing a split leather riding skirt, boots, blouse, vest, and Western hat. "I like it! I want an outfit just like that!"

"We can stop at the mercantile before we go out to the ranch, if you want," Jenny offered.

Jenny knew how fashion-conscious Rose was. Her friend was always certain to be wearing just the right clothes for any occasion. She was secretly pleased that Rose approved of her garb. Jenny wondered what

Rose would think if she ever saw her wearing her pants. The thought made her smile.

"Hello, Jenny."

Richard's deep-voiced greeting drew her attention away from Rose. She glanced past her friend to see Richard and Aubrey coming their way. She went to meet them.

"Richard—Aubrey. Welcome to Durango. How was your trip?" Jenny asked.

Richard took her hands and pressed a kiss to her cheek. "Long, but worth every mile, now that we're here with you." His gaze was devouring her.

Aubrey greeted her, too. "So this is Durango," he said, looking around with open interest.

"As we head out to the ranch, you'll see much more of it," Jenny told him.

"I'm impressed already. It's much nicer than I expected."

"What were you expecting?" She looked at him quizzically.

"Oh, I don't know—gunfight in the middle of the street—a lot of saloons and dance halls—maybe a lynching by a mob of angry townsfolk—"

"We have our fair share of saloons and dance halls, but generally, Durango is a pretty quiet town."

Aubrey looked a bit disappointed. "Maybe I've been reading too many dime novels."

They all laughed as Melanie and Aunt Tillie joined them. Tillie and Evelyn were delighted to be reunited and quickly fell into catching up on all that had happened since Evelyn had come West with Jenny.

"The carriage and buckboard are out front," Jenny told them now that they were assembled.

She led the way to where Tom was waiting. Once the luggage had been loaded, the men climbed up into the buckboard with Tom, while the ladies all rode with Jenny in the carriage. They made their way to the mercantile and spent the better part of an hour there while Rose and the others outfitted themselves.

Jenny found the shopping trip an adventure in itself, watching her friends pick out hats and boots and other more practical clothing. Rose took the longest and after the others had gone outside, Jenny stayed with her while she finished making her selections. They had often shopped together in Philadelphia and always had a good time.

"What do you think, Jenny?" Rose asked as she turned to her friend, modeling a white Stetson for her.

"Try the dark one on," Jenny suggested.

Her friend did, and they both smiled as they realized it was the perfect hat for her.

"I think I'll wear it now!" Rose announced, carrying her last selection up to the counter where Jenny had been standing with George Lansing, the owner.

"Now, Jenny, don't forget we've got the big dance and social coming up Saturday night. We'll be looking forward to seeing you and all your guests there," George told them.

"This is going to be so much fun. I'm madly in love with Durango already!" Rose declared as she paid for her purchases and then gathered up her bundles and started from the shop.

"Thank you, Miss Stanford."

"Thank *you*, George!"

Jenny had one thing to pay for, too.

Rose looked over her shoulder at Jenny to say something as she was making her way toward the open door. She wasn't paying any attention to where she was going, and she gasped as she ran into the solid wall of a man's chest.

"Oh!"

Rose's movements were less than graceful as her purchases went flying along with her new hat. She struggled just to stay on her feet, and she was thankful when a pair of strong arms came around her and steadied her.

"Are you all right, ma'am?" a deep voice asked.

Rose looked up into a pair of the most startlingly blue eyes she'd ever seen, and she was instantly mesmerized. A tingle ran though her as she became aware of the warmth of her contact with the hard body of the man gazing down at her He wasn't tall, but he was solidly built and very attractive. Words failed her. She could only stare at him.

"Ma'am?" he said again, this time sounding more concerned as if he truly believed she might have been injured in their collision.

"Rose?" Jenny called, hurrying toward her.

"Oh, dear—" Rose heard herself babble nervously as the man suddenly released her.

Rose wanted to sway toward her handsome stranger just so he would hold her again, but she realized that would be too outrageous and too obvious.

"Are you all right?" the man asked.

"Yes—thank you—I'm sorry—I'm the one who ran into you. Are you hurt?"

"I've survived worse," the man told her, grinning as he bent to start picking up her strewn parcels. "Here's your hat." He held it out to her.

Rose reached for it and only then realized that her hand was trembling. That reaction was very unusual for her.

Jenny looked on, amazed by what she was witnessing. She'd known Rose for a long time and had never seen her act this way around a man before. She hid a grin as she watched her friend struggle to compose herself.

"Can I help you out to your carriage?" the stranger offered.

"Why—thank you," Rose said breathlessly.

The stranger stepped back to let her pass before him. He waited for Jenny, too, then followed them outside.

The carriage and buckboard were waiting for them. He handed the packages up to Tom on the buckboard, then turned to help Rose into the carriage. Jenny had already climbed up to the driver's seat.

"Thank you, sir. You are a gentleman," Rose said in her most elegant manner.

"It was my pleasure, ma'am." He tipped his hat to

her and was gone, disappearing back into the mercantile.

"Who was that man?" Rose asked, looking back, craning her neck as they started to drive away.

"I don't know," Jenny answered. "I've never seen him before."

"Oh." Rose was disappointed.

"He certainly was handsome, wasn't he, Rose?" Aunt Tillie remarked.

"He certainly was," Rose agreed as she put her hat back on. If this was what the Wild West was like, she loved it already.

Dan Lesseg went back inside the mercantile, this time entering without incident.

"You have any more wild women in here, George?" he asked with a grin as he made his way down the aisle.

"No, it's safe now, Dan," the owner answered, laughing with him.

"Who was that woman?" Dan asked as he came to stand at the counter. "I heard the other woman call her Rose, but I've never seen her around town before."

"Her name's Rose Stanford. She's from back East," George explained. "That was Jenny Sullivan from the Lazy S with her. Jenny's turning the Lazy S into a guest ranch of some sort, and your Rose is one of her first visitors. She was a pretty one, wasn't she?"

Dan glanced back toward the doorway, hoping to

catch sight of her again, but they'd already driven away. He thought of the dark-haired, dark-eyed beauty and gave an amused shake of his head.

"Yes, Rose was a pretty one."

"So how are things at the High Time?" George asked. He knew Dan was the bartender at the saloon.

"Busy as usual," Dan replied. "I'm heading there now. It's about time to get back to work."

"I know the feeling," George agreed as more women came in to do their shopping.

Dan purchased the few things he needed, then started out of the shop. It was as he made his way toward the door that he noticed one of Rose's packages that he'd missed earlier. He picked it up, frowning as he tried to decide what to do.

"George—" He returned to the counter and explained the situation. "Do you think they'll be back in town for the dance, or should I take it out to the ranch?"

"I'll take care of it. Don't you worry about it," George assured him.

Dan left the package with George, thanked him, and went on his way. Still, he couldn't help feeling a little disappointed that he had no excuse to see the lovely Rose again.

Chapter Fourteen

With Jenny driving the carriage and Tom driving the buckboard they made the trek to the Lazy S in good time. Rose had moved up to sit with Jenny on the driver's seat.

"The scenery is so beautiful. I never dreamed it would be this wonderful," Rose said as they drew near the ranch. "No wonder you wanted to come home."

"I know. There's just something about Colorado that I love."

"I understand, and I'm beginning to think I should have told the others it would be two hundred dollars a week instead of just one hundred."

"What are you talking about?" Jenny asked, puzzled.

"I guess I forgot to mention it in my letter but I

told Richard and Aubrey that it would cost them one hundred dollars a week to come here. I'm sure they'll be paying you once we get to the house. I have our money right here," she said, patting her purse.

"I didn't expect any of you to pay," Jenny protested.

"Don't be ridiculous. We're going to be eating your food and living at your ranch. It's costing you money to keep us. It's only fair that we should pay for our room and board."

"But—"

"Hush!" Rose cut her off. "If you won't let me pay, we'll leave right now. Although, I have to tell you, I don't think I want to leave. Just look at this scenery. I can't wait to try to capture that feeling in my photographs!"

"So you brought all your equipment with you?"

"Yes. The more pictures I take, the better I can convince people when I get back home of just how wonderful the Lazy S Guest Ranch is. If this ride out to the ranch is any hint of how beautiful things are here, it's going to be easy to sell. Easterners will be flocking to Colorado just to visit you."

Jenny looked thoughtful. "You know, I enjoyed the time I spent living in Philadelphia, but my heart has always been here."

"I can certainly understand why. The scenery is breathtaking, and if all the cowboys look as good as the one I ran into at the mercantile, single women will be beating a hasty path to Durango!" Rose laughed. "If I can manage it, I'm going to track that man down and take a photograph of him."

"I don't know if he's from the area or not," Jenny said thoughtfully, trying to remember if she'd ever seen the man around town.

"Well, I'll just have to go looking for him. You said there were going to be hunting trips," Rose said, grinning wickedly. "I'll go hunting, but the game I'll be after won't be four-legged!"

Jenny laughed out loud. "You'd better be careful Aunt Tillie doesn't hear you. She might lock you in your room and not let you out without a chaperon the whole time you're here."

Rose affected an innocent look. "There would be no need for that. I'm going to behave myself."

"That'll be unusual," Jenny teased.

"I want to capture the true flavor of the area. I want to let everyone know what it's really like here," she declared primly. "And my cowboy would be perfect."

"*Your* cowboy?" Jenny questioned.

Rose grinned at her. "I'm calling him mine until I find out he belongs to somebody else."

As they drew closer to the house, Tillie leaned over to speak to Jenny.

"So this is your home?" Tillie asked.

"Yes, and—" Jenny started to explain that they would be staying in the newly renovated guest house when she saw Cole come out onto the front porch.

She stopped talking, startled by his unexpected appearance. Her pulse began racing, and she was suddenly nervous. Jenny told herself she was certain he was there only for some business reason, but she couldn't deny that her heart had skipped a beat at the sight of him.

"And just who is that splendid example of Western manhood?" Rose asked breathlessly as she, too, caught sight of Cole. "I tell you Jenny, you do know how to grow good-looking men out here."

Jenny knew there was no avoiding telling Rose the truth. She had confided in her friend about her broken engagement, and so she blurted out. "That's Cole Randall."

Rose swung around and stared at Jenny in open disbelief. "*That's* Cole Randall? *The* Cole Randall? *Your* Cole Randall?"

"Yes."

"Oh, my," she breathed. "Cole gives *my* cowboy some real competition."

"I agree with you," Melanie put in. She'd been quiet for most of the ride, but was eyeing Cole with open interest now, too. "He's the man you were engaged to once, isn't he, Jenny?"

"That was a long time ago." Jenny tried to sound nonchalant, though she was still a bit breathless. "I think I may have mentioned in my letter to you, Rose, how my father appointed Cole to be the executor of the estate, so we're working together now to keep the ranch going."

" 'Working together,' are you?" Rose's eyes were twinkling with devilish delight.

"Yes, *working*," Jenny insisted with dignity, although the memory of his forbidden embrace lingered in the back of her mind. She mentally pushed it away, wondering why he had to pick today of all days to show up at the ranch. "Ours is a 'business only' relationship."

"He's been very helpful to Jenny," Evelyn put in. "He even approved of her idea about the guest ranch."

"Your Cole must be smart then, too. I like that combination in a man," Rose said with delight.

All laughed, except Jenny, though she did manage a slight smile. She was tempted to correct her friend's idea that Cole was in some way "hers" but didn't bother. Any protest she offered would probably have drawn even more notice than just letting the remark pass.

Jenny reined the carriage horses in before the house and quickly jumped down.

"Hello, Cole. Are you here to meet my first guests?" she called out as she looped the reins over the hitching post.

"Actually, I rode over because I had some papers from Andrew Marsden to deliver to you, but I'm glad to meet your friends," he responded, descending the porch steps to help the other ladies out of the carriage.

"I'm Rose," Rose announced as she put her hand in Cole's and allowed him to assist her.

"It's nice to meet you, Rose," Cole said.

"Why, thank you, sir." She eyed him appreciatively

and thought he looked even better up close if that were possible.

Cole grinned at her.

Rose found herself automatically smiling back. She instinctively liked this man and found herself wondering how her friend could ever have left him standing at the altar.

Had she been physically stronger, she would have been tempted to throw him over her shoulder and march off to a preacher with him. Rose wondered where all these wild ideas were coming from. She knew that a lot of people thought her outrageous, but she'd never been this outrageous before. She decided there must be something about Western males that appealed to her, and whatever it was, she liked it—a lot. This was definitely proving to be a wonderful trip, and they had only just arrived.

"Let's go inside the main house," Jenny directed. She didn't know why watching Rose flirt a little with Cole bothered her, but it did. "Tom, will you see that the luggage is taken over to the guest house?"

"Yes, ma'am." The ranch hand hurried off to do as he was told.

Jenny quickly made the introductions. Cole shook hands with Richard and Aubrey, and then they all went inside.

"I've been expecting you!" Frances announced with delight as she met them in the parlor. "Welcome to the Lazy S. I'm Frances. If you need anything, anything at all, you just let me know."

As Frances served refreshments, they settled in around the dining room table, and Jenny explained all she had planned for their visit.

"Do we ever get to rest?" Tillie asked, smiling in amazement at all the activities they could participate in.

"Don't worry, Tillie," Evelyn laughed. "You and I can just sit up here on the porch of the main house and watch the rest of them having their fun."

"Now that sounds more like a wonderful, relaxing vacation to me," Tillie agreed.

"You two can relax all you want, but there's a whole new world out there that I want to explore!" Rose told them, then looked at Jenny. "And I'm very serious about taking a lot of photographs, Jenny. I want to use them to convince everyone back home that they should come to the Lazy S for a visit. Will we be going back into town any time soon?"

Jenny knew exactly what and who her friend was thinking about. "If you'd like to, we can go to the dance this next weekend."

"That would be wonderful," Melanie said. She wasn't averse to all the outdoor activities that had been planned, but she would definitely enjoy going to a dance much more.

"Richard? Aubrey?" Jenny looked at the two men and found Richard's gaze upon her.

"Of course," Aubrey answered, pleased that there would be something civilized to do.

"Any time I can take you to a dance, I'm delighted," Richard told Jenny in an intimate tone that did not go unnoticed. "It gives me an excuse to hold you in my arms."

She found herself blushing a bit at his bold statement. "We'll plan on going, then."

Rose casually glanced Cole's way just then and noticed that, although his expression never changed, his jaw tensed during Jenny and Richard's exchange. Since Cole hadn't said a word yet, Rose decided this was as good a time as any to draw him into the conversation.

"Cole? Will you be attending the dance?"

"I usually do unless ranch business interferes," he answered.

"Then I will be expecting to dance with you," Rose declared.

Cole couldn't help smiling at her. He'd never met anyone quite like Rose before. "I'll be looking forward to it."

"Why don't we go over to the guest house and let you get settled in while Frances fixes a late lunch?" Jenny suggested.

They all agreed. As they started to get up, Rose looked over at Cole.

"Will you be staying to eat with us, Cole?"

Jenny was surprised by her friend's question, but knew she shouldn't have been. Rose was always straightforward, and Jenny had long found it one of her most endearing qualities. If Rose wanted to spend more time with Cole, far be it from Jenny to stand in her way.

"Cole?" Jenny asked.

"Thank you, but no. I've got some things I have to attend to. If you'll excuse me, I'll be heading out now." He looked over at Jenny. "I left the envelope with the paperwork from the lawyer in it on the desk in the study. If you've got any questions about it after you've had a chance to read it over, just let me know."

"Thanks."

With that, Cole was gone.

Rose and the others were slower leaving the house, but Rose could still see Cole in the distance as he rode away. She stood for a moment, admiring the powerful yet solitary figure he made. Cole was certainly an intriguing man, and she was determined to learn more about what was going on between him and Jenny.

"There's a rider coming in!" one of the hands on the Jameson spread shouted to Wayne Jameson when he spotted Cole coming up the road toward the main house.

Wayne hurried out of the barn to take a look.

"Shit!" he cursed. "It's that damned Randall!"

"Miss Mira's going to be happy to see him," the man chuckled.

"Shut up," Wayne snarled. "Randall's timing is terrible."

"What do you want us to do?"

Wayne glanced around to see if anything looked out of place. "Just go on about your business. Where is Mira? Have you seen her lately?"

"She was up at the house last time I talked to her, but that was a while ago."

Wayne nodded and headed for the ranch house. No doubt Cole had come to see Mira. From what his sister had been telling him, he had been sniffing at her heels pretty regular lately, and that was good. Cole was rich, and they could use his money.

Mira heard the shouts outside that someone was riding in, and she rushed to the window to look out. She recognized Cole immediately. Cole had come to see her! Her plan just might work after all. She only hoped that the men went on with their work as if nothing unusual was going on. Dropping what she was doing, she went out to meet him.

"Afternoon, Mira," Cole said as he dismounted and tied his horse out front.

"Hello, Cole," she replied.

She was tempted to throw herself in his arms and kiss him full on the mouth, but didn't. After the rebuff she'd suffered the other night at his house, she was going to be a little more aloof from now on. Besides, she could see her brother coming up to speak with Cole.

"It's so good to see you," she told him. Doubts had been haunting her about the possible success of all that she was planning, but now Cole had come to her. Mira's confidence returned.

"It's good to see you, too." Cole smiled as he looked over at Wayne. "Afternoon, Wayne."

"Cole." Wayne nodded and shook hands with him. "What brings you out our way? It's been a while."

"This is strictly a social call. I just stopped by to see if your sister would do me the honor of going to the dance with me in town next weekend."

"I'd be delighted," Mira answered without hesitation. "Why don't you come on inside and have a cool drink?"

"Sounds good to me," he agreed, following Mira and Wayne indoors.

It was nearly an hour later when Cole finally rode for home. He was feeling quite satisfied that Mira would be his date for the dance in town. He tried to keep his thoughts focused on the conversation he'd just had with Mira and Wayne, but his thoughts kept drifting back to his visit to the Lazy S.

From the first, he hadn't liked the looks of the guest named Richard. When he'd heard the man's remarks about going to the dance with Jenny, he'd known his gut reaction to him had been right. He definitely didn't like the man, and he considered himself a good judge of character.

Not that it really mattered what he thought about him. He didn't have to deal with Richard. Richard was Jenny's problem.

* * *

The opportunity for Rose to talk with Jenny about Cole didn't come until much later that evening. Rose lingered behind at the main house to speak to Jenny privately after the others had gone to the bunkhouse to retire.

"I'm just not ready to go to bed yet," Rose told her as they stood on the porch staring out at the night sky.

The night was clear and beautiful, with just a sliver of a moon on the horizon.

"Are you as excited about being here as I am about seeing you?" Jenny asked.

"Absolutely. The trip was long and tiring, but worth every minute."

They shared a secret smile, much like they used to do when they'd been roommates at school.

"So, tell me. . . ." Rose began.

"Tell you what?"

"You know—everything about you and Cole."

Jenny cast a quick glance at her friend, wondering at her interest in Cole. "There's not much to tell. We were engaged when I was very young. I received the letter from the academy telling me that I had been accepted only four days before the wedding."

"And you wanted to go to school more than you wanted to marry Cole?" Rose was shocked as she said it.

"I was so young—and so alone. I didn't have a girlfriend like you to talk to, and Aunt Evelyn and I weren't close back then," Jenny said, remembering all the heartache of the day.

Rose's expression was sympathetic. She could just imagine how pressured Jenny must have felt.

"I guess I was lucky that way. My mother and father always encouraged me to be outspoken and go after what I wanted." Rose paused and grinned conspiratorially. "I must have caused them endless grief."

"I know I caused my father grief," Jenny said sadly. "He did so want me to marry Cole. But I didn't know what I wanted then. I was marrying Cole for the wrong reasons—or at least I thought so at the time."

"I'm proud of you," Rose said with conviction.

"You are?" Jenny was completely taken aback. She had thought Rose was going to tell her she was crazy not to have gone through with the wedding.

"Don't you realize how brave you were? How much determination that took? There aren't many women who could have done what you did. Most would have gone ahead and gotten married and been miserable the rest of their lives married to a man they couldn't stand—" She said the last deliberately, wanting to provoke Jenny.

"Oh, it wasn't that I couldn't stand Cole—" Jenny protested quickly.

"So you did care for him?" Rose asked archly, glad that her instincts had been right about the two of them.

"Cole was wonderful."

"He was?" Rose repeated, wanting to make Jenny think about what she was saying.

"Yes. He was. It was just that I . . ."

"Wasn't ready to get married."

"Exactly."

"But what about now?"

"What about now?" Jenny looked at her in confusion. She wasn't sure where this conversation was going.

"Cole Randall is one handsome man, Jenny. Are you sure you want to keep a 'business only' relationship with him?"

"After what I did to him, Rose, he must hate me. If Cole hadn't been named Papa's executor, he wouldn't have anything to do with me right now."

"How can you be so sure about that? You didn't see the way his expression changed when Richard talked about going to the dance with you."

"It did?"

"That's right. Are you really certain that he hates you?"

"Well, I . . ." The memory of Cole's kiss burned vividly in her thoughts.

"What's that look all about?" Rose asked perceptively.

"What look?"

"The one you just had on your face."

Jenny was certain she was blushing, though it was dark. There were moments like this when she regretted that her friend knew her so well. "I . . . uh . . ."

"Has something happened between the two of you since you've been back?"

"Well . . ."

"Jenny." Rose said her name in a stern tone that demanded the truth.

"Well, Cole did kiss me once," Jenny told her quickly, "but he was mad when he did it."

Rose laughed in utter delight at the news. "I love it! How romantic!"

"Romantic?"

"Absolutely! It's no wonder Cole was mad. What flesh-and-blood man wouldn't have been mad at the woman who left him at the altar? Now here you come marching back into his life, more beautiful than ever, and he's been appointed by your father to take care of you! This is wonderful!"

"What are you talking about?"

"I'm talking about you and Cole."

"There is no 'me and Cole'!"

"Jenny, Cole must have loved you to have proposed to you in the first place, and haven't you been curious as to why he hasn't married someone else in the years you've been apart?"

"Well—yes," she admitted to her best friend.

"Aha! Do you still love him?" Rose asked, wanting to get to the truth of her feelings. She hadn't known the full story of their relationship until now, and she was intrigued.

"I don't know. . . ." Jenny answered.

"You didn't say you didn't!" Rose pointed out and

was pleased when she saw the surprised look on her friend's face.

"But—" Jenny's thoughts were in chaos.

"You've got a lot to think about, Jenny. What do you say we call it a night? Sleep on this. We'll talk again in the morning."

Without giving Jenny time to say any more, Rose left her to her thoughts.

Jenny stood alone on the porch for a long time, then reluctantly went back inside and up to bed. She knew sleep would not be quick in coming that night. She should have been excited about her guests' arrival and the plans she had for them for the next day, but instead, her thoughts centered on Cole.

Today had been the first time she'd seen Cole since their encounter in the pasture, and for some reason, as she lay in her bed the memory of his passionate embrace could not be banished. The night was a long one.

Chapter Fifteen

It was still dark outside the following morning as Frances made her way up to the big house to begin cooking breakfast for all the guests. As she drew near, she was surprised to see that a lamp was burning in the kitchen. She wondered who could be up already and realized it must be Jenny. She could just imagine how excited Jenny was about the guests' first full day on the ranch.

Frances let herself in the back door and found Jenny already dressed, sitting at the kitchen table having a cup of coffee.

"You're up mighty early this morning," Frances said as she joined her.

"Good morning," Jenny greeted her with a smile. "I had a feeling you'd be up earlier than usual, too."

"I want to make sure everything is perfect for our

guests," Frances explained. Then getting her first good look at Jenny, she realized that in spite of her smile, she looked tired. "Are you feeling all right? You aren't getting sick, are you?"

"I didn't get a whole lot of sleep last night."

"Why not? Are you worried about the guests?"

"No . . . nothing like that." She hesitated, still confused in her mind and not quite sure how to address the subject.

"Is it Cole?" Frances asked astutely.

Jenny's eyes widened. "How did you know?"

"I was wondering how things have been going between the two of you. Are you getting along?"

"Oh, yes. There's no problem that way. He's handling the estate just the way Papa would have wanted him to."

"Then—?" Frances urged her on, knowing she needed to talk about her feelings.

Jenny had often confided in her as a young girl, and Frances had always wanted to help in any way she could. The only time she'd failed to really pay attention to what Jenny was telling her had been just before the wedding. Jenny had tried to explain what she'd been feeling about marrying Cole, but Frances had told her it was just bride's nerves, that everything would turn out all right. To this day, she regretted that she hadn't been more attentive. She would never make that mistake again. If Jenny wanted to talk, she was going to listen and be supportive.

"Well, it was something Rose said to me last night.

We stayed up later than everybody else, and we were talking . . ." Jenny frowned.

"What was it?"

She finally just blurted it out. "Rose seems to think I'm still in love with Cole."

"Really?" Frances hid the smile that threatened. She had always believed Jenny and Cole were perfect for each other, and she had hoped Jenny was mature enough now to recognize her true feelings. "What do you think?"

"I don't know," she said miserably. "Even if I did care about him—and I'm not saying I do—I'm sure Cole hates me."

"Love and hate are not so far apart," Frances said wisely.

"Did I make the right decision when I went back East? Or should I have married Cole and not gone away to school?" The question had haunted her for two years.

"Looking back, I think you were wise in what you did."

"You do?" Jenny was shocked by Frances's answer.

"You were so young, and even though I know you cared for Cole, I don't think you loved him the way a woman is supposed to love her husband."

Jenny looked at her, puzzled. "How is that?"

Frances blushed a little, but decided it was time to talk plainly. "Why, when Louie and I first met and we were courting, I couldn't wait to sneak off with him so he could steal a little kiss or two."

"Frances!" Jenny laughed in delight at her story, trying to imagine the serious ranch foreman actively pursuing Frances. "You mean Louie was that romantic?"

"Oh, yes," she sighed. "We were young and so in love. Why, we almost couldn't keep our hands off each other—"

"Like in a few of the dime novel romances I've read," Jenny said thoughtfully.

And like Cole's kiss the other day.

The revelation came to Jenny in a flash of understanding.

"Yes, something like that," said Frances. "Only in real life a good girl is virtuous until her wedding night. And I was virtuous, although I have to admit, it was hard sometimes. I loved Louie a lot, and I was thrilled once we were wed."

"You're right—Cole and I never were alone much."

"I'm sure he loved you. Maybe he was deliberately keeping a distance between you back then to protect you."

"To protect me from what?"

"From what he was truly feeling for you, dear."

Jenny was suddenly seeing Cole and everything that had happened between them in a whole new light. Was the angry passion Cole had revealed to her when they were alone in the pasture just a hint of his true feelings for her?

"So he deliberately was never alone with me to keep me safe, and in keeping me safe, he lost me." She looked up at Frances in shock. "I never understood."

"You were so young and full of dreams." Frances wanted to ease her guilt.

"And he loved me so much—"

"But what about your feelings? Did you love him then? Do you love him now?"

Again Jenny fell silent, remembering. Memories of her childhood blossomed in her mind—memories of the first day she'd met Cole.

"I think I've loved him forever," she finally said, acknowledging what was in the depths of her heart.

"How old were you when you first met? Eight or nine?" Frances remembered that day very clearly.

"I was nine. It was the day that Papa and I went into Animas City and—"

"And Cole rescued you from the middle of the street." Frances vividly recalled how distraught Paul had been when they'd returned to the ranch and he'd told her what had happened.

"That's right. Papa and I were crossing the main street when I dropped my doll. I didn't even think about danger. I didn't even look to see if anyone was coming. I just ran back out to get it, and suddenly there was a buckboard bearing down on me." She shuddered involuntarily at the memory. "Cole appeared out of nowhere. He grabbed me up and carried me to safety."

"It seems like Cole was always there whenever you needed help. He's always been your hero, hasn't he? Your champion—"

"He has, hasn't he? Like that time when my horse got away from me and he raced up and caught the reins and saved me. And then there was the night in town at that dance when Will Baker cornered me and tried to kiss me—"

"I remember that night. Will was sporting quite a shiner for a while," Frances laughed. "How old were you then?"

"Barely fifteen, I think." Jenny was suddenly serious. "Do you suppose Cole loved me even back then?"

"It's possible." Frances was thoughtful.

"He's being my hero again, you know, supporting the guest ranch idea the way he has," she said softly.

"Yes, he is."

Jenny drew a ragged breath as she accepted the truth. "I do love him, Frances. I never realized until now just how much."

"So what are you going to do about it?"

"There's not much I can do—not knowing how he feels about me."

"He may very well be angry with you over what happened. A man does have his pride. But Cole is definitely worth fighting for, don't you think?"

"Well, I—"

"Jenny, I have never known you to back down from a challenge."

Jenny's spine stiffened at her words, and she smiled. "You're right, Frances. Thank you! I love Cole Randall, and I'm going to figure out a way to win him back."

"Don't thank me. Thank your friend Rose. She sounds like a very perceptive woman."

"That's why I love her. She never ceases to amaze me. I think I'll go tell her so right now!"

"Do you think she's awake?"

"Even if she isn't, she'll want to hear my news. And then we have to start planning—"

"Planning?"

"I have to figure out the best way to convince Cole that he still loves me and can't live without me!"

Frances was chuckling as Jenny rushed from the house on her way to awaken Rose.

Rose was not in the least upset by Jenny's excited entrance into her small sleeping room. She sat up in bed, yawning and rubbing her eyes.

"What time is it?" she asked sleepily.

"Time for you to help me finish what you started," Jenny told her.

Rose eyed her curiously. "What are you talking about?"

"I'm talking about Cole."

"What about him?"

"You were right, Rose. I love him. It took me all night, plus a long conversation with Frances, to finally realize it, but I do love Cole and I want him back."

"What about Richard?" Rose asked slyly, lowering

her voice just in case someone could overhear their conversation.

"What about him?"

"How does he compare to Cole?"

"There's no comparison," Jenny declared. In her mind, Richard paled to insignificance next to Cole.

"Exactly!" Rose laughed gaily. "I knew it! You do love Cole! So how are you going to win him over?"

"I don't know. That's why I came in here to wake you up early so we could figure out what I should do."

"We need to make a battle plan," Rose said thoughtfully, her expression turning serious as she began to plot.

"A battle plan?" Jenny's eyes widened.

"That's right. You're going to have to storm Cole's defenses."

"You sound like a general going to war."

"Sometimes love is like war. He's hardened himself against any tender emotions, and you've got to find a way to get past the barriers he's put up. You have to lay siege to his heart."

"I like the sound of that. When do we get started?"

"How soon will you see him again?"

"Probably not until the dance in town."

"So we've got a little time to plan." Rose was excited as she started to think of ways to reach out to Cole. "This is going to be so much fun!"

"I hope you're right," Jenny said. Then, suddenly afraid that it might be too late to win him back, she asked, "But what if he really doesn't love me anymore?"

"Then we'll just have to make him fall in love with you all over again. We will not be denied! I don't want to hear any more doubts from you, Jenny. You love Cole, and you've made up your mind that you're going to do everything in your power to catch him. Right?"

"Right."

"Then failure is not a possibility."

They huddled there on Rose's bed in the predawn darkness, plotting the best ways to seduce a cowboy. They had four days to formulate a plan of action.

"This certainly makes me appreciate Philadelphia and a well-sprung carriage," Aubrey declared under his breath to Richard as they jolted along on a cross-country horseback ride with Jenny, Melanie, and Rose later that day.

"You're not giving up already, are you?" Richard taunted his friend.

"Hardly. I'm no quitter. I just prefer a more civilized way of life, that's all. One of these days I'm going to have to stop following you on these adventures."

"But think how boring your life would become."

"Boring might be quite pleasant right now. You see, I don't have a reason for being here as you do."

"You're here as my moral support."

"As if you'd heed my advice anyway," he scoffed.

"It all goes back to what I told you before we left: if you'd proposed to Jenny a month or two ago, we wouldn't be stuck here in the middle of nowhere now."

"You need to learn how to relax and have some fun, Aubrey."

"I know very well how to relax and have fun," he groused, "and this isn't it. It's bourbon and cigars at the men's club and then playing high-stakes poker until dawn."

"I will do my best to find a saloon for you in town, my friend."

Aubrey only grunted in response as the group slowed near a scenic viewpoint.

"Rose—I thought you might want to get a picture from here," Jenny said as she stopped her horse. "What do you think?"

The vista before them was magnificent. The mountains rose in majestic splendor over the lush valley below.

"Each time I look in a different direction, I see a scene more beautiful than the last," Rose told her.

Rose dismounted and, with Tom's help, started to unpack the eighty pounds of photography equipment that was loaded on a packhorse. This would be the sixth photograph she'd taken since they'd ridden out that morning, and she firmly believed that each one was better than the last.

"I guess the rest of us can take it easy for a while," Jenny suggested.

Rose was getting to be quite professional in her handling of the delicate equipment. She carefully assembled her camera and then insisted that her friends pose for her.

"I want proof that you really were here," she explained.

While they all held perfectly still, she took the photograph. She smiled with satisfaction when she'd finished.

"That will be the best one so far."

"If you want to take more than just photographs of the great outdoors, you could take the camera with you when we go into town for the dance."

Rose suddenly smiled brightly at the prospect. "Cole said he was going to be there. Maybe I can get a picture of him to take back East with me, and maybe I can find my mystery cowboy and take his picture, too."

"Still thinking about him, are you?"

"Yes. He was the first real cowboy I ever ran into," Rose said with a grin, remembering her encounter with the handsome mysterious stranger. "I want to see if I made as big an impression on him as he did on me."

"It will be interesting trying to find him. I guess we could start by asking George at the mercantile. He might remember what happened and know who he is."

"You're right! We'll go there first," Rose decided.

"And while you ladies are taking your photographs,

Aubrey and I will take the time to explore the more manly entertainments in your town," Richard told them.

"I'm sure you'll have a wonderful time," Jenny said.

"The trip into town is still a few days away yet," Melanie said. "What are we going to do tomorrow?"

As they got ready to ride again, Jenny told them of the day-long hunting trip Louie had scheduled for the men and the three-mile hike she'd arranged for the women. She was looking forward to having time with just Rose and Melanie. They had a lot to talk about and a lot of plans to make before the night of the dance.

Chapter Sixteen

Richard was not a happy man. His whole purpose in coming on this expedition was to spend some time with Jenny, but it wasn't turning out that way. Every minute of his time had been filled with carefully scheduled activities.

He had gone horseback riding.

He'd hunted.

He'd hiked.

He'd ridden along on a roundup and helped repair a damaged fence line.

Now as they were finally heading back to the ranch for the night, Richard decided that he'd had enough. He had not had a minute of privacy with her in all the days they'd been there.

He intended to rectify the problem that very night.

"Why are you looking so grim?" Aubrey asked as

they rode along together a short distance behind the others.

"I've been trying to get Jenny alone, but there's always somebody around. And now tomorrow we go into town for the dance."

"That'll be the time for you to make your move."

"I hope so. The only reason I made the trip out here was to be with her."

"Talk to her tonight. You don't have anything to lose, and it's not as if she's being courted by anyone else. She's just really serious about making the ranch a success and probably isn't thinking too much about romance—or anything else, for that matter."

Richard grunted in reluctant agreement. Jenny certainly had no social life to speak of, and the only other man who'd been around was her ex-fiancé. Richard was certain Cole posed no threat.

"I've been thinking. If you tell Jenny that she can use your money to fix the place up once she marries you, she'll probably rush you to the altar."

"But then that would mean we would have to live here," Richard complained. He was more than ready to head back to civilization.

"Maybe for only part of the year," Aubrey offered hopefully. "You do love her, don't you?"

Richard didn't answer. He knew he desired Jenny and wanted her badly. But love and marriage? That was a far bigger commitment than he wanted to make. He would have to see how things went between them during the next day or two. He was definitely going to seek her out tonight.

Mira gave a lot of thought to what she would wear to the dance the following night. Since Jenny was back in the area, she might very well show up, too, so Mira wanted to look her absolute best. She didn't want Cole to have any reason to look at another woman. She selected a dark blue gown with a low-cut bodice. She hoped the revealing decolletage would keep Cole's attention focused on her all night long—and maybe a few other men's, too. A little competition from other men might spike his interest in her. She was ready and willing to do whatever it took to make him her own.

When they returned to the ranch from the ride, Rose accompanied Jenny to the main house.

"I want to take a look at your gowns. Whatever we choose for you to wear tomorrow night has to be really special," Rose advised her. "It's got to be romantic, yet exciting."

"I hope I've got something like that," Jenny said, trying to think of what was in her wardrobe. When she'd packed so hurriedly to come back to the ranch, she hadn't worried about bringing any of her fancier gowns.

"If you don't, I brought two gowns with me, and one of them just might work for you. We'll find something, don't worry. We are going to be staying overnight in town, right?"

"Yes. It will be late when the dance is over, so we'll take rooms at one of the hotels."

"Good. That will give us a place to fix your hair before the dance."

"My hair?" Jenny was surprised. She'd always worn it tied back or she'd let it fall freely about her shoulders.

Rose looked pensive. "I've been studying you today, and I think your hair would look wonderful if we styled it up some way. I'll experiment with it and see."

"But—"

"You love Cole and you want to win Cole over, don't you? You have to remember, this is war, and this will be our first attack. We have to make you look so gorgeous that he won't be able to take his eyes off you. Trust me in this."

"If you're so good at capturing men's hearts, why haven't you married yet?" Jenny asked. She knew that Rose saw quite a variety of men, but she'd never gotten serious with any of them.

Rose looked thoughtful, then finally answered, "I've never been in love. I've liked a lot of men, and I've enjoyed their company, but no one's ever swept me off my feet. I guess I'm still looking for that handsome prince to woo me."

"A prince?"

"Every girl can have her fairy tale to believe in, can't she?"

Jenny laughed. "If you say so."

"I do. Now, back to you and Cole. We have to figure out a way to get him to dance with you."

"I don't think he'll want to."

"We'll make him want to," Rose insisted. "After all, he can't snub you in public. When he asks you to dance, there must be some way you can maneuver him into a quiet corner somewhere."

Jenny smiled at Rose. "I like the way you think."

"Good, but do you know what you're going to do with him once you get him alone?"

"I've got a pretty good idea."

"That's my girl. That will be assault number two."

"How many 'assaults' is it going to take?"

"Does it matter? I think you're going to be enjoying every one of them."

"You're right!"

They made their way up to Jenny's room and spent the next hour going through her wardrobe. When they didn't find the perfect gown, Rose went out to the guest house and returned with one of her own. A few minutes later, Jenny was standing before her wearing a rose-colored gown that was stunning on her.

"I never looked this good in it!" Rose protested good-naturedly as she surveyed her friend. "You're beautiful." She said the last a bit reverently.

Jenny turned to look at herself in the full-length mirror and was surprised by the vision she made. The gown fit her perfectly, and the color highlighted her fairness. The neckline was revealing without being too daring.

"Thanks, Rose." Jenny turned back to her friend, her eyes aglow with the realization that she truly did look lovely.

"When we go into battle, we have to be prepared," Rose said with a grin as she stepped behind Jenny and unfastened her hair, freeing it to fall around her shoulders. She then lifted the heavy mass up and twisted it into a stylish knot, leaving a few tendrils loose to fall softly about her face. "And that's what I want to do with your hair. What do you think?"

"I almost look like a different person."

"Let's hope your intriguing new look works on Cole. I guarantee you're going to have every man at the social wanting a dance with you. They'll be standing in line."

"As long as Cole is one of them, I'll be happy."

They shared a conspiratorial look of eager anticipation.

"What time do you think we should start into town tomorrow?" Rose asked.

"You're the one who wants to take pictures around town and try to find your mystery cowboy. How early do you want to get there?"

"Early," Rose said with conviction. "Because once I find him, I'm going to want to spend as much time with him as I can."

"We'll leave right after breakfast."

"I'll be ready, there's no doubt about that."

Richard was ready when it was finally time for the evening meal. He'd cleaned up and changed clothes and felt almost civilized again. It was a pleasurable sensation.

He and Aubrey left the guest house just as Melanie, Tillie, and Rose came out, too. They all walked up to the main house together.

Frances's cooking was delicious, as usual, and the conversation centered on the next day's trip to town.

"So we'll be staying the night?" Richard asked, liking the prospect.

"Yes. Then we'll return to the ranch the following day."

"We'll be ready to leave whenever you are," Aubrey said, equally glad to be going into town. He was eager to explore some of the saloons he'd heard about. He was looking forward to a serious round of poker and a strong drink.

Everyone was tired from the activity of the day, so no one lingered too long after eating.

Jenny walked out onto the porch to say good night to everyone as they started back to the guest house to retire. The night was clear, crisp, and cool with a slight breeze stirring in the trees. She stood at the railing, inhaling deeply of the sweet air. This was her heaven.

"It is a beautiful night, isn't it, Jenny?" Richard

said in a low voice. He knew Evelyn had gone back inside to go to bed, but he spoke softly for he wanted to keep their conversation as private as possible.

Jenny was a little surprised to find that Richard had lingered behind.

"Yes, it is," she agreed. "Aren't you tired? Everybody else sounded as if they couldn't wait to call it a night."

"I was just regretting that my stay here is nearly half over and we really haven't had the chance to spend much time together," he remarked, thinking how pretty she looked in the moonlight. Her remark about calling it a night had excited him. He would love to go to bed—if she would go with him.

"Things have been busy," she agreed, suddenly feeling a bit awkward. She knew Richard was interested in her, but her feelings for him were not amorous.

"You haven't had a moment's peace in a long time, have you?" he sympathized as he came to stand beside her.

The porch was dark except for the glow of the lamplight coming through the front parlor windows.

Jenny wanted to step away from him to keep some distance between them, but she felt foolish backing away. She could handle Richard.

"It's been a difficult time."

"I'm sorry about your father's death, Jenny," he said sincerely. "But once you get things straightened out here, you can go back to living your life again."

She glanced at him, realizing he didn't understand her at all. "This is my life, Richard."

"What about Philadelphia? You had a good life there with your Aunt Evelyn. You were happy there, weren't you?"

"You're right. I was happy, but once I came home, I knew—This is where I want to be."

"With all that you've just been through recently, you can't be really sure of that, can you?" he said, reaching out to Jenny.

Richard's tone was soothing enough, but his attitude irritated her. She allowed him to touch her shoulder, but did not move any closer to him.

"I know you're trying to be kind, Richard, but I do know my own mind. I won't be going back to Philadelphia. This is my home. I'm staying here."

"Jenny—" he said softly.

When she glanced toward him, he moved quickly to take her in his arms and kiss her.

Jenny didn't fight him. Richard seemed overly attentive tonight, and so she was not surprised by his ploy. She accepted his kiss. The whole while his lips moved over hers, though, they evoked no response from her at all. She felt no physical attraction to Richard. She was remembering another kiss—Cole's kiss.

Cole's kiss had been wild and passionate. It had seared both her heart and her soul, and had awakened within her the truth of her feelings for him.

Richard's kiss aroused no desire in Jenny other than the need to move away from him. When he tried to draw her closer and deepen the exchange, she broke off the embrace and distanced herself from him.

"It's been a long day, Richard. I'd better go in now," she said, smiling a little to soften her hurried exit.

As Richard watched her disappear inside and close the door, his jaw locked in anger. *Damn the woman!* Jenny was as elusive as ever. He was not used to being denied. He was Richard Donathan III, and he didn't like her attitude one bit.

Richard believed he could use his money to entice Jenny, but he wasn't accustomed to having to buy a woman's affections. As a Donathan, he was guaranteed entry to the best homes and the attention of most of the marriageable females in his social class. He didn't understand why Jenny was proving to be so hard to win over. He wasn't about to quit, though. That would be admitting defeat, and a Donathan was never defeated.

Richard stalked off into the night, not quite ready to return to the guest house. Tomorrow they would go into town for the dance. Surely he would get another chance to be with Jenny there, and perhaps it was time that he gave some serious thought to Aubrey's suggestion. . . .

Maybe he should think about marrying her.

Chapter Seventeen

Rose's excitement was even greater than usual the following day as she and Jenny left the hotel and began their search for "her cowboy," starting at the mercantile. Because she wanted to take the camera with her, Tom had been recruited to come into town with them and help carry things. He trailed after them now, weighted down by the expensive equipment.

"I'm ready. Are you?" Rose asked.

"We'll give it our best effort," Jenny promised. "I hope George remembers the man we're talking about."

"Even if he doesn't, I'm going to find a way to track him down."

"Why is this cowboy so important to you?" Jenny was curious. She hadn't noticed anything unusual about the man.

"I'm not sure," Rose said thoughtfully. "There was just something about him—I mean, the moment our gazes met, I . . ." Rose stopped talking, realizing how ridiculous she sounded.

"From the moment your gazes met, what?" Jenny prodded. This wasn't a normal conversation with Rose. She'd never known her friend to give in to romantic flights of fancy.

"Oh, nothing. I'm probably just imagining things, and that's why I want to see him one more time—to find out."

"Well, if he's in Durango, we'll find him. I promise."

"I'll hold you to that."

They reached Lansing's Mercantile.

"Here we are," Jenny announced as they stopped out in front.

"I hope the same gentleman is working."

"George should be here. He's the owner."

They entered the store to find the older man hard at work behind the counter.

"Why, Jenny! It's good to see you again. Are you in town for the big dance tonight?"

"We sure are, George. You remember my friend Rose, don't you? And this is Tom; he works for me."

"Of course. Nice to see you, too, miss." He was staring with open interest at the camera equipment. "Is one of you a photographer?"

"I am," Rose told him, "and I was wondering if I could get you to pose for me, George? I've been taking pictures out at the ranch and I wanted some from around town. I'd love to get one of you standing in front of the store."

George was thrilled. "Why, yes, ma'am." He started to take off his apron as he came around the counter.

"Don't take off your apron. I want to capture the feel of Lansing Mercantile."

"You sure?" He wanted to look his best for her.

"Yes. I like you just the way you are," Rose insisted.

George nervously smoothed down his hair as they went outside. Rose quickly set about arranging her tripod and camera. She directed George exactly where to stand for the best light and was pleased with the final pose—George centered on the porch in the front of the store with the big "Lansing Mercantile" sign hanging above him.

"That's wonderful," Rose told him when she'd finished. "Thank you."

"Oh, it was my pleasure, believe me. It isn't every day that I can get the chance to have my picture taken."

He was feeling quite special as they walked back indoors. Some of the townsfolk had gathered around to watch, curious as to what she was doing.

Tom stayed outside with the equipment.

"I'll make sure you get a print. And by the way, I wanted to thank you for sending that other package I dropped out to the ranch. I hadn't even realized it was missing."

"Dan found the package after you'd gone," George answered easily.

"Dan? Is he the man I ran into?" Rose asked.

"Yes, that's Dan. Dan Lesseg. He found it in one of the side aisles when he was leaving that day. I told him I'd see to it that you got it."

"I appreciate your help, and I'd like to thank Dan, too, if I could. Do you know if he's still in town?" She tried to sound casual, but her heartbeat had quickened when she'd learned his name. *Dan. Dan Lesseg.* She thought Dan was a wonderful name.

"Oh, sure, Dan's in town, but I don't know about a lady like you going to find him. . . ."

Jenny heard the hesitation and awkwardness in George's voice and wondered at it. "Is there a problem, George?"

He looked a bit sheepish. "Well, Jenny, you see, Dan works at the High Time. He's the bartender there."

"He's a bartender?" Rose was amazed. Of all the things she'd imagined him doing, working in a saloon wasn't one of them.

"That's right, and a darned good one, too. I can attest to that," George told them with a smile.

"Where is the High Time?" Rose asked.

"It really ain't no place for a lady to go," George cautioned.

In good humor, Rose was tempted to ask him why

he thought she was a lady, but she controlled the impulse. "But a picture of a real saloon and a bartender would be wonderful! What says 'Wild West' better than a saloon? Besides, we'll have Tom along with us."

"Well—um—I suppose it would be all right." George glanced outside to where the young hand was waiting and guessed the boy could help the women out if they got into any trouble. He hadn't run into anyone like Rose before and was completely charmed by her vivacity. His common sense was telling him to discourage her interest in the saloon, but her excitement erased his fears. "The High Time's just past the railroad tracks . . ." He gave them the directions.

"Thanks, George," Jenny told him.

"You be careful," he cautioned, wondering if he'd done the right thing.

"We will, don't worry."

Jenny, Rose, and Tom started off toward the High Time.

"This is so exciting!" Rose said. "I'm going to a real saloon!"

"You're sure you want to do this?" Jenny asked.

"Of course I'm sure. That's why I came out here. I wanted to experience this kind of excitement."

"All right. Let's hope your Dan is working."

"If he isn't, maybe we'll just stay at the bar and wait for him to show up," Rose said smiling.

Jenny laughed. She could only imagine the reaction

around town if the news got out that they had frequented the High Time.

As they made their way toward the saloon, a very handsome couple came out of one of the buildings and started walking toward them.

"Jenny?" the woman said in delight when she saw her. "It's so good to see you!"

"Elise—Trace—it's good to see you, too!" Jenny said as she hugged Elise. She hadn't seen her old friends since she'd returned. She quickly turned to Rose to make the introductions. "Rose, these are my friends Elise and Trace Jackson. They're the owners of the *Durango Weekly Star*. This is Rose, my friend from Philadelphia."

"It's a pleasure to meet you," Rose said.

"You're a photographer?" Trace asked, noticing the equipment Tom was carrying.

"Yes. I'm taking as many pictures as I can here in Durango. Your town is so beautiful—I'm going to use them to help promote Jenny's guest ranch when I go back to Philadelphia."

"So it is true, then?" Elise looked at Jenny. "I had heard talk that you were considering taking in visitors."

"Yes. Rose brought the first group out this week. I have a total of five guests staying at the Lazy S right now."

"And we're having a wonderful time!" Rose put in.

"We'll have to do an article on your success," Trace said.

"That would be wonderful."

"Are you staying in town for the dance tonight?" Elise asked.

"Yes."

"Then we'll see you there."

"And you'd both better save a dance for me," Trace said.

"Our pleasure," they responded.

Jenny and Rose moved on with Tom following, still on their quest to find Dan.

"Jenny, are all the men in Colorado good-looking? Your friend Trace is every bit as handsome as Cole and Dan."

"I guess we just know how to grow 'em right out here," Jenny laughed. She had to admit, though, Rose was right. Trace was very attractive. "Trace and Elise's story is a most interesting one. He used to be a lawman. . . ." She went on to tell Rose how the two had met and fallen in love.

"That is so romantic," Rose sighed. "Elise had her hero right there with her the whole time, and she didn't even realize it. What a wonderful story."

"Yes, it is."

They saw the sign for the High Time ahead, and Jenny stopped and looked at her friend.

"How do you want to do this?"

"I'm just going to walk in and ask for Dan. That's the easiest way, don't you think?" Rose knew it was a little late for her to start playing the role of the shy, retiring female.

"To tell you the truth, I've never gone into a saloon before."

"I can go in for you," Tom offered. He knew how rough saloons could be and didn't want anything to happen to them.

"That's sweet of you, Tom, but I'm going to do this myself," Rose declared. "When I want something, I go after it."

Rose marched ahead and Jenny followed her. She bravely pushed the swinging door open and went inside, her head held high. She stopped just inside the door and let her gaze sweep over the room, looking for Dan. This was her first ever view of a real saloon. It was cleaner than she'd expected, though the scent of cigars and whiskey did hang heavy in the air. There was a small area that must serve as a dance floor, an upright piano in one corner, and a bar that ran across the entire width of the back wall. A few customers were seated at the tables, and more stood at the bar with a woman wearing a revealing dress. But she saw no sign of Dan.

"I don't see him, do you?" Jenny asked.

"No."

Several of the customers at the tables noticed them and started elbowing their companions. One man got up and approached them, his gait a bit unsteady.

"Say, girlies, are you here for a good time? Did you just start working for Fernada? I ain't seen you here before, have I?" he asked, grinning at them hungrily. Though they obviously weren't dressed like the normal bargirls, he didn't care as long as they took care of business—and that meant pleasuring him.

Just then Tom came into the saloon behind them carrying all the equipment. The man peered at him in confusion.

"What the hell's goin' on?"

Fernada had been standing at the bar when the two women entered the High Time. Since Dan was in back, she hurried forward to take care of the situation, not wanting any trouble. She knew how obnoxious Jimmy Hogan could be after a few drinks.

"Is there something I can do for you ladies? Are you lost?" Fernada asked.

"No . . . no, we're not lost," Rose said, still looking for some sign of Dan. "Actually, we're looking for—"

And then Dan emerged from the back room.

"Someone—" Rose's breath caught in her throat when she saw him.

Dan was every bit as good-looking as she'd remembered. He was carrying a case of liquor, and she could see how his shirt stretched taut across his powerful shoulders. She found herself actually growing a bit nervous about talking to him again. Her reaction amazed her. Nothing had ever made her nervous, but this man did. She found it thrilling and a bit unnerving.

Fernada followed the direction of Rose's gaze and frowned, puzzled. "You're here to see Dan?"

"Yes," she breathed.

The men at the bar had alerted Dan that something unusual was going on, and he set the liquor aside and glanced toward the front of the saloon. It took him only an instant to recognize Rose and Jenny. He smiled and quit what he was doing to go and speak with them.

"Well, hello," Dan said.

He'd tried not to think about Rose too much after their encounter. He had not expected to ever see her again. But instead of forgetting her, he couldn't shake her from his mind ever since. Seeing her again now, he realized why. She was as beautiful as he remembered. He didn't know why she'd dared to come here, seeking him out, but he was real glad that she had.

"Hello, Dan." Rose smiled at him and him alone. Although there were others with them, she felt as if they were by themselves, intent only on each other.

"You know my name. . . ." He was even more surprised.

"I asked George at the mercantile. He told me where to find you."

"I'm glad he did," he said, still grinning.

"You know these ladies, Dan?" Fernada interrupted. She could not imagine why these two obviously well-bred women had dared to enter the bar.

"Fernada, this is Jenny Sullivan from the Lazy S and her friend Rose. I ran into them the other day over at the mercantile." As he said it, his gaze met Rose's and they both smiled.

"So you two don't work for Fernada?" Jimmy Hogan said in confusion.

"No, Jimmy, they don't," Fernada explained. "Why don't you belly up to the bar and I'll buy you a drink in a minute."

"Why, I'll just do that," he said as he staggered off, disappointed, but happy to be getting free liquor.

"So is there something we can do for you?" Fernada asked. She wanted to get the women out of the High Time as quickly as possible.

"Actually, I needed to speak with Dan," Rose said, looking up at him.

"I'd better go take care of Jimmy, Dan. You hurry it up here, all right?" She gave him a look that spoke volumes and let him know that she wanted the women out of the saloon fast.

"What can I do for you?" Dan asked sincerely.

Rose could come up with a list a mile long of what she'd like him to do for her. First on the list would be "kiss me."

As she realized the direction of her thoughts, Rose chastised herself.

"I just wanted to thank you for seeing that the package I dropped at the mercantile got delivered to me."

"I was just glad I found it for you."

The moment seemed to be growing more and more awkward. Rose knew she should leave, but she didn't want to. "I've never been in a saloon before."

He knew that. She was a lady through and through, and she had no business being in a place like this. He knew he should encourage her to leave, but he wasn't ready to say good-bye to her yet. "What do you think of the High Time?"

"It's a world unto itself, and that's the other reason why I came here," she told him. "I've brought my camera, and I wondered if I could get a picture of you standing out in front of the saloon near the sign."

"You want to take a picture of me and the High Time?" He looked from her to where Tom stood with the equipment.

"Yes. I'd like one of you, and Fernada, too, if she'd be interested. I'm going to use them when I go back home to Philadelphia to show everybody what Durango and the Lazy S are really like. I hope the pictures get people excited about visiting the West. I'm sure there are any number of men back East who would love to come to a place like this," Rose explained, looking around once more. She didn't tell him that she planned to keep at least one copy of his photograph for herself.

Dan looked back toward the bar. "You boys all right on your drinks for a while?"

"Yeah," they answered, all watching him with open interest. They couldn't wait to find out what was going on.

"Fernada? Can you come here a minute?"

She didn't know what Dan wanted, but she served Jimmy his drink and followed them out of the saloon. "What's going on?"

"Rose wants to take our picture," he told her.

"She does?" Fernada was thrilled. She'd never had her photograph taken.

Jenny and Tom stayed out of the way as Rose went to work setting up the tripod, adjusting her equipment, and making sure there was enough light to get the best shot.

"I'd like to take one with you together, and then I want to take two more—one of each of you individually."

When she'd finished setting up her camera, she directed them where to stand and made sure the exposure was right. That done, she took the pictures.

"Can I get a copy of your photographs?" Fernada asked, eager to see how they turned out.

"I'll be sure to develop an extra print for you."

"Thanks. Are you both staying in town tonight for the big dance?" Fernada asked.

"We wouldn't miss it," Jenny told her.

"It should be a good time. Almost everyone turns out."

"What about you, Dan?" Rose asked without a bit of embarrassment. "Will you be at the dance?"

She was hoping he would be there. She wanted to dance with him—to have his arms around her and . . . The image in her mind was wonderful, until he answered her.

"I have to work tonight."

Dan had never, ever resented his job before. He had always put in long hours and usually enjoyed it, but right now, it irritated him that he had to work that night. He'd never wanted to go to a dance before, but tonight he did. And he knew very well what the reason was. Rose would be there.

"Oh. Well, I'll see you when I get the photographs developed, then."

He brightened at the thought of being with her once more. "I'll look forward to it."

"I can't wait to see them!" Fernada added, still excited about the photographs and missing completely the underlying tension between the two. "I'd better get back to work."

"Thank you for your help," Rose told her as Fernada disappeared inside.

"And I'll see you again later?" Dan asked Rose, his gaze meeting and holding hers.

"Yes," she answered firmly. "Should I bring the photographs back here?"

"Yes. It's not very often that I'm anywhere else."

"Then I'll find you."

Dan went back to work as Rose carefully packed up her things and gave them to Tom. They started back to the hotel.

"That went nicely, don't you think?" Rose asked Jenny.

"Actually, I'm surprised that it went as well as it did."

"You were really worried?"

"If my papa had been alive, he would have had a

fit if he'd found out I'd been in there," Jenny told her with a grin.

"I guess I'm a bad influence on you," Rose laughed.

"Yes, and I'm enjoying every minute of it."

Chapter Eighteen

Jenny stood before the mirror in the hotel room, critically studying her reflection.

"Do you think I look pretty enough?" she asked Rose.

"You are gorgeous tonight. I wish I'd looked this good in that gown. I may just have to let you keep it. It's absolutely wonderful on you."

The gown was enticing. It set off her figure to perfection, and Rose had arranged her hair up in an artful style that bespoke elegance. Jenny looked sophisticated and worldly.

Jenny nodded at her reflection, her expression determined. "Cole Randall, here I come."

"There will be no way he'll be able to ignore you—and neither will any of the other men who are there," Rose told her with confidence. "Who knows? Maybe

Richard will propose to you tonight." Her grin was wicked.

"I don't even want to think about that. Richard's nice enough, but I'm not attracted to him—not the way he'd like me to be."

"And I'll bet the more aloof you are with him, the harder he pursues you," Rose said thoughtfully. "It's obvious Richard loves challenges. You're probably the only woman who's ever denied him anything—and that makes him all the more determined to have you."

"I'm sure that's why he and Aubrey are here. He was getting quite serious back in Philadelphia just as I got word about my father and had to leave."

"Well, I'll keep an eye on you tonight. If you look like you need rescuing, I'll find a way to save you."

"You are a true friend." Jenny laughed as an image of Rose trying to save her from Richard played in her mind. "Although I don't know how you'd manage to take on Richard."

"He may be bigger than I am, but I'm more determined."

Somehow, Jenny knew Rose was right.

"By the way, you look very pretty tonight, too," Jenny told her. "It's a shame your cowboy has to work all night and won't get to see you."

"I know. The thought occurred to me that I ought to go back over to the High Time and spend the evening at the bar with him, but that's probably not such a wonderful idea."

"This is unusual for you," Jenny remarked thoughtfully, casting her friend a sidelong glance. "I've never known you to react to any man the way you're reacting to Dan."

"I know. I don't quite understand it myself," Rose said, a bit perplexed; then she smiled. "But I'm enjoying it. Let's just hope that I get to see him at least a few more times before I have to go back home."

"You will."

"I hope so." The possibility of not seeing Dan again troubled Rose, and the fact that she was even worrying about it surprised her. She turned her thoughts away from her cowboy and back to Jenny's dilemma.

"So, are you ready?"

"I'm as ready as I'll ever be, but there is one more thing I have to warn you about."

"What's that?" Rose was surprised.

"Not what—who. His name is Clint Parker."

"And just who in the world is this Clint?"

"Clint is a hand at one of the other ranches, and he loves to dance."

"Yes, so?"

"So, he can be hazardous to your health—if you're not careful." At Rose's puzzled look, Jenny went on to explain. "He's not exactly graceful, so watch your toes."

"Just be sure to warn me if he shows up, so I'll know it's him," she said.

"As your best friend, I could do no less. We'll have to tell Melanie, too."

They left the hotel room, moving gracefully along the hall and then down the steps to the lobby. Tillie and Evelyn were already there with Melanie, waiting for them, as were Aubrey and Richard.

When Jenny saw Richard standing there, his gaze devouring her as she descended the stairs, she stifled a groan. It was going to be a long night, she could feel it. Jenny forced herself to smile.

Richard had always believed that Jenny was one of the most beautiful women he'd ever known, but tonight she looked more stunning than ever. After spending these last days with her on the ranch, where she'd practically been dressing like a man every day, he was delighted to see her looking like a lady again.

"Good evening, Jenny," he said as he went forward to greet her.

"Is everybody ready to go?"

"We've been waiting for you and Rose, and I must say, you were worth the wait."

"Why, thank you, Richard."

In gentlemanly fashion, Richard offered Jenny his arm.

There was no way she could refuse politely, so she took it and allowed him to escort her from the hotel.

As they made their way to the dance, Richard attempted to make small talk with her, but she found herself watching for Cole, hoping to catch a glimpse of him. She saw no sign of Cole anywhere, though, and was forced to endure Richard's undivided attention. Jenny knew if this kept up, she would actually look forward to Clint Parker asking her to dance.

The outdoor dance floor that had been erected for the evening was crowded with couples as the music played on into the night. Brightly colored lanterns cast their muted glow over the scene. The evening was perfect, the sky clear, the moon bright.

Cole pretended to be enjoying himself as he squired Mira around the dance floor. It wasn't that he was having a bad time. It was just that he found himself watching for Jenny and worrying about her. She had said she was going to be there, and he had not yet seen her.

"Cole, this is so much fun," Mira said, gazing up at him with open adoration. "Thank you for inviting me."

"My pleasure, Mira," he responded.

It was at that moment that Jenny and Richard reached the side of the dance floor. Jenny immediately spotted Cole and Mira dancing together. She dared not let her expression slip at the sight of Cole smiling at the other woman as if he were having the most wonderful time in the world.

Jenny unconsciously squared her shoulders, mentally preparing to do battle.

"Richard," she said, turning to him without preamble, "let's dance."

She'd been so elusive and almost indifferent to him as they'd made their way to the dance that Richard was a bit taken aback by her unexpected invitation. He didn't waste any time worrying about it, though. All he wanted to do was hold Jenny in his arms.

"Your wish is my command," Richard replied gallantly. He swept her out among the other dancers.

Jenny kept her gaze focused on Richard.

But she wanted to be watching Cole.

Jenny forced herself to smile at Richard politely.

She wanted to scowl.

To all the world, Jenny appeared rapturously happy as she danced with her Eastern gentleman. They looked like a sophisticated couple, enjoying a dance and each other's company.

But that was far from the truth.

In her heart, Jenny was angry. Cole was with Mira! Jenny wondered if he had escorted her to the social, or if he was merely having a dance with her. She hoped it was the latter.

"I didn't realize there would be so many people here tonight," Richard said to Jenny as they continued to dance. "I'm impressed."

"These dances are very special events around town, and they're always a lot of fun. It isn't often that everybody gets a chance to relax and have a good time."

"And that's what I intend to have tonight—a good time—with you," Richard said, gazing down at Jenny.

He struggled to keep from ogling her, but the low-cut bodice did entice him. He could barely keep his eyes off the splendid display, but he knew it wouldn't do for him to be ogling her in public.

"What did you and Aubrey do all day?" Jenny asked just to make conversation. She could feel the heat of his gaze upon her, and it was making her uncomfortable.

"We found a few saloons that were to our liking. Aubrey got into a poker game and won quite handily. He was rather pleased with the outcome."

"I don't doubt that for a minute." It was common knowledge back in Philadelphia that Aubrey was quite an accomplished gambler.

"What about you? Surely you didn't just sit in your hotel room all day."

"Actually, Rose and I had quite an adventure on our own."

"Really?" He couldn't imagine what they'd done. It wasn't as if Durango was a center of any sophisticated activity.

"Yes. We went around town taking pictures, and we ended up at the High Time Saloon."

"You and Rose went into a saloon?"

He almost stopped dancing, his shock was so great.

"Yes, and we found it quite interesting."

His expression turned a bit condemning. A saloon was no place for a woman! He quickly amended that thought, for he had passed quite a pleasant afternoon with a young woman in one of the rooms above the bar while Aubrey had been playing poker. But that was different. Women like Rose and Jenny had no business being there.

"I'd never been in one before, and—"

"There's a good reason why," he said tersely. "A saloon is no place for a lady."

"Well, Rose wanted to take a photograph of a saloon to show everyone back in Philadelphia, and since we discovered that the man she met the other day at the mercantile was the bartender at the High Time, we decided to go there."

"I wish you had said something before you went. Aubrey and I could have accompanied you. I don't like you putting yourself in danger that way."

"We weren't in danger. Besides, we had Tom with us the whole time."

"Even so, he's little more than a boy. You would have been much safer if Aubrey and I had gone along."

"Our reputations emerged unscathed," she replied.

She was going to be very glad when this dance was over so she could get away from Richard. He was no relation to her. He had no claim on her whatsoever. She didn't need advice from him on how to conduct herself, and she certainly didn't need any lectures from him on how to behave.

The music finally stopped, and she was thrilled at the opportunity to escape. It was difficult enough watching Cole with Mira. She didn't need Richard being dictatorial and condemning and monopolizing her time.

Jenny glanced surreptitiously Cole's way as Richard walked her to the side of the dance floor, and she found that Cole was still with Mira. It rather surprised her. From what she'd heard since she'd returned, Cole had never gotten serious with any woman while she'd been away. Yet tonight, Mira seemed to be the center of his attention.

Jenny had never formed an opinion about Mira one way or another. They had known each other since they were young, but had never really been friends. She decided right then and there, though, as she watched Cole lead Mira from the dance floor, his hand familiarly at her waist, that she didn't like the other woman much at all. And the way Mira was clinging to him irritated her greatly. If they were so caught up in each other, Jenny wondered if she was ever going to get the chance to have Cole to herself.

Richard walked her over to where Rose was standing.

"Richard, I would love a cup of punch," she told him sweetly. She wanted a moment alone with Rose.

"I'll be right back." He went off to do her bidding.

"Having fun?" Rose asked.

"Hardly. I may never get the chance to be with Cole, judging from the grip Mira has on him."

"So you know her? I was wondering who she was."

"Oh, yes. She's one of the neighboring ranchers."

"She's quite pretty."

"She looks very nice tonight."

"But you look even better," Rose insisted. "Has Cole even seen you yet?"

"I don't know."

"Why don't I see what I can do to stir things up a bit?"

"What did you have in mind?"

"You'll see." Rose gave her a wicked grin as she started off casually toward the place where Cole was standing, seemingly deep in conversation with Mira.

Rose was delighted when her timing proved perfect. Just as she reached them, the music started again.

"Cole, I know this isn't Sadie Hawkins day, but would you dance with me?" she asked without the slightest bit of coyness.

Mira gasped and glared at her. She didn't know who this woman was, but she was tempted to hit her.

"Evening, Rose," he said. "Mira, would you mind?"

"Of course not."

Mira gritted her teeth, though, as she watched Cole take the other woman out onto the dance floor. She knew he'd been put on the spot, but if he'd really wanted to stay with her, he could have refused. After all, he was with her tonight.

"Thank you, Cole," Rose said, sweetly smiling up at him. "Jenny warned me earlier about dancing with Clint Parker, and I thought I saw him heading my way."

Cole chuckled out loud. "Poor Clint."

"From the way Jenny tells it, you should be feeling

sorry for the ladies. Has anyone suffered any lasting injuries from her encounter with him?"

"I don't think so," he answered, still smiling. He liked Clint as a friend, but understood the ladies' concern. What Clint lacked in grace, he tried to make up for with enthusiasm.

"But there could always be a first time. Thank you for being my hero and saving me."

"It's a pleasure."

"And I promise not to step on you." She grinned at him.

"I never thought you would." He grinned back. "Are you enjoying your stay at the Lazy S?"

"Absolutely. I'm growing quite fond of the area, and with all the photographs I've been taking, I think I'll be able to create a lot of interest when I go home."

"That will certainly help Jenny's business."

"I know. The more I get the word out, the better."

"Do you plan to come back regularly?"

Rose was quiet for a moment. "I haven't really thought about it," she admitted. "I've just been enjoying the time I have here now."

She realized then that she would have to go back home soon, in little over a week, and she had only just found Dan. She took a quick glance around the crowd, hoping against hope that he might have come. But there was no sign of him anywhere. She was certain that he was dutifully tending bar at the High Time. She wondered if he thought of her at all. She noticed Cole do a double take and suddenly start grinning again.

"What is it?" Rose asked, trying to see what he was looking at.

"I just saw Clint."

"So?"

"Guess who he's dancing with."

"I have no idea," she replied as he swung her around just in time to glimpse Jenny in Clint's arms. "Oh, no—Cole, you were my hero; now you have to be Jenny's."

"She could have said no."

"It's too late for that. She was probably cornered, and since I'd already claimed you, there was no escape for her. You have to save her, Cole. She doesn't have anybody else."

"What about good old Richard?"

"Richard and Jenny have been seeing each other for a while," Rose said, and she was secretly pleased when she noticed that Cole tensed at her words. She'd have to let Jenny know that he seemed a bit jealous. She quickly continued on, "And they've had some good times together in Philadelphia, but I don't see him anywhere around right now. You're here. You could be the one to save her."

"She'll be all right. She's danced with Clint before and survived unscathed."

"Maybe she has in the past, but you're responsible for her now. Just think of her feet! If she's maimed and can never walk again, how will she be able to work and save the ranch? And then what would you do? You'll be responsible for her finances. Think of the expense of medical care if Clint injures her. . . ." Rose exhausted all the reasons she could think of to push Cole toward Jenny. "Dance me over there, go ahead. I'll sacrifice myself to save Jenny. You take Jenny. I'll take Clint. That's what best friends are for."

Cole wasn't quite sure which of the arguments Rose had used convinced him to intercede, but he swung them expertly toward where Clint was tromping around in great spirits, enjoying the fast-paced melody.

"Do you mind if I cut in?" Cole asked Clint, surprising the other man.

"You want to trade?" Clint asked, not stopping his dancing but looking straight at the woman he'd heard was named Rose. She was a pretty one, and he'd wanted to dance with her earlier, but she'd disappeared on him. He smiled broadly. "Sure, Cole. I'll trade you. Thanks, Jenny."

"You're welcome, Clint," Jenny said, not quite sure what was going on. She wondered what Rose had said to Cole to get him to come for her. "Thank you for asking me to dance."

Rose gave Jenny a secret wink as she went willingly into Clint's arms, and he danced her off into the crowd.

Chapter Nineteen

Jenny and Cole did not have time to stand there awkwardly and stare at each other. They were in the middle of the dance floor and had to keep moving.

Without a word, Cole took Jenny in his arms and swept her away. They moved gracefully together, matching each other's rhythm, their bodies instinctively attuned. There was no need for them to speak. Words would only have destroyed the moment.

Cole held her close while memories of other dances years before played in his mind. Jenny had fit against him perfectly then, and she did so now. He glanced down to find her gazing up at him. She looked lovely tonight, and he had a great desire to dance her off somewhere private, miles and miles away from here, where it would be just the two of them alone. Then he was going to kiss her—not a chaste kiss, but a passionate, hungry kiss that would tell her all that he was really feeling.

Just thinking about kissing Jenny stirred his body to life.

The sensual awareness that filled him surprised Cole. He tried to ignore it.

This was not the time.

This was not the place.

And this was definitely not the woman.

Cole had offered to dance with Jenny only to save her from Clint—nothing more.

Jenny found herself practically floating in Cole's arms. Cole was such a contrast to Clint in so many ways. Where Clint had been rough, Cole was smooth. Where Clint had been wildly enthusiastic about his dancing, Cole was controlled in his moves. Where Clint had been open and good-natured, Cole was reserved and seemed almost cautious with her.

Jenny realized vaguely that dancing with either man could prove dangerous to her, but for far different reasons. Dancing with Clint had been physically risky, but dancing with Cole was more threatening to her peace of mind.

The music continued, and she was glad. She didn't want the dance to end. She reveled in the feel of Cole's hard, powerful body in fluid motion against hers as they circled the dance floor. The moment was heavenly for her. This was where she belonged. There was nowhere else she wanted to be but with Cole.

As soon as the music ended, Cole would be gone—

back to Mira. She had to find a way to make this moment last. She wanted to get Cole alone—someplace away from the crowd—away from Richard—away from Mira. Someplace much more private. . . .

Try as she might, Jenny wasn't sure where that would be. She'd been surrounded by people ever since they'd arrived. Richard had rarely left her side, and just when she'd managed to escape him, Clint had appeared and would not be denied his dance. Jenny had been thrilled when Cole cut in on Clint, but she couldn't help thinking that Rose had used some kind of subterfuge to get him to do it.

A sense of futility threatened Jenny's determination. It seemed she was making no progress at all in winning Cole back, but then she realized she couldn't just give up. She loved Cole, and Cole had loved her once. She intended to make him love her again.

"That's my girl." Her father's voice seemed to ring out in her mind.

Tears welled up in her eyes. Her determination returned full force, and with it, the courage to do what needed to be done.

"Jenny?" Cole noticed the tears in her eyes and couldn't imagine what was troubling her. "Is something wrong?"

"No. No, I was just thinking . . ." Jenny replied hesitantly, still feeling quite emotional.

"Thinking about what?" he pressed.

Just then the music stopped. They stood there as other couples milled around them.

"It was nothing . . . I know you have to go back . . . Mira's waiting for you," Jenny said. She tried to force a smile. "Thanks for saving me from Clint."

With that, Jenny turned and walked away from him. She deliberately went in the opposite direction from where she'd last seen Mira waiting for Cole's return. She was taking a chance by leaving him this way, but she prayed that Cole would come after her. It was the only hope she had of getting to be alone with him that night.

Cole hesitated. Mira was waiting for him, but Jenny was about to disappear in the crowd. He made his decision.

He followed her.

What Rose had said to him in partial jest earlier had made an impression on him. Jenny was his responsibility, she had no one else. Though he knew Jenny was a strong woman, if something was troubling her deeply enough to reduce her to tears, he had to go to her and make sure she was all right.

Cole forgot about Mira.

Jenny needed him.

"Jenny—wait—" he called out softly as he closed the distance between them.

She glanced back, thrilled that he had come after her. She took care, however, not to let her pleasure show in her expression. "What do you want?"

"We need to talk," he said seriously as he took her arm and guided her away from the lights and the people.

Cole sought a secluded spot. He led her on until he found a quiet place about a block away from the festivities. It was deserted and dark, close enough so they could hear the music, but far enough away so they had some privacy to talk. He stopped and faced her, looking down at her in the darkness, trying to read her expression in the heavy shadows of the night.

"Why were you crying?" he asked gently. "Why are you so upset?"

She drew a ragged breath. "I'm sorry. I was just thinking about how strange life can be."

"What do you mean?"

"I was thinking about how you can have something so very precious and not realize it until you've lost it." Her voice was a husky whisper.

Cole stared down at Jenny. Her words had touched him and torn at the defenses he'd erected against her. He thought she was talking about losing her father so unexpectedly, and he was allowing himself to feel sorry for her. He wanted to soothe her somehow.

Jenny decided to take a lesson from Rose and blurt out the truth. "I was thinking about us, Cole—and what we could have had together. . . ."

He was caught completely off guard by her confession. He wasn't sure what to think or say, or what to feel. He just knew that he wanted to hold Jenny and kiss her and never see her cry again.

"Jenny—"

He reached out to draw her near, wanting to tell her with his embrace that the past was over and they couldn't change it, but they could have a future.

"Cole! There you are!" Mira's voice was piercing as she appeared out of nowhere, closing on Cole and Jenny like a hound hot on the scent. "I've been looking for you."

Cole stopped, his hands dropping away from Jenny even before he could touch her.

Mira marched right up to them, a woman determined. She took Cole's arm in a possessive grip as she turned a cold, dismissive glare on Jenny.

"You will excuse us, won't you, Jenny?" she said indifferently, then gazed up at Cole, her expression one of open adoration. "Cole, darling, I was so worried about you. I didn't know where you'd gone."

She tried to press his arm to the side of her breast as she held on to him, but he resisted her efforts.

"Jenny—I—" Cole began.

Jenny just smiled and walked away from them. She didn't look back. She was concentrating too hard on keeping her expression blank. She didn't know that Cole's gaze followed her until he lost sight of her in the crowd.

"Jenny! What happened? Did dancing with Cole help? Where is he?" Rose came hurrying toward her, eager to learn all the details of their time together. She had seen Jenny leave and had watched as Cole followed her.

"Well, I'm not sure," Jenny told her as they stood together a little ways from the dance floor and out of sight of Cole and Mira. "Cole did come after me, and

I really think he was about to kiss me, but then Mira showed up."

"Oh, no," Rose groaned in sympathy. "I should have thought of that. I should have suggested to Clint that he dance with Mira next! I didn't think she'd be keeping such a close watch on Cole."

"Obviously she was, but at least I did get one dance with him," Jenny said triumphantly. "That's more than I would have gotten a week or so ago, and I'm certain it's all because of you."

"Me?" Rose tried to look innocent.

"Yes, you. How did you convince Cole to cut in on me and Clint? What did you say to him? Whatever logic you used, it must have been good."

"All I told him was that it was up to him to keep you safe and that I'd heard how dangerous it could be for any woman to dance with Clint."

Jenny couldn't help herself. She laughed out loud. "I guess he must at least care about my physical welfare."

"He could have refused, you know. So I think the fact that he did save you from Clint means a lot."

"We can only hope," Jenny said, still smiling. "And just how did you fare, taking on Clint for me and putting yourself in harm's way like that? That's the mark of a true friend, you know. I owe you."

"I suffered no lasting damage. My quick reflexes kept me safe and sound."

"I'm proud of you," Jenny declared.

"And so am I," Aubrey put in as he walked up to

join them. "But just what am I proud about?"

"Of how good a dancer Rose is," Jenny told him.

"Then I think it's time I found out for myself. Rose, may I have the honor?" he asked gallantly.

"It will be my pleasure."

Rose and Aubrey moved out onto the dance floor, leaving Jenny alone with her thoughts.

Jenny tried to forget what had just happened with Cole and Mira, but it proved difficult to do. She was certain that Cole had almost been ready to kiss her, and she'd been ready, too. But then Mira had come. . . .

Jenny was almost glad when Richard appeared before her and invited her to dance. It would distract her for a while. Accepting his offer, she allowed him to lead her out onto the floor, but as he twirled her expertly around, she saw Cole and Mira join the dancers, too.

"Where did you go?" Richard asked. "I was looking for you but couldn't find you."

"I had to talk with Cole for a minute."

"It must be difficult for you to have to deal with him so much. After what happened between you, I know how you both must feel about each other."

He sounded very confident of his opinion.

"What do you mean?" Jenny bristled at Richard's assuming he knew anything about her or her life.

"Well, when you think about it, if it hadn't been for your father's will, you two probably wouldn't even be speaking to each other right now. I know I certainly wouldn't want to have anything to do with a woman who'd broken an engagement with me."

Jenny was tempted to tell Richard that he didn't have to worry, he would *never* have that problem with her, but she controlled herself. "That was a long time ago. Cole and I have both gotten past that. We're mature adults, and we deal with one another as such."

Richard definitely didn't want to spend his time talking about Cole. He sensed there was still something between Cole and Jenny, despite her denials. He decided to use the rest of the evening to his advantage. He was going to find a way to have a romantic moment with her and make her forget all about the other man.

Earlier when Richard had seen Jenny with Cole, he'd actually felt a twinge of jealousy. That was very unusual for him. As he danced with her now, he pondered even more deeply Aubrey's advice to propose to her. This might just be the night—if he got the opportunity.

He would see.

It was a little after ten p.m. when Sam, the owner of the High Time Saloon, stopped in to talk with Dan for a minute.

"Fernada said she thought you weren't feeling too well tonight," Sam said. He was concerned about his bartender, for he'd never known Dan to be less than the best when it came to his job.

Dan glanced toward Fernada standing farther down

the bar. He understood what she was trying to do for him, but he didn't like to lie. He'd always found that the plain truth served him best.

"I have to tell you, Sam, I'm not glad to be here tonight, but it's not because I'm sick." He served another drink to a thirsty cowboy as he spoke with his boss.

"Is something wrong?"

"There was something I wanted to do tonight, and it looks like I won't be able to do it."

Sam frowned thoughtfully. In all the years Dan had worked for him, Dan had never taken advantage or done less than his full share of work. "Do you want me to take over for you here?"

Dan was surprised by his offer. "You wouldn't mind?"

"How long do you need to be away?"

"Just a couple of hours should do it," Dan said, suddenly excited about the possibility of seeing Rose again.

"Go. Just be back here by twelve-thirty," Sam growled good-naturedly. "What's got you so agitated? A woman?"

"Not just any woman," he answered. "A very special woman."

With that, Dan handed Sam the towel he'd been using to wipe the bar. It seemed almost a ritual passing of arms.

"I'll be back."

"And I'll be right here serving drinks."

Dan hurried home and quickly washed up. He shaved and changed clothes. He spent an extra minute in front of the mirror, checking to make sure he'd shaved close enough. Then, realizing he was wasting time, he made his way to the dance.

The sound of the music came to Dan from several blocks away, and his anticipation grew as he drew closer. Though he had only seen Rose twice, there was something about her that set her apart. He was looking forward to having a dance with her tonight and spending as much time with her as he could.

Dan reached the dance floor and stood quietly at the side, scanning the couples, looking for Rose. He heard her before he saw her. From somewhere behind him near the refreshment table, the lilting sound of her laugh came to him. His reaction surprised him. It was almost as if his soul recognized the sound.

Turning away from the dancers, Dan was drawn to her. He found her surrounded by three other men, and all were laughing at something she'd said.

"Are you sure you have to go back to Philadelphia, Rose?" one of the men asked.

"Oh, yes. Philadelphia's my home, but I must tell you, I'm enjoying my time in Durango very much."

"We're enjoying having you here," another man replied.

"Can I have this dance?" the first man asked as a new melody began.

"Of course," she accepted, taking his hand and allowing him to draw her away.

As Rose was being led to the dance floor, an unusual feeling came over her. She looked back over her shoulder, wondering what it was that was troubling her. It was then that she saw Dan standing off to the side, watching her.

For an instant across the distance, their gazes met.

Dan had come to her!

Rose knew the dance she was about to dance was going to be the longest in her life. She didn't want to be with this man, she wanted to be with Dan. . . .

Rose was spun away then and lost sight of Dan. She kept trying to locate him in the crowd, but couldn't find him. She felt almost bereft.

"Are you all right?" her dance partner asked, noticing that she seemed to be looking for someone.

"Oh, yes. I thought I saw Jenny, but I was mistaken."

"Jenny's over there," he said, nodding behind her.

Rose cast a glance that way and saw Jenny dancing with Richard again. She pretended to be satisfied with spotting her girlfriend, but in truth, she still longed to know where Dan had gone.

When the music ended, Rose thanked her partner and started back to the side of the dance floor. She didn't have long to worry about Dan. He appeared by her side.

"May I have the next dance?" he asked in a courtly manner.

"Yes," she breathed, her eyes aglow as she gazed up at him. "You came."

"I couldn't stay away," he answered, surprising himself when he realized it was the truth.

As the music began again, he swept her into his arms without another word, and they moved out among the other dancers. It was a slow, lilting melody, and they circled the floor in perfect union.

Rose had often heard of love at first sight, and thought it a fantasy. She had now become a believer. She didn't know how or why this was happening to her, but Dan was the man she'd waited her whole life for. It didn't matter that they were so different. What mattered was that they were soul mates.

Gazing up at him as they continued to dance, Rose studied the hard, lean line of his jaw and felt the hard-muscled strength of him against her as they moved as one. His shoulder beneath her hand was powerful. She didn't want to speak, for she didn't want to break the spell. This dance, this moment, was too magical, too special.

Dan had come for her.

The music ended, and Rose felt almost lost when his arms dropped away from her.

"Would you like a cup of punch?" he asked, wanting to keep her by his side, fearful that some other man would try to take her away from him.

Rose found herself smiling at his offer to serve her. "I thought if you were here, you were off work," she quipped.

At her quick wit, Dan grinned back. "My job is to

make people happy, and that's what I want to do for you."

Her expression turned serious as she told him, "If you want to make me happy, then let's go for a walk, just the two of us—somewhere where we can talk—somewhere away from here." Rose knew she was being brazen, but it didn't matter. She just wanted to be with him.

Dan wondered how Rose had managed to read his thoughts. All he wanted was to be alone with her. He held out his hand to her in unspoken invitation.

Rose took it without hesitation and felt a surprising jolt of excitement at that simple contact. She had a distant thought that she should check on Jenny and see how her friend was doing, but dismissed it. Jenny was a grown woman, and she could handle herself quite nicely. Rose knew she would never have another night like this one—another chance to be with Dan. She wanted to take advantage of every minute they had together. She didn't want to waste a second.

Chapter Twenty

Dan led Rose off, away from the glow of the lanterns, away from the notice of any townsfolk. He needed to have her to himself for what was left of his two-hour reprieve.

"How did you get away from work?" Rose asked, surprised and delighted that he was there.

"I told my boss I had something very important to take care of."

"You did?"

"Yes." He paused and looked at her. "You." Dan started off again down the street toward a quiet park-like area.

Rose went willingly, smiling the whole while. She had a fleeting thought that Aunt Tillie might miss her, but quickly put it from her. She was with Dan. Nothing else mattered.

When they reached the secluded grove, Dan stopped, but he didn't release her hand.

"I've always liked it here," he said simply.

"It's quiet."

"Very."

"And private."

"That's what I like about it most," Dan said as he took her in his arms.

Above them the moon shone brightly in a starry sky. The faintest of breezes stirred the trees. It was a haven, a romantic retreat made just for them.

"I've wanted to do this ever since the first time I saw you."

There was no need to say more as Dan bent to her and claimed her lips in a kiss. It was a gentle, testing exchange, as if he thought her fragile and feared he might harm her. But when she shifted closer to him and wrapped her arms around him, urging him on, he eagerly deepened the kiss.

Rose was shocked by the power of her reaction to Dan. It was elemental and undeniable. Excitement shivered through her. The instincts that had been driving her came fully to life as she found herself caught up in the ecstasy of his embrace. She had never known a man's kiss could be so arousing.

Lost in a rapturous storm, they shared kiss after hungry kiss.

Dan had never known anyone like Rose before. She was open and warm and giving and loving. He wanted her more than he'd ever wanted any woman, and she was there, in his arms.

Unable to resist the temptation, his hands began a restless foray. He wanted her—he wanted to make love to her—he wanted to lose himself within her—

When he sought the soft curve of her breast, Rose gasped and tensed. No man had ever taken such liberties with her—but this was Dan. She relaxed, wanting him near, needing him near—

Her initial reaction stopped Dan cold and made him realize just how truly innocent she was.

Dan knew he had to stop the madness between them now, before things got out of control and they both forgot who they were and gave themselves over to the power of their desire for each other. Dan went still, breaking off the kiss, just quietly holding her.

"Dan?" Rose whispered his name as she drew back to look up at him in the moonlight.

He gave her a quick, gentle kiss, then only held her quietly, waiting for his passion to cool.

In her innocence, Rose didn't understand why he'd suddenly stopped kissing her. His kisses had been wonderful, and she didn't want him to quit. If she could have had her way, she would have stayed in his embrace forever.

"I like kissing you," Rose said, lifting one hand to caress his cheek. "Why did you stop?"

Dan gave a guttural groan as he captured her hand and pressed a kiss to her palm. "I have to stop."

"But why?"

He smiled gently at her. "Because if I don't stop now, your virtue would be in danger."

Had there been enough light, he would have seen her blush.

"Oh."

Dan kept his arms around Rose, cradling her close, enjoying the scent of her perfume. She'd worn a fragrance of roses, and the scent would forever be emblazoned in his mind—and his heart—after this night.

Rose had kissed a number of men during the less-than-exciting courtships she'd endured through the years, but no man had ever thrilled her the way Dan did. She wondered what she was supposed to do next. She had no idea, and it was completely out of character for her to be helpless. She always took charge and forged ahead. She always knew what she wanted and had a plan how to get it. Right now, though, she was at a loss. She realized she wanted to get to know him better, to spend as much time with him as she could until it was time for her to go.

Go—

It suddenly occurred to Rose that there would have to be an end to their relationship. She had to go back to Philadelphia. She didn't like that thought at all, so she put it from her mind. She would take each day as it came and enjoy to the fullest what time she did have there in Durango—with Dan.

"I guess we'd better head back," Dan finally said. Regret sounded in his tone. He didn't trust himself to stay there alone with Rose any longer. She was too tempting for his peace of mind.

"I know," Rose sighed, not wanting to see this moment end, either. As disconcerted as she was by her tumultuous emotions, she always believed that if she wanted something, she should go after it. Resuming her normal ways, she gave him a slow smile as she asked, "But before we go back, could you kiss me one more time?"

Dan realized she didn't know what she was doing, but her smile was so inviting, hinting at the undeniable pleasure he knew would be theirs if he obeyed her request, that a shaft of heat seared straight through him.

"It would be my pleasure," he told her, and he meant it. Still, he knew he had to keep a tight rein on the passion he felt for her. Otherwise it would shatter his most honorable intentions.

Dan crushed Rose to him as his mouth moved hungrily over hers, plundering her delicious sweetness and branding her as his.

It was with an effort that he finally put her from him.

"I think we need to go back and dance some more," he said with gruff good nature.

"I like kissing you better," Rose said forthrightly.

"Trust me, I like kissing you better, too."

They started back, each regretting the loss of their intimacy. They walked slowly, for they were in no hurry to return to the crowd. They liked being in each other's company better.

"Dan—" she said his name softly. "How did you come to be here in Durango? Did you grow up around here?"

"No. Actually, I'm from St. Louis. When I was young, I had heard a lot about Colorado and the mountains. All the talk fascinated me. I knew I had to see for myself. As soon as I was old enough, I came West, and all it took was one trip. I made the move permanent about eight years ago. I started off in Denver and then came here with the railroad. I've been here ever since. Durango is right for me. It's where I belong."

"But why did you become a bartender? Didn't you ever want to do anything else?" She'd never known anyone else who'd worked in a saloon, and his choice of jobs intrigued her.

Dan was quiet for a minute. A lot of people looked down on him because of where he worked, and usually sophisticated women like Rose would have nothing to do with him, considering him to be beneath them socially. Dan considered the possibility that Rose was toying with him—that he was a lark for her—an adventure and nothing more. Someone she could enjoy being with while on vacation in the Wild West, but who she'd soon forget once she'd returned home. It surprised him that the possibility had the power to disturb him.

"I've asked myself the same thing occasionally, but

I like what I do and the pay is good," he told her simply.

"Do you have any family back in St. Louis?"

"My mother and sister are there. What about you?"

"I live with my parents, but I enjoy traveling. This trip to Durango has convinced me of that." She didn't add what she was truly thinking—that her travels had brought her to Dan and that was the real reason she was enjoying this particular trip so much.

"Do you plan to organize more groups to come to the Lazy S?" he asked, hoping she'd be returning to Durango regularly, so he could see her.

"I want to help Jenny as much as I can. That's why I was so excited about taking the photographs today. I know my photographs can show how beautiful everything is much better than words. But as far as being in charge of any more of the groups that come, I don't think so. My lifelong dream has been to have my very own photographic studio, and I think with the pictures I've taken on this trip, I can do it."

"Have you developed them yet?"

"Not yet. I'm going to do that when I get back to the ranch."

"Won't it take a lot of money to open a studio?" He wondered where she'd find the financing to do it.

"Once my father sees what I've accomplished, he'll realize how good I am. He'll know that I'm not playing, that I'm really serious about photography, and he'll help me. He's always supported my decisions in the past, so there's no reason why he shouldn't back me now."

Dan had known from the beginning that Rose was a lady, but he'd never thought about the possibility that she came from a wealthy family. The revelation emphasized how impossible any real relationship would be between them.

Rose lived a moneyed, sophisticated life in the East.

He was the bartender at the High Time.

"Let's just hope Fernada and I didn't break your camera when you took our photograph today," he said with a smile, trying to lighten his own mood. "I'd hate to end your career before it started."

"As handsome as you are, that would never happen," she replied.

Then on sudden impulse, she grabbed his hand and tugged, wanting him to follow her into a dark alleyway. Dan wasn't about to resist her. Alone for a moment, Rose looped her arms around his neck and brazenly kissed him.

It was a wild thing for her to do.

It was a crazy thing for her to do.

And she loved every second of it.

They were quite near the dance and might be discovered, but Rose didn't care. She didn't know when she'd ever see him again after he left her tonight.

Dan reveled in her spontaneous embrace. His grin was lopsided when she released him.

"I don't know what I did to deserve that, but whatever it was, I'll gladly do it again."

He noticed when he stopped speaking that Rose looked a bit sad.

"What if we never get to see each other again?" she asked, lifting her troubled gaze to his.

Dan grew very serious. He knew there was no future for them. They were worlds apart. They were two very different people, and yet he also knew that he couldn't just let her go.

"We will," he said seriously. He drew her gently to him. "I promise you."

His mouth sought hers in a soft, cherishing kiss. Then he slowly and regretfully let her go.

"We'd better go back."

"I know," she agreed.

They returned to the social and joined the other couples on the dance floor. They remained together, dancing every dance, dreading the moment when Dan would have to leave and return to the High Time.

Cole was beginning to believe the night would never end. All he wanted was for it to be over. Ever since he'd tried to talk to Jenny and Mira had interrupted them, Mira had not let him out of her sight. He had made the mistake of inviting her, so there was no way out of it now, but after tonight he would make sure he never got himself in this situation again.

Cole had learned a lot about himself tonight, and what he'd learned had been a revelation to him. He wasn't quite sure what he was going to do about it, but he had to do something.

"I'm having such a wonderful time, Cole," Mira told him. "Thank you for bringing me."

"It's been an enjoyable evening," he lied.

"I think so, too," she agreed.

Certainly, Mira knew things could have gone better, but there had been no way she could have prevented Jenny from showing up. Even though Cole had stayed with her since the incident, it infuriated her that he'd gone chasing after Jenny in the first place. This was the woman who'd dumped him at the altar, and Cole had acted like a lovesick fool! Mira was certain that if he got involved with Jenny again, he would be the laughingstock of the whole town, and that would be very humiliating to her—knowing that he wanted Jenny more than he wanted her. There was no way she was going to stand by and let herself be embarrassed like that.

"Would you like more punch?" Cole offered. At least, if he went after refreshments, he might have a moment away from her.

"That would be nice." She noticed her brother Wayne making his way toward her. She wasn't sure if she was glad to see him or not. When he drank, he could be trouble. "Where have you been all evening?"

"Just having a good time, sis." He grinned at her, revealing that he'd had too much to drink. "Evenin', Cole."

"Wayne." Cole nodded in return. "I'll be right back

with your punch, Mira." He was glad her brother had shown up, for it gave him the opportunity to escape.

Mira was tempted to go with him, but stayed to talk with her brother.

"I can't believe Jenny showed up tonight."

"So?"

"So Cole went after her earlier, and I got there just in time."

"In time to do what?" Wayne was curious.

"He looked like he was about to kiss her, and ever since we came back to the dance, I've caught him glancing her way."

Wayne heard the unspoken fury in his sister's voice and knew trouble was brewing. "What do you plan to do about it?"

"I've been thinking about that, and right now seems to be the perfect time to have a little talk with her. I'm going to put an end to this right here and now. I'll see you later."

With steely determination, Mira made her way to where Jenny was standing alone on the far side of the dance floor.

"Good evening, Jenny," Mira said with fake sweetness.

"Hello, Mira," Jenny said with little enthusiasm, wondering what the woman wanted.

"You know, Jenny, you had your chance to marry Cole and you chose not to," Mira said, getting straight to the point. "While you've been gone, Cole and I have grown close—*very* close. Why, I've even enjoyed a good night's sleep in his bed—if you know what I mean." She looked at Jenny, her gaze piercing and hard as she watched for her reaction.

Somehow, Jenny managed to keep her true emotions hidden. She'd suspected that the other woman wanted Cole badly, but she'd never thought they were really lovers.

"I am very happy for you, Mira," Jenny said coolly with a slight smile. "You just need to understand that any dealings Cole and I have are strictly business. Since he is the executor of my father's estate, we are being forced to work with one another on ranch business."

"Good. He's mine, and I intend to keep him."

With that, Mira gave her a victorious smile and walked away.

Jenny watched her go and couldn't decide if she was angry or heartbroken. She knew she had no claim on Cole. She had no right to be jealous of him. But the thought of Cole making love to Mira was devastating.

Chapter Twenty-one

Richard was as ready as he would ever be. His frustration had grown as the evening passed and Jenny continued to dance with other men. Each time he'd been forced to stand aside and watch her being held in another man's arms, he'd grown more angry.

Now that he had finally decided she was the woman for him, he wanted her all to himself. He had made up his mind at long last. Tonight, he was going to propose.

Richard knew he would have to convince Jenny to give up any ideas she had about living in Durango for the rest of her life, but he was certain that would be easy once she realized how wealthy she would be as his wife. In Philadelphia, as Mrs. Richard Donathan III, she would be sought after; she would command respect and attention. He was certain she would love every minute of it.

"Jenny? May I have this dance, please?" Richard asked. He'd waited until the woman she'd been talking to had walked away before approaching her.

"Of course, Richard," Jenny said, needing and wanting to be distracted from her thoughts of Cole and Mira.

Richard took Jenny in his arms and danced her out onto the floor. He held her closer than usual, wanting to feel her against him. He had made his plan, and he was ready. At a strategic moment, he was going to waltz her away from everyone. He'd been looking around and had found a private spot close by. Once he got Jenny where they could speak without being interrupted, he was going to propose.

Richard's eagerness grew as they danced. Jenny didn't seem to notice that he was trying to dance them toward a particular side of the floor. When he reached the spot where he could sneak off with her, he stopped dancing and took her hand.

"Richard—what are you doing?" Jenny balked, resisting a bit as he drew her away.

"I want to talk to you alone for a moment."

"What's wrong with right here?" she asked.

"I wanted our conversation to be private, Jenny."

He did not relent and grew more than a little annoyed when she still held back.

"You can talk to me here," Jenny said.

Her refusal to cooperate with him enraged Richard.

His anger and his passion came together, and strong emotion rushed through him. He tightened his grip on her hand and pulled her with more effort. He was not accustomed to being denied. He was used to women falling at his feet.

Jenny didn't want to cause a scene, but she didn't want to be alone with Richard, either. Still, short of screaming, there was no getting away from him, so she finally went along. When he led her to a darkened corner, she hesitated again.

"Richard—whatever it is you have to say—" she began.

"Needs to be said right now." he finished for her.

And with that, Richard grabbed her and kissed her. It was a hot, savage kiss that reflected exactly the way he was feeling. His mouth ground down on hers punishingly. He wanted her to be his—his wife, his lover and his possession. He meant to have her—one way or another.

Evelyn was standing with Tillie, happily watching all the dancing couples. Rose was with her cowboy, Melanie was dancing with one of the men from town, and Jenny was dancing again with Richard. Everything seemed fine, but then Evelyn grew worried when she saw Richard stop dancing and practically force Jenny off the dance floor. She knew Jenny was capable of taking care of herself in most circumstances, but there was something about the look on Richard's face that troubled her.

"Tillie, did you see that?"

"What?"

"Richard. It looked like he was practically dragging Jenny off somewhere that she didn't want to go. I'd better go after them and see what's going on."

"I'll come with you."

They were following the couple when Evelyn noticed Cole standing with Mira. Thinking she just might need his help, she sought him out.

"Cole! Could I speak with you privately for a moment?" Evelyn asked.

"Mira, if you'll excuse me?"

"Of course," she answered, but she wasn't pleased. She knew this woman was Jenny's aunt.

Cole moved a few steps away with Evelyn and Tillie.

"What is it?" he asked.

"I'm sorry to bother you, but I didn't know who else to ask for help."

"Is something wrong?"

"It's Jenny. She was dancing with Richard when suddenly it seemed he was forcing her to leave the dance with him," she explained. "I'm worried about her and wanted to go check on her."

"You stay here. I'll handle it."

"Oh, thank you, Cole."

"Which way did he take her?" Cole asked in a tight voice.

He'd seen the two of them dancing together and had deliberately looked the other way. He remembered far too well what Richard had said that day out at the Lazy S about holding Jenny in his arms.

"They went off that way." Evelyn pointed in the direction they'd gone.

"You wait here in case there's trouble," he dictated.

Without a backward glance or a word to Mira, Cole went after Jenny.

Richard was enjoying the kiss, even though Jenny didn't seem to be fully responding to him yet. He knew it was just a matter of time. There wasn't a woman in the world who could resist him.

The hand that clamped down on Richard's shoulder was iron, the grip unyielding. With brutal force, Richard was physically torn away from Jenny.

"What the—" Richard protested as he was spun violently around.

He had no time to say more. Cole's fist caught him squarely in the face, and he collapsed, moaning on the ground.

"Cole!" Jenny gasped.

Cole was filled with blind rage. The sight of the other man kissing Jenny so forcefully infuriated him. He'd hit Richard hard enough to make sure he didn't get back up right away. He was standing over him now, his hands still clenched into fists, ready and waiting for more trouble if Richard wanted to give him any.

"Jenny, are you all right?" Cole asked, his voice tight as he glanced her way.

"Yes—yes, thanks," she breathed.

Cole nodded, then looked down at Richard again, who was starting to stir. Blood was streaming from his nose, and his left eye was starting to swell. Cole felt Richard deserved more, but he controlled himself.

"Don't ever put your hands on Jenny again. Do you hear me?" he snarled.

Richard was cursing under his breath as he slowly gathered his wits. He looked up at Cole and nodded, just wanting him to go away. His humiliation was great, and his own fury was barely in check.

A crowd was gathering as word spread that there had been a fight. Everyone was gawking at them.

Cole's expression was thunderous as he looked at Jenny again, but when he realized she wasn't hurt in any way, the look on his face softened. He held out an arm to her.

Jenny hurried to his side. She felt calmer as soon as his arm came protectively around her shoulders. She went with him willingly as they turned away from Richard, still lying miserable and bleeding on the ground.

Jenny was emotionally numb. She couldn't believe what had happened. One minute she was being forced to suffer Richard's unwanted attentions, and the next, she was safe with Cole.

"The show is over, folks," Cole announced to the gathered crowd.

A murmur of interest went through the onlookers

as they talked among themselves, trying to figure out what had happened.

Evelyn, Tillie, and Melanie came rushing up.

"Jenny! Are you all right?" Evelyn asked.

"She's fine," Cole answered. "She's mine. I'll take care of her."

"Thank you, Cole," Evelyn told him.

Cole and Jenny went on only a little farther before they came face to face with Mira and her brother. The two had been hurrying over to see what all the excitement was about.

"Cole!" Mira cried as she saw him and ran to him. "What happened?"

"There was some trouble," he offered, not wanting to talk to her right now.

"Someone said you were in a fight. Are you all right?" She'd been worried about him, but the sight of Jenny by his side left her outraged.

"I'm fine." Cole looked dismissively past Mira to her brother. "Wayne, I have to help Jenny right now. Could you see that Mira gets home tonight?"

Wayne could just imagine how his sister was feeling to be so ignored in front of the entire town. "What the hell happened?"

"There was some trouble." Cole nodded toward Richard. "And I stopped it."

Cole didn't even wait for Wayne to answer, but shepherded Jenny away from the scene.

* * *

As Mira watched them walk away, her fury was boundless. She wanted to scream her frustration, but she waited, fire flashing in her eyes, murderous emotions burning in her heart. Instead, she began to plan in earnest what she was going to do to get even with Jenny. She'd been upset earlier that evening by the way Cole had acted around Jenny, but now she was furious.

"Come on," Wayne told her. He knew she was mad and wanted to get her away before she did something she might regret. "You ready to head back home?"

Mira shook off his hand when he touched her arm.

"There's something I want to do, but it isn't head back home," she snapped at him.

"This ain't the time or the place," Wayne cautioned her, and he started to walk away.

"You can go if you want. I'm not through here yet." Mira was barely in control of herself as she waited a moment, then followed Cole. She wanted to see exactly where he was going and what he was going to do with Jenny.

"Are you sure about leaving Mira that way?" Jenny asked as Cole guided her back toward her hotel.

"I'm sure." He was terse. "I want to make sure you're safely back in your room."

"But Richard would never—"

Cole's look her silenced her, and she realized sadly that he might be right. Richard had been acting strangely, and things might become even more difficult with him after this.

"Thank you for stepping in when you did. I wasn't quite sure what to do. Richard has never done anything like that before."

"You're lucky."

"I'm lucky that you came after me when you did. Richard was acting like Will Baker did all those years ago. Do you remember that night with Will?"

"I remember."

There was no way Cole would ever forget that night. It was the first time he'd realized he was in love with Jenny. The other boy had been trying to steal a kiss from her, and he'd defended her honor. But that had been a long time ago.

"You were my hero then, when you saved me from Will, and now, tonight, you've saved me from Clint and from Richard," she told him with a smile.

"I think I just have bad timing. I'm always showing up when you're in trouble."

"Well, your timing's not bad for me. I think I'm lucky to have you around." Jenny was sorry that the unfortunate incident had occurred, but she was glad it had brought her and Cole together.

Cole was startled by her declaration. He would have liked to believe her, but he didn't. He glanced down the street toward the hotel and realized that they were going to the same hotel where she'd stayed on what was to have been their wedding night. He remembered how he'd gone back that second time to see her, flowers in hand, only to discover she'd gone. He hadn't been in that hotel since, but he was going there now. He scowled.

"I guess it is lucky that I was around to help you. Rose reminded me earlier that, as I am your father's executor, you are my responsibility."

Jenny was stunned and hurt by his unexpectedly cold response.

She didn't want Cole to think of her as a responsibility.

She didn't want him to resent her.

She just wanted him to love her again.

Cole made no effort to initiate any further conversation during the rest of the walk. Each step he took closer to the hotel heightened his recollection of that miserable night—a night he wished he could forget.

He tried to concentrate instead on sorting out exactly what he was feeling for Jenny right now. The rage that had possessed him when he'd seen Richard hurting Jenny had been real—very real—and he wondered why he'd reacted with such ferocity. The power of the feelings that had surged through him had been overwhelming.

Logically, he understood why he cared. It was simple. As Rose had said, Jenny was his responsibility.

He just didn't understand why he cared so much.

Jenny had left him at the altar.

Jenny had ended their relationship.

Jenny had left town without even saying good-bye.

Yet now she almost seemed as if she regretted what had happened between them.

His mood turned cautious. He was unsure of his own strong emotions and unsure of what Jenny was doing.

They reached the hotel.

"Is something wrong?" Jenny asked when she noticed a hardening of his expression.

"No."

"You can go on back to the dance if you want," Jenny told him. "I'll be fine now."

"I want to make sure you get upstairs all right."

"It's not necessary," she insisted.

Cole looked so annoyed that she wanted to give him the chance to get away from her. There was no doubt in her mind that she loved him, but as he'd said, he thought of her only as a responsibility. Knowing he felt that way about her troubled Jenny, and she wondered, even loving him as she did, if there could be a future for them.

"I'll see you to your room," he said.

Jenny stopped arguing and started up the steps. When they reached the hall, it was deserted. As they passed the room that had been hers on what was to have been their wedding night, she noticed that Cole glanced sharply at the door. It was then that it dawned on her what he was thinking about. She deeply regretted right now that she had chosen to stay in this hotel.

Memories of that night returned to Jenny, too. She

remembered how Cole had come to her and told her he still loved her and wanted to marry her. She realized now how hard it must have been for him to seek her out again after she'd just publicly rejected him.

She intended to make it up to Cole.

They reached the room that was hers tonight, five doors farther down the hall. She unlocked the door and started to go in.

"Wait." Cole stopped her.

He took charge, stepping inside ahead of her to light the lamp and take a look around. Once he'd made sure the window was locked, he turned back to her and found that she was waiting in the doorway, watching him.

"Is it safe?" Jenny asked.

The question hung heavily in the air between them as he stared at her. The bed was in his line of vision, and in his mind's eye he could see her lying upon it. He forced the image aside.

"Yes," he answered, his voice deep and gruff. "You're safe."

Suddenly, staring at Cole across the room, Jenny didn't want to be safe. Cole looked dangerous, his expression guarded, yet dark. His physical presence was nearly overpowering. She was drawn to him. She wanted him, and she wanted to make him believe it.

Recklessness and determination filled Jenny.

She stepped inside the room and closed the door. She wondered what Rose would do if she had the man she wanted alone in her hotel room. A slow smile curved her lips. She didn't need to ask Rose. She knew what to do.

"Cole—I'm not so sure I want to be safe—"

Chapter Twenty-two

Cole watched Jenny warily as she walked slowly toward him. He wondered what she was doing—what she wanted from him. Something told him to leave now that he was certain she was all right, but something else, a more basic, more primitive need, held him there.

"The last time we were in this hotel together . . ." she said in a soft voice.

"You told me our wedding was off," he finished in a flat voice.

"I know," Jenny said gently as she stopped before him and lifted her gaze to his in a plea for understanding. "I was young. I wanted to see the world, to experience life and live it to the fullest."

Cole's jaw tightened as he looked down at her. When she rested one hand on his chest a jolt of sensual awareness shot through him. He tensed even more but said nothing.

Jenny continued, "What I didn't realize then was that I had the best of the world right here in Durango—with you."

When his expression still didn't change, Jenny realized that actions spoke louder than words. She rose up on tiptoes to press her lips to his. She knew she was being brazen. She didn't care. She had to convince Cole that she loved him. She had to make him believe her. If her words couldn't do it, she'd let her actions speak for her.

Cole held himself in rigid control as Jenny kissed him. He accepted her kiss, but did not allow himself to react. When she slipped her arms around his neck and shifted even closer to him, though, his composure started to slip. A shudder of desire wracked him.

"Kiss me, Cole—Please," Jenny whispered against his mouth.

It was her plea that shattered the iron grip he had on his desire. He reacted on pure instinct, crushing her to him, his mouth slanting passionately over hers in a fiery brand.

Jenny whimpered in ecstasy at his unbridled response.

Cole gave a low-throated growl as he pressed kiss after hungry kiss on her lips. Jenny was his heaven and his hell. He knew it was crazy to be holding her and kissing her this way, but right now, nothing mattered but the glory of having her in his arms. He wanted her. He desired her more than any other woman he'd ever known. There had never been anyone for him but Jenny.

The bed was so close, it was a simple matter for Cole to pick Jenny up in his arms and lay her down upon its softness without ending their kiss. Jenny did not release him, but drew Cole down with her. It was pure sensual delight to have his hard-muscled body covering hers. She reveled in the pleasure of his nearness as she returned his kisses in full measure.

This was what she'd longed for.

This was what she'd always needed.

When he began to caress her, she was shocked by the intensity of the excitement his touch aroused within her. He slipped her gown from her shoulders, baring that tender flesh, and she gasped at the sensation so new and so thrilling.

Cole was hungry for Jenny. All the time he'd spent denying himself, controlling himself, protecting her—it didn't matter now. She was here in his arms, willing and eager, and he wanted her.

Jenny hated that she couldn't caress Cole as he was caressing her. She began to work feverishly at the buttons on his shirt, wanting to bare his chest and shoulders to her touch. She wanted to be as close to him as she could. Cole shifted slightly away from her, giving her easier access, and she made fast work of freeing him from his shirt. His chest was hard and hot to her touch, yet he shivered as she caressed him.

The knowledge that her touch had the power to

affect Cole that way emboldened Jenny. She traced fiery paths over his shoulders and down his back as she held him close. Wild emotions filled Jenny as she clung to him. She thrilled to his touch and returned his kisses with abandon.

At long last, she was where she belonged.

She never wanted to let him go.

"I love you, Cole." Caught up in the ecstasy of the moment, she whispered what was in her heart.

She had thought he would declare his love, too, and they would live happily ever after.

She was wrong.

At her declaration of love, Cole went still. Reality painfully returned and jarred him from the sensual fever that held him in its grip. Cole was forced to realize just where he was, what he'd been about to do, and who he'd been about to do it with—Jenny.

In an almost violent move, Cole tore himself away from her and stood up beside the bed.

Jenny was shocked by his sudden desertion. She lay upon the bed staring up at him, still on fire with her need to be one with him. She didn't understand why he had left her. She didn't understand why he wasn't there on the bed, holding her.

"Cole—" she said softly and lifted one hand to him in an invitation to return to her. She wanted him back in her arms, kissing her and loving her.

The sight of Jenny, her clothing in disarray, her cheeks flushed with passion's glow, seared Cole. She looked beautiful—desirable. He wanted to make love to her—Lord, how he wanted to make love to her! But that was all it was, he told himself—a physical desire.

Cole took a step back to distance himself from Jenny even more. He couldn't think straight standing that close to her.

After Jenny had left him, he'd sworn never to fall in love with another woman or to care about another woman the way he'd cared about Jenny. Up until now he'd managed to keep that vow. But now, Jenny was back, and she was wreaking havoc in his life.

"I have to go," he muttered as he turned away from her and headed for the door, buttoning his shirt as he went.

"Cole! Wait—" she called out.

But it was too late.

He had gone and shut the door silently behind him.

Jenny stared after him. She remembered another time when he'd walked away from her and closed the door in exactly the same way. A shiver ran through her at the memory.

Mira was shocked to see Cole come out of Jenny's hotel room buttoning his shirt. She held her breath and stepped back quickly to hide in the shadows at the far end of the hallway. She was fearful that he might catch sight of her and realize she'd been spying on him. Cole seemed too distracted, though, to even bother looking her way.

Mira waited, watching him walk off down the hall,

and as she did, the fury that was burning within her grew hotter. Cole had been in Jenny's room with the door shut, and he'd come out fixing his clothing!

She wanted to rage and rant. She wanted to scream at the injustice of it all. She wanted to kill.

But Mira waited, biding her time. Only when Cole had gone down the steps did she emerge from hiding. She was slow in leaving, not wanting to risk rushing after him and being discovered.

"What did you find out?" Wayne asked in drunken good humor when his sister emerged from the hotel a short time after he'd seen Cole leave. He'd been waiting for her outside, trying to blend in so no one would notice him, and he'd done a good job. Even Cole had walked right past him, unaware of his presence.

"Everything I suspected is true. That woman is a slut!" Mira told him venomously.

"How do you know that?"

"What the hell do you think he was doing up there in her room for so long?"

"You don't know that for sure."

"He was fixing his clothes when he came out of her room."

"Damn, maybe I'd better go get me some of that." Wayne glanced toward the hotel entrance. The thought of Jenny Sullivan warm and willing beneath him left him hot.

"Shut up, you idiot!" Mira had had enough. "If it

wasn't for you, none of this would be happening right now."

"What are you talking about, woman?"

"I'm talking about you! If you hadn't been so stupid and almost got yourself caught rustling up in their high pasture, you wouldn't have had to kill her father and Jenny would still be back East. Then Cole would be mine—all mine." Her fury at her brother was unbounded.

"How was I supposed to know that stupid old man was going to show up right then?"

"He wasn't the one who was stupid! It was his property! When you're stealing from somebody, you've got to be smart enough to make sure you don't get caught!" Mira seethed. "Do I have to take charge of everything out at the ranch?"

Wayne shrugged. He didn't care who did what, as long as he had money enough for liquor and women. He was very much like their father that way. He couldn't remember the last time he'd seen their father sober. That was why he and Mira had had to take over the ranch and start running things. "So what do you want to do now?"

"I want to get rid of Jenny, that's what I want to do. I don't have a chance of getting Cole to marry me with her around."

"What do you mean, 'get rid of'?"

"What do you think I mean?" She shot him a hate-filled look that spoke volumes.

"How are you going to do that? You aren't planning on doing anything here in town, are you?" Wayne was worried. It had been difficult enough making Paul's death look like an accident. He didn't know how he would cover up murdering Jenny.

"No, but believe me, I'd like to—right here and now," she told him coldly.

Glancing back toward the hotel, Mira envisioned Cole making love to Jenny. Her jealousy and anger grew. When she'd gone to Cole's house to see him and ended up spending the night, he'd taken great care not to be in a compromising situation with her. Yet here tonight with Jenny, he'd been willingly and eagerly alone with her in a hotel room.

Silently, Mira vowed that one day—come hell or high water—Cole was going to be hers. She didn't care what it took—she was going to have him.

Cole didn't even consider returning to the dance. He went straight to the High Time. He got a drink from Sam, who was still tending bar, then settled in by himself at a back table. He stared at the bar girls, contemplating bedding one of them just to ease the ache in his body, but as quickly as the thought came, he put it from him.

Cole didn't want just any warm body.

He wanted only Jenny.

He remembered another night when he'd sat there in the High Time, thinking about Jenny and generally being miserable. Fernada had convinced him to fight for Jenny that night. He had taken her advice and had tried, only to discover that she had already gone.

But that had been a long time ago.

He still loved Jenny that night.

He had wanted her back.

But now?

He wasn't sure what his feelings were for her.

Cole took a deep drink. He waited, wanting the tension to ease within him. Somehow, though, he knew there would be no relaxing tonight.

Tonight he could have made love to Jenny.

And yet he had walked away.

It made no sense that he'd left her. She'd certainly been willing. Hell, she'd called him back to her, almost begging him to come to her.

But he had walked away.

Cole tried to understand his own actions. Jenny had had only to kiss him, and he'd forgotten himself. He had wanted her badly, desired her deeply. But he knew there was more to a relationship than desire. He had to trust the woman he loved, and from experience he'd learned that he couldn't trust Jenny. Not after what she'd done to him.

Or could he?

In disgust and frustration, Cole took another drink.

Dan knew the time had come to leave. He had hoped the night would last forever, but Sam was waiting at the bar for him. He'd promised Sam he'd be back, and he had to go.

"It's that time, isn't it?" Rose sensed the change in

Dan's mood as they stood together in a quiet spot near the refreshment table.

"I have to get back. Sam could only cover for me for a couple of hours," he told her regretfully.

"Will I get to see you again?" she asked. She didn't care if she was being brazen or not. She wanted to spend as much time with him as she could while she was in Durango.

"When are you heading back to the ranch in the morning?" Dan hadn't even left her yet, and he was already trying to figure out a way to see her again.

"Around ten. Why?"

"How about we meet for breakfast?"

"I'd love to," she said, her eyes aglow.

Rose wanted desperately to kiss Dan again, but she couldn't, surrounded as they were by others.

"Shall I take you back to your aunt?" Dan offered.

"Please."

She took his arm, and he accompanied her to where Tillie, Evelyn, and Melanie were talking to a group of ladies.

"I'll see you first thing in the morning," Dan told her, regretting that he had to leave her, regretting that they would be apart for even a few hours.

"I'll be ready and waiting for you," she answered.

"Good night, ladies," he said to the others and then took his leave of Rose.

"Good night, Dan." Rose watched him go, thinking him the most handsome man in the world.

"Aren't you being a little too eager, dear?" Tillie asked.

Rose smiled at her. "Not with Dan—no."

"Is he as nice as he seems?" Tillie had watched her niece and Dan for most of the evening and wondered at Rose's reaction to him. She'd never known her to be so excited about or interested in anyone before.

"He's nicer," Rose sighed.

"But he's a bartender, isn't he?"

"Yes. So?"

"I'm sure your father would have a few things to say about his daughter spending time with someone of that caliber," she cautioned her.

"If my father got to know Dan, he'd like him," Rose said, coming quickly to Dan's defense.

"That could be, but since nothing's going to come of this flirtation of yours, I guess we don't have to worry too much about your father approving or disapproving." Tillie deliberately tried to provoke Rose, wanting to see how she would react.

Rose went quiet at her words.

Nothing's going to come of it—

Was nothing going to come of the feelings she had for Dan? Rose was so drawn to him, so enthralled by him—Was it because they were so different? From such different backgrounds?

Rose found it hard to believe that in just a few days she would leave Durango and never see him again.

"Maybe and maybe not," she finally responded.

"Are you planning to continue a relationship of

some sort with that young man?" Tillie asked astutely.

"I don't know," Rose said slowly. "I only know that I've never met anyone quite like him before. I like him, Aunt Tillie. I really like him, and I enjoy spending time with him."

"Well, enjoy what time you have with him, but remember we will be going home soon.

"I know. The time has passed far too quickly." *And especially tonight*, Rose added in her thoughts.

"It does seem to have gone by fast for us, yes, but I'm not so sure about Richard and Aubrey," Tillie said.

"Why?"

"Didn't you hear about what happened tonight between Richard and Cole?"

"No, what?" Rose had been so wrapped up in Dan that she hadn't paid any attention to what was going on around them.

"I can't believe you missed it." Quickly, Tillie told her about Cole and Richard fighting over Jenny.

"Oh, my," Rose breathed. "Where are they now?"

"Cole took Jenny back to the hotel a while ago."

"Should we check on her and make sure she's all right? I wonder what she's going to do about Richard."

"I don't know, but I'm sure he's a very unhappy man right now. You're right about checking on Jenny. Let me get Evelyn and Melanie, and we can all go back to the hotel together."

A short time later, they were on their way. They reached the hotel and went upstairs and stopped at Jenny's room.

Evelyn knocked quietly, not wanting to disturb the other guests. When there was no answer, she knocked a little harder, but there still was no response.

"I guess she's asleep," Evelyn told the others.

"We'll have to wait and see how she is in the morning," Rose said, but she was a little concerned. It wasn't like Jenny to sleep so soundly.

Chapter Twenty-three

Jenny had listened in silence as her aunt and Rose tried to rouse her. She waited, not responding, until they gave up for the night. She was glad when the women finally went away and left her alone. She didn't want to talk to anyone about what had happened that night—not yet.

Jenny was deeply upset. She had hoped to win Cole's love, but she'd failed miserably. She'd made a complete and utter fool out of herself. She had thrown herself at him. She had had him right there in that very bed with her, and he had simply walked away from her without a backward glance.

Jenny groaned in humiliation at the memory. She wondered how she was ever going to face Cole again. No matter when it happened, it was going to be very embarrassing. She couldn't wait to get back to the Lazy S.

Sleep was long in coming that night.

Rose undressed and got ready for bed, but she wasn't sleepy. Feeling restless, she went to stand at the window and gaze down at the street below. She couldn't see the High Time from there and was sorry. If she'd been able to see the building, she would have felt closer to Dan.

After a long moment, Rose turned away and sought the comfort of her bed. She hugged a pillow to her breast as she remembered the glory of Dan's kisses. The evening had been wonderful, and she could hardly wait for the morning so she could have breakfast with him.

Rose sighed as she closed her eyes. She invited sleep eagerly, wanting the night to hurry by, and she hoped all her dreams would be of Dan.

Jenny was not in the best of moods as she got up and dressed early the next morning. She had tossed and turned all night, thinking of Cole.

Jenny had never been one to handle rejection well. She'd allowed herself the night to be upset, but now with the dawn of the new day, she was determined to start planning again. She was not going to give up. She would find a way to claim Cole's love.

Descending the stairs, Jenny planned to rendezvous with the others in the lobby and then go on to breakfast together. She thought she'd have a few minutes of peace and quiet before everyone came down to join her, but just as she reached the lobby, Richard and Aubrey entered the hotel.

"Richard—" She stopped at the foot of the staircase, startled to find that he and Aubrey were only now returning to their rooms. She'd thought the two men would be breakfasting with them.

"Ah, my dear Jenny. What a pleasant surprise," Richard drawled sarcastically.

Jenny couldn't believe how bad Richard looked. One eye was swollen shut and discolored. His clothes were disheveled. He reeked of liquor and was obviously very drunk. Though Aubrey hadn't been injured, he didn't look much better. It was plain that he, too, had been drinking heavily all night.

"Richard—good morning. Are you just now returning to your rooms?"

"Oh, yes, my dear. Aubrey and I wanted to sample the real night life of your town, and it seems the night life turned into morning at some time." He laughed at his own witticism.

"I thought you would be joining us for breakfast this morning before we ride back to the ranch."

"As you can see, breakfast is not what I have in mind right now. However, I did want to speak with you. It's fortunate that you're here. Do you have a moment?"

Jenny felt a bit uneasy about talking to him alone, considering the way they'd parted the night before, but it was daylight and they were in a public place.

"Of course, Richard. What did you want to talk about?"

"If you two will excuse me, I'm going up to my room." Aubrey quickly took his leave of them. He wanted to give Richard some time alone with Jenny, for he knew that what he wanted to say to her had to be said in private.

Richard was glad when Aubrey had gone. He wanted Jenny all to himself. There was a small, rather private sitting area off to the side of the lobby, and he gestured in a gentlemanly fashion for Jenny to precede him. He followed her, and they sat down across from each other in two wing chairs.

"I wanted to let you know that Aubrey and I won't be returning to the ranch with you today," Richard announced. "We'll be spending the rest of our time here in town until the departure date."

Jenny was at once relieved and saddened. She had been dreading seeing Richard again. It would definitely be easier if he stayed in Durango, but she regretted the necessity. "Are you sure, Richard?"

He turned a cold look on her. "I'm very sure, my dear. I'll ride out with Aubrey later this afternoon so we can pick up our luggage."

"I'm sorry things turned out this way. I've always considered you to be a good friend, Richard."

At her words, his expression hardened. Her rejection had not sat well with him, and it would take him quite a while to come to grips with it. "I have never wanted to be your friend, Jenny."

"I hate for us to part on these terms." She was sincere.

He shrugged indifferently. "I have never been one to fantasize about living in the wilds like some kind of savage. I prefer civilization. Philadelphia is far more to my taste than Durango. Its women are far more to my taste, too."

Though he had just passed a wild night in drunken revelry, sampling a number of bar girls at one of the saloons in town, he looked forward to returning home. He couldn't get to Philadelphia fast enough to suit him.

"Is your eye going to be all right?" Jenny asked, ignoring the sting of his words.

"Actually, I am seeing far more clearly today with one eye than I previously had with two." He stood up. "I think we've said all that needs to be said, my dear."

"We'll have your bags ready for you when you come out to the ranch today."

"On second thought," he added, deciding that he would prefer never to see her again, "why don't you have them brought into town for us? There's really no reason for Aubrey and me to make the trip out there if we don't have to."

"I can arrange that."

"Fine. Well, good-bye, Jenny." Richard gave her a mocking half bow and left her sitting there.

* * *

"It will be better this way, trust me. Especially when Cole comes out to the ranch to see you," Rose assured Jenny, relieved upon hearing of Richard's decision to stay in town.

Rose had come down early, passing Richard on the stairs, and had hurried over to find out what had happened.

"I'm just sorry there was a fight," Jenny said.

"Are you really?" Rose asked, a twinkle shining in her eyes. "Look at the reaction you got out of Cole! You won a major battle in your war."

"You are so optimistic. I'd love to think you're right, but I don't. Cole's hitting Richard didn't mean anything."

"Of course it did," Rose insisted. "Cole strikes me as a very controlled man. Someone like your Cole doesn't just hit another man for no reason."

"My Cole?" Jenny repeated.

"That's right," Rose said with great satisfaction. She was very pleased with the way things were going.

"You don't understand," Jenny argued. "Cole told me on the walk back to the hotel that the only reason he'd been watching over me was because you had reminded him that I was his responsibility."

"Don't believe that for a minute. If Cole thought of you merely as a responsibility, he might have tried to interrupt Richard as he tried to kiss you, but he would never have assaulted him that way. Cole was angry when he hit Richard—very angry."

"I'd like to think you're right, but he certainly didn't act like it when we were alone together."

"What happened?" Rose sensed there was a lot more to the story than Jenny was revealing.

Jenny was glad that no one else was around so she could confide in Rose. "Cole insisted on making sure my room was safe for me before he left."

"Yes. So?"

"Well, we did kiss, but . . ."

"But what?" Rose was excited.

"Well, I thought it was time for the truth between us. So I told him I loved him."

"And?"

"He walked out on me."

Rose frowned thoughtfully. "Cole didn't say anything?"

"Only something like 'I have to go,' and that was it."

"Ah, but he did kiss you," she pointed out, taking some satisfaction in that knowledge.

"Yes."

"And he did insist on coming inside and checking the room for you."

"Yes."

"He was worrying about you, that's for sure. What are you going to do now?"

"I'm not sure what I should do." Jenny's expression saddened. "After last night, I understand exactly how Cole felt when I walked out on him at the altar. I hurt him badly, Rose, and I'd like to spend the rest of my life making it up to him—if he'll give me the chance."

"He will. You just shocked him last night, that's all. He has a lot to deal with—a lot to think about where you're concerned. He'll come around."

"I hope you're right," she said. "But enough about me, what about Dan? How did things work out for you last night?"

"Great, and he's supposed to be coming to breakfast with us this morning."

"That's wonderful." Jenny was truly happy for her friend. "So, what do you plan to do about your Dan?"

"Do about him?"

"I caught a glimpse of you together last night. You looked very happy."

"I was."

"So are you just going to pack up and go home and forget all about him?"

Rose frowned. She'd been trying not to think about that. "Well, I—"

"How do you feel about him?" Jenny pressed.

"I'm not sure. He's certainly nothing like any of the other men I've known."

"What do you mean?"

"He's not concerned with the things that men like Richard and Aubrey think are important. Dan's more—"

"Down to earth?"

"I guess that would be a good way to phrase it, and he's very interesting, too. He intrigues me."

Jenny glanced past Rose just then and saw Dan enter the lobby.

"Speak of the devil," she teased in a low voice as she nodded in his direction.

"He's here?" Rose said quickly, excitement evident in her voice. She turned and smiled brightly at the sight of Dan coming their way. "Good morning."

"Good morning, ladies. Am I late?" he asked, smiling at them both and then turning his full attention to Rose.

Jenny thought he looked as delighted to see Rose as she did to see him, and she hid a knowing smile as she watched the two of them together.

Tillie, Evelyn, and Melanie came down the stairs then, and it was time to go to eat.

They made their way to the small restaurant. Once they'd settled in at a table and their orders had been taken, Evelyn spoke up.

"Where are Richard and Aubrey? Aren't they eating with us this morning?"

"No," Jenny answered.

"Why not? Is Richard still upset over what happened last night?" her aunt asked.

Jenny knew there was no avoiding the truth, so she quickly related her conversation with Richard. "Richard is very upset. He and Aubrey have decided not to return to the ranch. They've requested that I send their luggage to them here at the hotel."

"Oh, my. He is angry, isn't he?" Evelyn said. "How bad did he look this morning?"

"It wasn't pretty. He'll probably still have quite a black eye when he heads home."

"Good for Cole," her aunt said with a small smile. "I always knew he was a gentleman. I'm proud of him for defending your honor that way. If I'd been doing a better job of chaperoning, though, he wouldn't have had anything to worry about. I'm going to keep a closer eye on you."

How Rose kept from blushing as she thought of her stolen moments with Dan, she never knew. Especially when she looked up to find Dan's gaze warm and knowing upon her. As their eyes met, they shared the unspoken thought that they were glad Aunt Tillie hadn't been too earnest in her chaperoning the night before.

"What do you have planned for the rest of your stay at the Lazy S?" Dan asked.

"I think we're just going to stay at the ranch and relax and enjoy ourselves," Rose told him, hoping against hope that he could find a way to see her again.

"Would you like to come out for a visit, Dan?" Jenny asked. "You could take Rose on a trail ride or a picnic or something."

"I'd like that," he answered, looking at Rose.

"I'd like that, too," she agreed.

As Evelyn and Tillie looked on, they knew their jobs as chaperons were not over yet.

Chapter Twenty-four

"I can't wait," Rose said eagerly as they traveled the last few miles to the ranch.

"Can't wait for what?" Jenny asked glancing over at her friend. "You were so sad before because you didn't want to leave Durango, and now you're excited about getting back to the ranch?"

Rose blushed a little bit. "Well, I've been thinking, and as soon as we get there, I can start developing the photographs."

"Ah, that explains it." Jenny laughed good-naturedly. "You want to see how your pictures of Dan turned out. What will you do if they aren't right?"

"I'll be forced to go find him so I can take another one," she answered, ready to use any excuse to see him again.

"Dan did say he'd try to come out to the ranch to see you this week."

"If he can make it."

"Rose—" Jenny began a bit hesitantly, not wanting to pry but feeling curious about her friend. "What's going on between the two of you? I mean, I know you like Dan, but are you getting serious about him?"

Rose glanced at Jenny, her expression both elated and perplexed. "I do like Dan—very much, and there is something special about him."

"Are you in love with him?"

Rose looked a bit guilty as she answered, "I think so. But how can that be? I've known him for less than a week, and I've only been with him a few times."

"How does he feel?"

"He hasn't said. We've just been enjoying what time we've had together."

"Well, I hope he can get out here to the ranch and spend some more time with you before you have to go home."

Rose sighed. "I hate the thought that we'll be leaving so soon."

"I know. In a few more days, you'll be gone. I'm going to miss you."

"I'm going to miss you, too. I'll tell you who else is going to be missing somebody," Rose added in a conspiratorial tone.

"Who?"

"Melanie," she said with a smile. "Did you notice

how quick she was to offer to ride back to the ranch in the buckboard with Tom?"

Jenny looked over her shoulder toward the buckboard which was following a short distance behind them. She could see that Melanie and Tom were deep in conversation as the young hand drove the team.

Jenny smiled. "Interesting. I guess it's unanimous: we all like Western men."

The two women shared a laugh as they pulled to a stop before the ranch house.

"Why don't you use our extra bedroom to develop your pictures?" Jenny offered.

"I'll do that. I can't wait to see how they turned out."

The photo developing was a lengthy process, but worth every minute—especially to get to see her picture of Dan.

As soon as everything was unpacked, Rose went to work while Jenny arranged for Richard's and Aubrey's luggage to be delivered to them in town.

Dinner time came and went, but Rose did not join them to eat. She worked on, not emerging until much later when all her photographs were finished. She was smiling as she came downstairs to where they were all waiting for her in the parlor.

"Well?" Jenny asked excitedly when Rose appeared in the doorway.

"Come take a look," Rose invited.

They all followed her upstairs.

At their first look at her work, they were in awe of

her talent. The photographs were magnificent. She had captured the mountain scenery expertly, and the portraits from town had turned out better than she'd ever hoped. The picture of George in front of the mercantile was wonderful, and the photographs she'd taken at the High Time with Dan and Fernada were perfect.

"Are you happy with them?" Jenny asked.

"Very."

"Your father's going to be impressed, too. Once he's seen them, I bet he'll help you set up your own studio in no time."

"I hope so," Rose said excitedly. "That's been my dream for ages."

As she thought about it, though, she wondered for the first time if that was what she really wanted to do. All her dreams about a studio back in Philadelphia had been before she'd met Dan.

It had been late when Cole had finally ridden home the night of the dance. He'd arrived back at the Branding Iron long after midnight and didn't get much sleep, rising at dawn to take care of ranch business. He deliberately worked hard all day long, concentrating on getting things done, wanting to tire himself out so he'd get some rest that night. It seemed that no matter how busy he kept himself, it was impossible to ignore the image of Jenny reaching out to him, inviting him to her bed.

"You all right, boss?" Fred asked late that afternoon, noticing how distracted Cole had become.

Fred's question interrupted Cole's deep thoughts, and he forced his attention back to the business at hand.

"Yeah, I'm fine. I'm just a little tired, that's all," he answered shortly, irritated with himself.

"Too much partying in town last night, huh, boss?" the ranch hand joked.

Cole wished that had been the case, but the one thing he hadn't been doing was having fun. "You finish up here. I'm going on back to the house."

He wheeled his horse around and rode away.

Cole was angry with himself. He'd always taken pride in his self-control, and the fact that Jenny could haunt him this way day and night disturbed him. He had known working with her might be awkward, but he'd considered himself a mature man who could handle it smoothly. Ever since he first set eyes on her the day she'd returned, though, his life had not been the same.

He had believed he was over her.

He'd believed he didn't care about her.

He'd believed he didn't love her anymore.

He'd been kidding himself.

He still loved Jenny.

Cole was shocked as he finally admitted the truth to himself. He wondered how he'd had the strength to walk away from her last night.

Damn, but she'd looked gorgeous lying there on the bed waiting for him. He could only imagine how wonderful making love to her would have been if he'd given in to his desire for her.

Cole cursed under his breath in frustration as he continued to ride toward the house. Sometimes pride was a good thing, but sometimes a man's pride could stand in the way of his true happiness.

He would not let that happen to him.

Jenny had already told him she loved him. Now it was his turn to acknowledge the truth of what was in his heart.

He made up his mind.

It was too late to go to Jenny tonight and profess his love, but he would ride for the Lazy S first thing tomorrow.

Cole reached the house and passed an uneventful night. He got little sleep, but didn't mind so much this time. It was his excitement about the prospect of seeing Jenny and telling her he loved her that kept him awake.

He was in a good mood in the morning when he rose and got cleaned up, ready for his trip to see Jenny. He was certain that after today, his life would never be the same.

"Cole!" Shorty Parkins came running up to the main house.

"What is it?" Cole asked, hurrying out on the porch to see what the trouble was.

"Word just came in—the rustlers have hit us again."

"Where?"

Shorty quickly told him everything he knew. "Down in the south range. It looks like about fifty head are missing. Some of the boys are trying to track them down, but I don't know if they'll have any luck. Every other time this has happened, they've gotten clean away."

Cole was furious, but realized there was nothing more he could do right now. His men were already on the trail.

"I've got to ride over to the Lazy S this morning, so I'll check to see if any of their stock are missing, too. I'll tell them to keep a look out for anything suspicious. Let Fred know that I'm going, and ask him to keep an eye on things while I'm away. I should be back tonight."

"I'll tell him."

Cole rode off to see Jenny. But his excitement was tempered by the news that the rustlers had returned.

"It looks like the boys did a fine job while we were in town," Wayne bragged to Mira as she came out to the stable. "They just told me they hit both the Branding Iron and the Lazy S again."

"Good," Mira said, glad that she was able to strike back at both Jenny and Cole in some way.

"Where are you going?" Wayne asked as she started to saddle up her horse.

"Not that it's any of your business, but I have a few things to say to Jenny that won't wait."

"You sure you should be doing this?"

"Oh, yeah." She smiled coldly at him as she tightened the cinch and swung the stirrup down. "I've had enough of her, and it's time she knows it. I'll be back."

"Rose! You've got company coming!" Melanie called out as she entered the main house. She had been down at the stables and had seen the rider coming in.

"I do?" Rose's heartbeat quickened. She hurried outside just as Dan reined in before the porch.

"Good morning, Rose," Dan greeted her, his voice warm and deep.

"What brings you out to the Lazy S?" she asked, smiling brightly at him. She'd feared that he wouldn't be able to get away from the High Time and was delighted to see him.

"There's this young lady who's staying at the ranch, and I needed to see her," he said as he dismounted and tied his reins over the hitching rail. As he took a step toward her, he dropped his voice and said in a more intimate tone, "I've missed you, Rose."

All she wanted to do was throw herself into his arms. How she controlled the impulse, she would never know.

"I've missed you, too, Dan. Would you like to come inside and see everyone?"

Truth be told, he didn't want to do anything but grab Rose and run away with her, but he behaved himself. "Of course."

Rose took his arm as he mounted the steps, and she

led him indoors. Dan doffed his hat when he entered the house and was greeted warmly by the ladies.

"I've developed all the pictures," Rose told him. "Would you like to see them?"

"Yes, I'd love to. When I saw Fernada this morning, she told me to ask you about them."

"I think she'll like the way they turned out."

They excused themselves from the others and made their way upstairs to the room she'd used for her work. The minute she opened the door for him, he took her by the wrist and drew her inside. Alone with her at last, Dan pulled her into his embrace and kissed her.

Rose had been anxiously hoping for just this moment, and she eagerly surrendered to his mastery. When he parted her lips, her tongue met his in a heated exchange. Her pulse was racing as his kiss ignited a fire of desire within her. They clung together, unable to get enough of each other, desperate for these few moments of privacy.

When Dan finally ended the kiss, he simply stood there, holding her close. He needed to let the fever of their nearly out-of-control passion cool.

"You had some pictures you wanted to show me?" he murmured. He did not want to let her go, but feared someone might happen upon them at any minute.

"I did?" she answered dreamily. She did not make any move away from him. She was perfectly content in his arms.

"That's what I heard," he said with a grin. "Of course, if you can think of something better to do while we're up here alone, I could forget the pictures—"

"You tempt me sorely, sir," Rose said, reluctantly moving away from him. "But come look at my work."

She had the pictures spread out about the room, and she took Dan's hand and led him to the first photograph of the mountains. He studied it seriously, then looked up at her. He was amazed by her ability to capture the beauty of the scenery with her camera.

"You really are very good."

He was sincere in his compliment. He had known Rose was an intelligent woman, but he'd had no idea she was so talented.

"Thank you."

He viewed the rest of her work, and his respect for her grew even more. Her portraits of people were as impressive as her landscapes.

They wanted to linger there in the room longer, but the sound of a rider coming up to the house at a gallop drew them back downstairs. They saw Jenny on the porch, deep in conversation with Louie. She looked so serious that they waited in the parlor for her to come indoors. When she did come back inside, it was obvious from her expression that she was angry.

"What's wrong?" Rose asked.

"I have to leave for a while. Some of the hands reported to Louie that there are cattle missing from up in the north pasture. I'm going to ride out and talk to them, and see what I can learn."

"Isn't that where your father had his accident?" Evelyn asked as she came in from the kitchen.

"Yes," Jenny answered tersely. She found herself wondering anew if there was any connection between the rustling and her father's death.

"Do you want me to ride with you?" Dan offered.

"No, Louie's getting one of the men to go with me. You two enjoy your time together. I should be back before dark."

Jenny hurried out to the stable to get her horse. She was angry at the news and wanted to get to the bottom of this trouble. Louie and Gene were waiting for her. They had already saddled her horse.

"Gene's going with you," Louie told Jenny.

"I appreciate the company."

Jenny's mood was determined as they mounted up and rode out.

It was early afternoon when Cole finally reached the Lazy S. He'd meant to get there earlier, but all the trouble on the Branding Iron had delayed him. As he tied up in front of the house, he was surprised when Frances came out to meet him. He'd been hoping Jenny would be the first one out the door.

"Is Jenny here?" Cole asked, eager to talk with her.

"No, not right now, but she should be back before dark, I hope," the older woman told him.

"Where did she go? Do you think I can catch up

with her?" He was ready to declare himself and didn't want to put it off any longer than necessary.

"She's been gone awhile. Louie heard from some of the hands that stock was missing from the north pasture. She rode out with Gene to see what happened."

"So you were hit, too. I'm missing about fifty head, myself," he told her. "That was one of the reasons I came to see her."

"Why don't you come on in and wait for her? Dan came out from town to see Rose today, and they went off on a picnic a while ago, but I expect them to return any time now. Evelyn, Tillie, and Melanie are all down at the stable watching Tom and another hand saddle-breaking horses."

Cole was greatly disappointed that Jenny wasn't there. He debated going back home. He certainly had a lot of work waiting for him, but he wanted to speak with Jenny too much to just ride off. He'd made the trip to the Lazy S to tell her he loved her. He was going to wait for her return—no matter how long it took.

Chapter Twenty-five

Mira's mood only worsened as she traveled the miles toward the Lazy S. She had always been jealous of Jenny, but that jealousy had now turned to deadly rage.

How dare Cole make love to Jenny up in that hotel room?

Mira was amazed that she'd managed to control her fury this long. But she would control it no longer. It was past time she and Jenny had a private little talk.

Riding cross-country to cut down the travel time, Mira topped a rise still some miles north of the Sullivan ranch house and reined in. There below her in the valley she caught sight of two riders. She watched intently and soon recognized that one of them was Jenny.

What luck! She'd wanted to talk to Jenny alone,

and now was the time. Mira started to ride down, then reined in again as an idea came to her—an idea that brought a feral smile to her face.

They were alone—there was no one else around for miles—no one who would hear the gunshots.

This was the woman who had stolen Cole from her, and she was within easy rifle range. She could pick them both off easily.

The choice was simple for Mira. If she acted right now, no one would ever know who'd shot them.

With slow calculation, Mira slid her rifle from its sheath and took aim. She had no second thoughts about doing it. The only thought in her mind was the memory of Cole coming out of Jenny's hotel room, his clothing in disarray.

Cole was hers! Jenny would never have him. Never!

Mira squeezed off the shot and smiled in vicious delight as the man fell from his horse. Jenny reined in and looked her way just as she fired again. Again Mira hit her mark. She laughed as Jenny fell from her horse and lay still, face down on the ground. The panicked horses raced off.

Mira stood up, watching and waiting to see if either Jenny or the man moved. She was tempted to go down and check on them, but when they continued to lie immobile in the dirt, Mira decided it wasn't necessary. She had earned her reputation as a good shot around the ranch and believed she hadn't missed.

Satisfied, she mounted up again and turned around to ride for home.

In a day or two, she'd make a trip over to the Branding Iron to see Cole. With Jenny out of the way, he would be all hers.

Cole settled in the study and started going over some of the ranch paperwork while he awaited Jenny's return. He'd been working there for nearly an hour when he heard a horse galloping up and shouts coming from the stable.

Certain that it was Jenny returning, Cole hurried from the study. He couldn't wait to see her again. He was smiling. This was the moment he'd been waiting for.

"Sounds like Jenny's back," Evelyn said as she emerged from the back of the house with Frances and Tillie. They went outside with Cole.

"Maybe she got lucky and found something out," Frances said, worried about the rustlers.

They started out onto the front porch, then stopped. There, running wild-eyed near the stable, was Jenny's horse, but there was no sign of Jenny.

"That's not like Jenny," Frances said, a cautious note in her voice as she stared at the lathered horse. "I wonder why she rode him so hard. And where is Gene?"

Tom came out of the stable and grabbed up the reins. "Whoa, boy. Easy there, fella," he said as he tried to calm the panicked mount.

"Where's Jenny?" Cole asked, looking around for her as he strode toward the stable.

"I didn't see her actually ride in," Frances said. "I only heard the horse."

Frances frowned as she and the other women trailed after Cole. She was suddenly remembering another time when a horse had returned to the stable riderless.

They hurried toward Tom.

"Is Jenny in the stable?" Cole called out.

Tom looked his way as he continued to try to calm the horse. His expression was troubled. "No. The horse came back without her."

"What?"

Cole was beside Tom in an instant, grabbing the reins and checking the horse over carefully.

"Where did Jenny say she was going when she rode out?" he demanded. She was out there somewhere, obviously injured in some way, or in trouble, and he had to go find her. He had to help her.

"She and Gene were riding for the north pasture," Frances answered quickly.

Cole remembered the north pasture all too well—how deserted and remote it was.

"Take care of the horse," he directed Tom. "I'm going after them." He handed the reins to Tom.

"What's going on?" Rose and Dan asked as they hurried over to see what all the excitement was about.

"Jenny's horse came back without her," Cole told

them quickly. "I've got to go look for her. She must be in trouble."

"This is just like what happened to her father," Frances pointed out worriedly.

Evelyn, Tillie, and Melanie were aghast at what had happened and shared worried looks.

"I'm coming with you," Dan declared.

Cole knew he might need his help. "Thanks."

"We'll come, too!" Rose said, "We want to help."

"No," Cole said sharply. "You women wait here." He looked at Tom and ordered, "Get the men together. We're riding out now."

Tom led the horse into the stable and ran off to gather the hands who were at the bunkhouse.

Cole and Dan went to get their horses while the women waited by the stable. The two men returned quickly.

"What should we do?" Evelyn asked in a shaky voice, looking up at Cole as she nervously clutched Tillie's hand for moral support. She was nearly in tears at the thought that something had happened to Jenny and Gene.

"Pray," Cole answered her, his tone solemn.

The ranch hands came running, and Cole quickly organized them and told them where to start searching. They rushed to get their mounts, and then rode out to check the areas Cole had assigned to them.

The women watched them go, horror etched in their faces. They knew Jenny and Gene were in some kind of trouble, and they hoped the men would find them quickly.

Jenny stirred and tried to open her eyes, but the pain in her head was too violent. She groaned and lay still, trying to remember where she was and what had happened. Even trying to think, though, made her agony worse. It took a superhuman effort to lift her hand to her forehead, and when she drew it away and peered at it, she was shocked to see her hand was covered with blood. Blackness overwhelmed her, and with the darkness came relief from the pain.

To Cole, it seemed he and Dan had been riding for hours, searching for some sign of Jenny or Gene. With each passing minute, he'd grown more and more worried. He remembered all too well what had happened to Paul. He could not allow himself to even consider that something like that could have happened to Jenny.

They rode on, determination driving them. They would not abandon their search. Cole just prayed that they would locate them before sundown.

It was nearly dusk when Cole caught sight of Jenny lying motionless on the trail.

"There!" he shouted and put his heels to his mount's sides.

Cole raced ahead, leaving Dan to catch up. When he reached Jenny he all but threw himself from the horse. Running to her side, he dropped to his knees beside her inert form.

"Jenny," he called in an agonized voice as he gently, carefully turned her over.

His heart was in his throat when he saw the blood on her face, and he feared she was dead. Only her groan reassured him that she was still breathing.

"She's alive!" he shouted to Dan, relief pouring through him.

Dan rushed to his side. "What happened? Was she shot?"

"Yes, and thank God, the bullet only grazed her," he told him.

"What do you want to do?"

"We've got to get her to the doctor." Cole's mind was racing as he tried to figure out the best way to transport her to the ranch house. He didn't want to wait for Dan to ride back and get the buckboard. That would take too long. He wanted to get her there as quickly as possible.

"What about Gene?"

They looked around and spotted him lying a short distance away. Dan ran to check on him.

"How is he?" Cole called out.

Dan shook his head and hurried back to Cole as Jenny stirred.

"Cole—" Jenny whispered as consciousness slowly returned. The pounding in her head was fierce, but the strong, warm arms holding her gave her comfort.

Cole was thrilled that she was coming to, but worried about her condition.

"Easy, love, I'm here," he said softly, knowing she must be in great pain.

"Gene—how's Gene?"

"I'm sorry—"

"Oh no—"

"Ah, Jenny—"

"My head—" she groaned and lifted her hand to her forehead again. "It hurts—"

"I know, darling, and we're going to get you help just as fast as we can."

"What happened?" Jenny asked in a weak voice.

"Someone shot you." Cole spoke quietly, but he was tense.

The mere thought that she had come so close to being killed tormented him. The urge to seek revenge was fierce within him.

"Why?" she whispered, lifting a tortured gaze to his.

"I don't know, but I promise you, whoever it was will pay."

Jenny's eyes drifted shut. Cole gently wiped the blood from Jenny's face with his bandana. She flinched beneath his careful ministrations, but she did not make a sound. The wound appeared to be a clean one, and he didn't believe it to be life-threatening.

Cole wished there was something he could do to make the trip back to the ranch easier on her, but there wasn't.

"Help me carry her. I'll mount up and hold her in front of me now that she's conscious. We won't be able to travel fast, but at least we can make steady progress."

"Do you want me to ride ahead for help? I can send someone back for Gene."

"Yes, and when you get to the ranch, send someone into town for the doctor. Then come back for us with the buckboard."

"I'll do it," Dan promised; then he lifted his gaze to scan the hills around them, searching for a clue to what had happened. He saw no disturbance, no sign of anyone around. "Who do you think did this? Who would have a reason to hurt Jenny or Gene?"

Cole's eyes narrowed as he remembered his fight with Richard at the dance. "When you send one of the men into town for the doc, make sure he stops at the marshal's office and tells Marshal Trent what happened at the social. I want him to find out where Richard Donathan was earlier today."

"You think he might be involved in this?" Dan was stunned by the thought, then realized Cole had good reason to suspect the other man after that night at the dance.

"I don't know," Cole said tersely as he held Jenny close and got to his feet. He moved as slowly as he could, not wanting to jar her. "But I want to find out."

Dan, coming to his aid, took Jenny from Cole to give him time to swing up into the saddle. Then he gently handed her up into Cole's keeping.

"Cole—" Jenny clung to him as he held her sideways before him, carefully cradling her to his chest.

"I'm taking you home, Jenny. Just hang on. I'll go as slow as I can to keep the pace steady for you," he told her quietly.

Cole kept an arm supportively around Jenny as he urged his horse back toward the ranch house—back toward safety.

Dan mounted up and rode to his side.

"You sure you'll be all right riding alone with her?" Dan asked worriedly.

"Yes. Just hurry up and get back here with the buckboard. I'll be watching for you."

Dan galloped off, determined to get to the Lazy S as quickly as he could.

Cole kept Jenny nestled against him, taking care not to make any sudden moves. He figured they had less than an hour of daylight left, and he hoped Dan made good time going back. Jenny rested quietly in his arms as they rode on toward home.

Chapter Twenty-six

Horror reigned at the ranch after Dan rode in and alerted everyone to what had happened. He quickly sent one of the hands who'd stayed behind at the house into town to get the doctor and to speak to Marshal Trent and directed another to bring back Gene's body. Then he loaded up the buckboard with pillows, blankets, and a lantern.

Evelyn and Rose insisted on going with Dan to help take care of Jenny. The three of them were solemn as they rode from the ranch. They knew the going would be difficult. Still, they were determined to get to Jenny as soon as they could.

Cole's progress had been slow and painful for Jenny. He'd tried his best to protect her and keep her safe, but any movement at all was hellish for her. He was tempted to stop and make a camp for the night, but he knew the sooner he got her back to safety, the better.

Though it appeared that whoever had done this to Jenny was long gone, Cole couldn't let his guard down. He was alert and watchful, ready for trouble, even as he tried to soothe Jenny and reassure her.

It seemed an eternity before Cole finally heard Dan's shout and saw the buckboard in the distance. He reined in.

"Dan's back with the wagon, Jenny," he told her gently.

Jenny rested against him, relieved that they weren't riding any more.

"We got here as fast as we could," Dan called out as he stopped next to Cole and Jenny. He handed the reins to Rose and jumped down to help Cole.

Jenny was trying to be brave, but a whimper escaped her as Cole handed her down to Dan.

Cole heard her cry and hurried to dismount. He took her back in his arms from Dan and carried her to the buckboard. As gently as he could, he laid her on the blankets. Evelyn and Rose were waiting and they were beside her in an instant. They lighted the lamp they'd brought along so they could see.

"Oh, God," Evelyn cried softly at the sight of Jenny so wounded. There was dried blood on her face and hair. She was pale and lying deathly still as they tended to her.

"Jenny?" Rose said as she took her hand in hers.

Both women waited breathlessly to see if she'd respond, and they almost burst into tears of joy when her eyes slowly opened.

"Aunt Evelyn—Rose—" she whispered.

"We're here, sweetheart," Evelyn said in a voice choked with emotion.

"Aunt Evelyn—"

It seemed Jenny had something to say that was important, so both women leaned close to hear her better.

"Cole saved me again—" Jenny finally managed. She tried to smile, but it hurt too much.

Cole was standing beside the buckboard, close enough to hear her words. Instead of feeling good, though, Jenny's words were like a knife in his heart. She might think he'd saved her, but to his way of thinking, saving her would have meant keeping her from harm. In that, he'd failed miserably. She could have been killed—

Cole was furious with himself and with whoever had caused Jenny harm. Once he married her, he was going to make sure that Jenny never came to any harm again.

"Cole was wonderful," Evelyn said gently. "We're just so relieved he found you. Now we're going to get you home safe and sound."

"Cole?" Jenny called out to him.

He quickly climbed into the buckboard to speak with her. "I'm here, Jenny."

"Stay with me, Cole—"

He remembered the last time she'd begged him to stay and he'd walked away. This time he knew that for as long as she wanted him, he would be there with her. "I won't leave you again, Jenny—ever."

Her heart sang at his words, but she was too exhausted to say any more. When he took her hand, she clutched his fingers and let her eyes close. Only now did she feel safe again. Cole was with her.

They put out the lantern, ready to finish the long, painful trip home. Dan tied Cole's horse to the back of the wagon, and with the women sitting up front with him, they started off.

No one at the ranch was able to rest. The hours passed with dreadful slowness. Some of the men who'd gone looking for Jenny and Gene had returned empty-handed and learned what had happened. They waited impatiently and worriedly with Frances, Tillie, and Melanie for Jenny's return.

It was very late by the time Dan drove the buckboard up to the house. At the sound of their arrival, everyone came running out to meet them.

Cole immediately jumped down when Dan stopped the buckboard. He carefully lifted Jenny from the wagon. His expression was stony, his manner rigid as he started inside with her.

"Bring her upstairs, Cole," Frances said from the porch, where she was holding the front door open for him.

He entered the house, and at Frances's direction he

carried Jenny upstairs to her room. Jenny mustered strength enough to loop one arm around Cole's neck, and just that little gesture relieved Cole's fears greatly.

Dan stayed with him in case he needed any help, and Rose and Evelyn went along, too.

Frances already had her bed turned down, so Cole ever so gently laid her upon the welcoming softness.

"Thank you, Cole," Jenny said quietly as she looked up at him.

Their gazes met.

Unable to help himself, Cole reached out and tenderly touched her cheek. He wanted to take her in his arms and hold her to his heart and never let her go, but he couldn't for fear of hurting her. He had to force himself to step away as Frances took charge.

"We've sent for the doctor. He should be here soon. Let me see what I can do to make you more comfortable. Cole, you go on downstairs. This is no place for you—or Dan either," she said, shooing the men from the room.

Cole went reluctantly, unaware that Jenny's gaze was upon him until Frances closed the door. He stood in the hallway with Dan, feeling totally useless.

"I guess we can go downstairs and wait for the doc," Dan suggested, feeling just as lost as Cole.

Evelyn and Rose had already gone down and were in the parlor with Tillie and Melanie. As Dan and Cole descended the stairs, they could hear Rose talking. Dan's heart lightened. He needed to see Rose right now. He needed her to smile at him. There was something about being with her that made everything seem all right.

But as they reached the bottom of the staircase, Dan could hear her crying.

"Aunt Tillie, I am sorry we ever came to this place!" Rose said vehemently, sobbing as she spoke.

"You don't mean that," Tillie said, trying to calm her.

"I do! I do! I wish Jenny's father had never had his accident. Then we'd all be back in Philadelphia where we belong! And Jenny would be safe and sound. What horrible thing is going to happen next around here? First there was the rustling, and now that ranch hand was murdered and Jenny is almost killed—shot down in cold blood for no reason! I hate it here! I want to go back to the city! I want to go back to civilization! I want to go home!"

Dan stopped where he was. He was shocked by Rose's revelation.

Rose hated it here—

She wanted to go back to Philadelphia—

Dan's expression grew grim. He'd thought they might have a future together, but now he realized the painful truth. Rose had never been serious about him. To her, he'd only been a diversion, someone to pass the time with while she waited to go back home.

In the study, Tillie opened her arms to Rose, wanting to comfort her. "Oh, darling."

Rose was sobbing as she went into her aunt's protective embrace.

Dan and Cole made their way to the parlor doorway and silently observed the scene before them.

Up until that moment Dan had believed that Rose was the woman of his dreams—the woman he'd been waiting for. He'd honestly believed he'd been falling in love with her and that they would live there in Durango happily together.

Now, though, having heard the truth of Rose's feelings, Dan knew they had no future together. His dream of a life with Rose was over. He would leave for Durango once he was sure Jenny was going to be all right, and then he would never see Rose again.

Cole and Dan spoke briefly with the women, then retreated to the porch to watch for the doctor's arrival. They said little. Both men were too worried about Jenny to speak of anything else.

Marshal Jared Trent strode into the Mother Lode Saloon, a man on a mission. He stood quietly just inside the doors, looking around the saloon. He'd just received the news from a Lazy S ranch hand about what had happened to Jenny Sullivan and her hired hand, and he was going to follow up on Cole Randall's suggestion to check on Richard Donathan's whereabouts at the time of the ambush. Cole didn't see the man anywhere in the saloon, so he approached the bartender, Gary Knehans.

"Evening, Gary."

"Marshal. Can I get you a drink?" the barkeep offered.

"No, I'm here on business. I'm looking for a man named Donathan, Richard Donathan. He's from back East."

"Oh, yeah—him."

"You know Donathan?"

Gary nodded. "He's been a regular here the last couple of nights. He's a big spender. The girls are enjoying him a lot."

"Where is he?"

"Upstairs with Caroline right now."

"Which room?"

"The last one on the right," the bartender directed. "What are you wanting him for?"

"There was some trouble out at the Lazy S. I just want to talk to him about it."

"What kind of trouble?" Gary was instantly interested.

"Jenny Sullivan was ambushed and shot and one of her men was killed.

"Is she alive?" He stared at the lawman, shocked by the news.

"Yes, thank God."

"Who'd be low enough to shoot a woman?"

"That's what I'm trying to find out," Jared said with fierce determination as he walked away.

Gary watched the lawman run up the steps. He knew what a good marshal Jared Trent was, and he knew it was not smart to mess with him. He hoped the Easterner had sense enough not to cause any trouble. Caroline wouldn't appreciate the interruption, but Gary supposed a lawman had to do what a lawman had to do.

Jared reached the door of Caroline's room and knocked.

"Go away!" came a woman's voice.

"This is Marshal Trent. I need to talk with Richard Donathan," Jared said tersely.

He could hear muted voices behind the closed door, but was unable to decipher what was said. It didn't really matter. Jared knew he was going to get his answers one way or another.

Jared waited another minute, giving them time to open the door, but he heard no one moving about inside. He knocked again. "I want to talk to you *now*."

Jared was almost ready to kick the door in when he heard the lock turn and the door was opened just enough to let the woman peek out at him.

"What do you want, Marshal?" Caroline asked. She was standing before him wearing only a red silk wrapper.

"Excuse me," Jared said, ignoring her state of undress as he pushed past her into the room. He wasn't there to worry about half-naked women. He was there to talk to Richard Donathan.

"You want something?" Richard asked in irritation, aggravated at having been interrupted in the middle of enjoying the pretty, young Caroline. He was still lying in the bed with the sheet drawn up to his waist.

Jared stared down at Richard, noting his black eye and bruised face. "You're Richard Donathan?"

"Yes."

"Where were you yesterday afternoon?"

"Here in town. Why?"

"Do you have any witnesses to that fact?"

"I could probably find some. Why, Marshal? What happened?"

Richard couldn't imagine what had happened. All he'd done since Jenny had returned to the ranch was drink, gamble, and take his pleasure of the girls in the saloons. It had been a rather relaxing time for him, actually, but he didn't feel very relaxed right now with the lawman glaring at him, demanding answers.

"Get dressed. I want you to come down to the office with me."

"You still haven't told me why," Richard insisted, growing worried and a bit angry at being a suspect.

Jared quickly explained.

"Jenny was shot?" Richard went still. He was completely shocked. "Oh, no! Is she all right?" His concern was real.

"The doctor's on his way out to the Lazy S."

"But what have you heard? How serious is it? She's going to be all right, isn't she?" Though he'd been furious at Jenny for her lack of interest in him, Richard had never wished any harm to come to her.

"I think so, but we probably won't know for sure until the doc gets back to town."

"Why do you want me?"

"Because right now you're a suspect, Donathan."

"Me!" Richard truly was in shock.

"That's right. Let's go. I want to question you some more down at the jail."

"Give me a minute to get dressed?"

"I'll wait in the hall for you."

Jared started from the room, but Caroline stopped him. She sashayed in front of him and let her wrapper gap open so he could see all her assets.

"You know, I do have a hankering for lawmen. If you ain't busy later, come on back here and see me," she said in a sultry voice, looking up at the handsome marshal with a hungry gaze.

Jared gave her a half-smile. "I appreciate the offer, but I'm a happily married man."

"There aren't many of those around," Caroline said, not giving up yet.

"I'm one of them. I'll be out in the hall."

He moved away from the predatory saloon girl and left the room, closing the door behind him.

Richard emerged from Caroline's room a few minutes later and accompanied the marshal downstairs.

As they reached the saloon, Jared noticed Wayne Jameson at the bar.

"Wait here," he directed Richard as he went to speak with the rancher. "Wayne—"

Wayne looked up, surprised by the marshal's appearance and wondering what he wanted. Fear stirred within him, but he kept it disguised. "Evening, Marshal Trent."

"I wanted to tell you rustlers hit both the Branding Iron and the Lazy S over the last couple of days. Have you had any trouble out at your place?"

"No. Everything's been quiet."

"Well, keep a look out. Things are getting dangerous out there right now."

"What happened?" Wayne was instantly worried as he remembered his sister's angry mood. When she'd left the house, he'd sneaked away into town to have some fun while she was gone. He'd never imagined he'd end up hearing news here.

"Somebody ambushed Jenny Sullivan, and one of her men."

"Oh, my God!" Wayne's eyes widened in horror. He recalled far too clearly his sister's hatred for Jenny. "How is she? She's not dead, is she?"

"She's alive, but her ranch hand was killed. I just thought you'd want to know about the rustling."

"Thanks for telling me."

Chapter Twenty-seven

Wayne was furious as he glared at Mira. He had ridden straight out to the ranch after talking to Marshal Trent and had roused Mira from a sound sleep. He could barely contain himself as he faced her down.

"What the hell did you do, woman?"

"What are you talking about?" she demanded, angry that he'd awakened her in the middle of the night.

"I'm talking about you shooting Jenny Sullivan!"

"I killed her and the man riding with her. So what?" she shot back at him, feeling quite pleased with herself.

"Like hell you did! You didn't kill her. She's still alive."

"What? Where did you hear that?" Mira was instantly awake, and suddenly she was more than a little frightened. She didn't know if Jenny had gotten a look at her or not.

"I heard it straight from Marshal Trent at the Mother Lode. He said she was still alive. He also knew all about the rustling at the Branding Iron and the Lazy S, and he was warning me to keep a look out for trouble here."

"Did he have any idea who shot them or why?"

"The barkeep told me the reason the lawman was in the saloon was to question that Eastern dude who was staying out at her ranch."

Mira started to tremble as relief flooded through her. "Good. They don't have any idea who did it."

"*Yet*" Wayne sneered. "I can't believe you did this. I can't believe you tried to kill Jenny after you called *me* stupid for killing her father! You've just made things even worse for us!"

"Damn that slut for being alive!" Mira was growing more and more angry with the situation. She'd always prided herself on her marksmanship, and she couldn't believe she'd missed such an easy target.

"You should never have tried to shoot her," Wayne said.

"If you hadn't killed her father, none of this would have happened in the first place!" Mira retorted, not about to take the blame for all that had happened.

"Hell, if you'd been a better shot, we wouldn't be in this mess right now! We just need to shut up and wait and see what happens. Maybe that Richard won't be able to prove where he was, and they'll arrest him."

Mira slowly got a grip on her fury. She began to plot what to do next. The fact that Jenny was still alive changed everything. Mira's expression grew devious as she considered what to do about Cole.

"Where was Cole? Did you hear anything about him?" she asked.

"No, no one said anything about him, other than the news about the rustling on the Branding Iron. If you want, after I get a couple of hours of sleep, I'll ride over to the Lazy S and see what's going on. I can tell them I heard what happened in town and came to see if I could help them out."

"You do that," she agreed.

"How is she?" Cole was the first one to meet Dr. Murray as he came down the stairs after examining Jenny.

Rose, Frances, Dan, and the others came out of the parlor, too, eager to hear the news. Evelyn had gone up with the doctor and had stayed upstairs to nurse Jenny once he had finished treating her.

"She's going to be just fine," he assured everyone.

"Thank God," Cole said out loud, not caring if anyone heard him. Ever since the doctor had arrived, he'd been sitting there in silence, waiting for his report on Jenny's condition and praying she would be all right.

"There may be a scar, but other than some initial weakness and headaches, she'll eventually make a full recovery. Jenny was one very lucky young woman," he told them earnestly.

"Thank you, Dr. Murray."

Everyone was immensely relieved that her wound was not more serious.

"Is there anything special we need to do for her?" Frances asked.

"I gave Evelyn the instructions upstairs. She knows what to do. Basically, Jenny just needs a lot of rest for a day or two." He looked at Cole. "Do you know who did this?"

"Not yet, but I sent word to Marshal Trent, so maybe he'll have something to tell us soon."

"I hope so," the doctor said. "Let me know if there's any change in Jenny's condition."

"We will," Cole promised.

"Is there anything else you need?"

"No. We're just thankful that Jenny's going to be all right, Dr. Murray," Frances said, smiling at him with heart felt gratitude. "Thanks."

"I'm glad everything is turning out this way. It could have been a far different story."

"Thank you," Rose said.

"I guess it's time for me to be heading back to town," the good doctor said, starting for the front door.

"I'll ride with you," Dan said.

He had only stayed around to make sure Jenny was going to recover. With the doctor's good news, he knew he could leave and not worry about her.

Dan noticed the quick, surprised look that Rose sent his way. He didn't care. He just knew that he needed to get away. Ever since he'd heard Rose declare her regret that she had ever come to Durango in the first place, he knew there was no reason for him to stick around. There had never been anything between them, and there never would be.

"Good night, Dr. Murray—Dan," Frances said as they left.

"Good night, Dan," Rose called out.

She was confused by the way Dan was suddenly ignoring her. On their picnic, they'd talked endlessly, and when he'd kissed her, it had been wonderful. His kisses had been arousing, and his touch had been heavenly. Now, though, he didn't even seem to want to talk to her, and she wondered what was wrong. She wondered if she'd done something to anger him.

Rose went after Dan, following him outside. She was determined, in her straightforward way, to find out what was troubling him. She didn't want to let him leave until she'd had a chance to speak with him.

"Dan? Do you know when I'll see you again?" she asked straight out.

Dan had already mounted up. He looked down at her, his expression unreadable.

"No," he answered and offered no more.

Dr. Murray stowed his bag in his carriage and climbed in. He picked up his reins.

"Are you ready?" He looked at Dan.

Dan nodded, then spoke to Rose one last time. "Good-bye, Rose."

With that, he wheeled his horse around and rode out, staying alongside Dr. Murray's carriage as they headed for town.

Rose was bereft as she watched them go. She didn't understand what had happened to change Dan so dramatically. Earlier, he had seemed as if he really wanted to be with her, yet just now, it had seemed as if he couldn't get away from her fast enough. She'd never felt this way about a man before, and she was at a loss to know what to do.

Rose remained where she was on the porch, staring after Dan long after he'd disappeared from sight.

Cole was not sure what to do after Dan and the doctor left. He wasn't certain if Jenny was going to be feeling well enough to see him anytime soon, but he wasn't going anywhere. He planned never to be apart from her again, and he wanted to tell her that as soon as possible. In fact, the sooner, the better.

Cole started out to the stable. He wanted to find Louie and talk to him about the shooting. He needed to know if Louie had any ideas about who might have done it.

"Cole—" Evelyn had just appeared at the top of the stairs as he was going out the door, and she wanted to stop him before he left.

He stopped and looked back to find Jenny's aunt hurrying down the steps toward him.

"Jenny wants to see you," Evelyn told him.

At her words, his spirits soared. He hurried upstairs to her room. He hesitated and glanced back toward Evelyn.

"Go on in," she told him, waving him inside. "If you need me, I'll be downstairs with Frances."

Jenny was lying motionless on the bed with her eyes closed. A white bandage swathed her forehead, and she was very pale. Cole had always thought Jenny a strong-willed woman, but in that moment he realized just how delicate and fragile she was. He realized, too, how close he had come to losing her. He loved her. Jenny meant the world to him, and he planned to spend the rest of his life proving it to her.

Cole stood immobile in the doorway staring at her, trying to deal with the turmoil of his own emotions.

Someone had tried to kill Jenny. Why?

He wondered if Richard had been jealous enough to want to do her harm, or if rustlers had been in the area and wanted her out of the way. He tried to figure out what anyone would gain by Jenny's death, but he could find no answer.

"Jenny?" he finally said quietly.

Her eyes opened at the sound of his voice.

"Oh, Cole—I'm so sorry about Gene—"

"We'll find whoever did this," he promised fiercely.

"Thank you." She smiled up at him. "I was afraid you had gone—"

He moved to her bedside and sat down in the chair there. He reached out and took her hand in his. His voice was husky with the power of what he was feeling for her.

"I'm never going to leave you again," he promised. "I love you, Jenny. I have always loved you, and I don't want to live without you."

Jenny's eyes widened at his words. "I love you, too, Cole. It just took me a while to realize it, but I do—with all my heart."

Cole leaned forward and kissed her. It was a gentle, cherishing caress that spoke of devotion and tenderness. When he ended the kiss, he shifted reluctantly away from her. He wanted to make love to her endlessly. He wanted to take her in his arms and never let her go, but in view of her condition, he had to go slowly. There would be time later for loving. Now, he was just thrilled that she was going to be all right.

"Cole?" Jenny looked up at him. Her eyes were aglow, and a gentle smile curved her lips. She still felt terrible, but she wasn't going to let that stop her. Nothing meant more to her than Cole's love.

"What, love? Do you need something? Is there anything I can get you?" he asked, ready and willing to do whatever she wanted if it would make her feel better.

"Yes, you can get me something."

"What?"

"You can send somebody into town to get Reverend Ford for me."

He looked worried at her request and couldn't imagine why she needed to see him. "You want to see the reverend?"

"Yes, right away. The sooner the better—but only if you agree to marry me," she said straight out. "Will you marry me, Cole Randall, and make me the happiest woman in the world?"

Jenny would forever remember how Cole's expression changed as she proposed to him. He went from worried to shocked to amused.

"In a heartbeat," he answered, leaning toward her to kiss her again.

When he finally ended the kiss, she smiled up at him lovingly.

"I thought it would be best if *I* proposed to *you* this time," Jenny told him.

"Are you sure you don't want a big wedding in town?"

"No, absolutely not. We'll be married here, privately."

"You aren't going to change your mind at the last minute again, are you?"

"There's no danger of that, Mr. Randall. I made a mistake two years ago, but I learned from it. I love you. I'm never going to let you go again."

"How soon do you want to have the ceremony? When do you think you'll be feeling well enough?"

"Let's plan on the day after tomorrow. Dr. Murray said I should be better by then."

"Good. I'll make the arrangements."

Cole kissed her yet another time, tenderly touching her cheek as he finally moved away from her.

"Jenny, there was one other thing I wanted to talk to you about," he began.

"What is it?"

"Have you remembered anything—anything at all about the ambush? Did you see anyone or hear anything?"

"It's all so confused in my mind," she said slowly, frowning as she tried to force herself to remember exactly what had happened on that fateful ride. "The shots came from up on the rise. Gene was hit first."

Jenny tried to concentrate, tried to recall if she'd seen anything that could help Cole find the ambusher, but she had no recollection other than hearing the first shot and seeing Gene fall. "I'm sorry, Cole. I wish I did know more, but that's all I can remember. I didn't see anyone. I wish I had."

"So do I," he said fiercely. He was frustrated that he had nothing to go on. "You rest now."

"You're not going to go—" Jenny clutched his hand, a little frightened.

"No, sweetheart, I'll stay right here if that's what you want me to do."

"Yes. Stay with me, Cole. Don't ever leave me."

"I won't, Jenny."

She gave him a small smile as her eyes drifted shut. She did not release his hand but held him tightly.

Cole settled in the chair beside the bed, watching Jenny rest. His gaze went lovingly over her, but it hardened when he stared at the bandage. The bandage reminded him all too forcefully of how very close she'd been to death.

The tenderness that had held him in its grip altered, and anger grew within Cole. He had vowed to find the one who'd done this to Jenny, and he would. If he didn't hear anything from Jared by tomorrow, he would ride into town himself and see what the lawman had found out.

Chapter Twenty-eight

Cole kept a vigil by Jenny's side throughout the day. She slept a lot, but every time she awoke, he was there with her. The only time he left her was to seek out Tom and send him into town with a letter for Reverend Ford. He returned to Jenny right away and stayed until Evelyn came up to the room near midnight to relieve him.

Frances had turned down the bed in the extra bedroom for him, and he slept there that night. His wasn't a deep, restful sleep, though, for he kept waking up, worrying about Jenny. Each time, the quiet of the house reassured him that all was well.

Cole was up with the sun, more than ready for the start of the new day. He had heard nothing from Marshal Trent, and he was almost ready to make the trip into town to find out what the lawman had learned.

He went downstairs to see if Frances had started breakfast yet.

"Good morning, Cole," the older woman greeted him as he came in the kitchen. "I'll have your breakfast ready in just a minute."

"Is Jenny awake yet?" he asked.

"I checked on her a few minutes ago, and she and her aunt were both still asleep. You go ahead and get yourself some coffee while I dish this up."

Cole poured himself a cup of hot, black coffee and settled in at the dining room table. He'd thought he would be eating alone, and he was surprised when he heard someone on the stairs. He got up to see who it was, expecting to see Evelyn. He was startled to find that Jenny was with her aunt.

"Jenny—you're up. Should you be out of bed this soon?" He was delighted that she was capable of moving around, but he was still concerned about her. He hurried to help her.

"Dr. Murray said I could get out of bed when I felt I was ready, and I'm ready," Jenny told him as she took his hand.

When she reached the bottom of the steps, Cole slipped a supportive arm around her waist.

"Have you got her, Cole?" Evelyn asked.

"Yes."

"Then I'll go help Frances with breakfast."

She went off to the kitchen while Cole guided Jenny into the dining room.

Cole kept Jenny close to his side as they made their

way toward the dining room table. Even though she was up and moving again, she still felt very fragile to him as he helped to support her. They reached her chair and he pulled it out for her, but she didn't immediately sit down.

"I am much improved this morning, but there is one thing that would make me feel even better," she said as she looked up at him and smiled slowly.

Cole was ready and willing to get her whatever she needed. "What is it?"

"A kiss," she said with a sigh as she looped her arms around his neck and drew him down to her.

"I think I can find one of those for you," he murmured.

"Only one?" she asked, lifting her lips to his.

Cole gave a low groan at her suggestive words and wrapped his arms around her as his mouth covered hers. Though he still had to keep a tight rein on his desire for her, this kiss was infinitely more satisfying than the chaste ones he'd given her yesterday. Only the sound of Frances and Evelyn coming tore them reluctantly apart.

As Cole helped Jenny sit down, he was pleased to see that some color had returned to her cheeks. He took the chair next to hers as the two women set down their trays of food. They all settled in and ate together.

It was only a short time later that Rose, Tillie, and Melanie came up from the guest house and joined them. All were thrilled to find Jenny up and about.

They were just finishing breakfast when they heard horses coming.

"I'll go see who it is," Cole offered, rising to go and meet the visitors. He was glad to see that it was the marshal riding in with Frank Goodwin, one of the neighboring ranchers.

"Morning, Cole," Jared said as he reined in before the house. "I'm glad you're still here."

"Good to see you, Jared—Frank. Have you got any news? What did you find out?" he asked quickly.

"Donathan wasn't involved. There were people all around town who saw him in Durango that day."

Cole nodded slowly, his mind racing as he tried to figure out who else could have been behind the shooting. "It must have been the rustlers, then."

"I'm sorry to hear about all your trouble, and I'm real glad Jenny's going to be all right," Jared said.

"So are we," Cole returned.

"Frank came along because he just found out yesterday that he had been hit, too," Jared explained.

"So that's three of us this time." Cole was thoughtful. "Why don't you two come on inside? Jenny's up and feeling much better today."

"That's good news. Thanks."

Jared and Frank followed Cole indoors. He introduced them to everyone; then they started to go to the study to talk.

"I'm coming with you," Jenny insisted.

"Are you sure you're strong enough?" Evelyn asked, not wanting her to overexert herself.

"Yes, Aunt Evelyn. This is my ranch." Jenny got up, and Cole was instantly beside her to help her.

Jenny sat in one of the wing chairs in her father's study, while Cole sat behind the desk. Jared and Frank sat on the sofa that faced the desk.

Cole quickly explained that he'd sent the men back up to the site of the shooting the following day, but they had found nothing.

"I'd expected as much, but it doesn't make it any easier to accept," Cole continued. "I've been trying to think of a way to track down Jenny's attacker, and I'm beginning to believe that the ambush and the rustling are somehow connected. We need to set a trap of some kind for these rustlers. There's got to be a way to stop them."

They discussed at length what could be done to lure the rustlers in and then trap them, and Jenny joined in. As they were talking, Frances knocked on the study door.

"Wayne Jameson just rode in."

"Bring him on in," Cole told her.

"I wonder why Wayne's here," Jenny said.

"I saw him in town the other night, and I mentioned to him what had happened. I told him to keep an eye out, so maybe he knows something," Jared offered.

Cole rose to meet Wayne at the door as Frances ushered him in.

"Glad to see you, Wayne." Cole shook his hand.

Wayne greeted everyone and looked at Jenny. "Jenny, it's good to know you're going to be all right.

I heard from Marshal Trent that you'd been shot. I rode over to see how you were and to see if you needed any help."

"That was kind of you, Wayne," Jenny told him. "We're all right, for now. Cole's helping me take care of things here on the ranch. We just need to find out who took a shot at me and who's been rustling all the cattle."

"Did you have any problems out at your spread, Wayne?" Jared asked.

"No. They left us alone this time. We were lucky."

"They hit Frank, too. That's why he's here. We're trying to put together a plan to trap the rustlers. I think it may be time to organize a cattlemen's association, too, and start patrolling the range ourselves."

"If need be, we can bring in a range detective," Cole said. "But I think we can catch them."

Wayne joined in the discussion, but grew more and more nervous as the other ranchers and the lawman laid out their plan for catching the rustlers. He realized that Cole was absolutely determined to bring them to justice, and he didn't want to be the man facing him when the truth finally came out. Wayne went along with everything they agreed on, and even offered to work with them. In the back of his mind, though, he was planning to get away as fast as he could. He had to get back to the ranch and warn Mira about what was going on. Their rustling days were over. It was time to cut and run while they still could.

Jenny grew weary as the men continued to plan their trap.

"If you'll excuse me, I need to rest for a while," she said, slowly getting to her feet.

"Jenny, it's just good to see that you're up and around already," Jared told her.

"Thank you, Jared," she said with a slight smile. "Frank, Wayne, I'll see you later."

"Take care, Jenny," Frank said.

Cole went to her and again slipped an arm about her waist to help her.

"I'll be right back," he told the men as he and Jenny left the study.

When they were in the hall, Cole simply picked Jenny up in his arms and carried her upstairs.

"You didn't need to do that. I could have made it," she protested, but her protest was halfhearted as she linked her arms around his neck. She liked having him hold her close.

"Yes, I did," he said, grinning at her. "It gave me an excuse to hold you."

"After tomorrow you'll never need another excuse."

Their gazes met and a fiery heat flamed to life within them both. They didn't say anything else as he carried her up to her room. Cole bent to lay her upon the bed, but Jenny deliberately didn't let him go. She drew him down with her, kissing him hungrily, wanting him near.

"I don't want to hurt you," he said quietly as he broke off the kiss.

"You'll never hurt me, Cole," she whispered against his lips, urging him back to her.

His mouth claimed hers possessively as his hands swept over her sweet curves. For long moments they lay together, starving for closeness, desperate to be near one another. Finally, as his passion threatened to wipe all logic from his mind, Cole tore himself away from Jenny.

"I've got to go back. They're waiting for me." He was breathing heavily as he shifted away to sit beside her on the side of the bed.

"Once we're married, you will never have to stop." She looked up at him, loving the look of burning desire that glowed in his eyes at her words.

"I'm counting the hours—believe me," he growled, kissing her one last time before he stood up. "You rest now. Save your strength," he teased. "You're going to need it tomorrow."

"I'll be ready," she answered.

"Will you be all right alone?"

"I'll be fine. You just hurry back once they're gone."

"Don't worry. I will."

Cole left without kissing her again. He knew if he did, he might not get back downstairs for some time, and he didn't want to have to explain the reason for his delay.

The meeting continued for over an hour before the

men finally had drawn up their plan. They were confident it would work, and as Jared and Frank rode for town, they were ready to recruit the other ranchers they would need.

Wayne rode out at the same time. He had said all the right things and acted as if nothing was wrong, but he was as close to panic as he'd ever been in his life. He rode at top speed for home. There was no time to waste.

Cole was still working in the study when Tom rode back in from Durango with the answering letter from the reverend. Cole opened and read it immediately. He was pleased to learn that the preacher would be there to perform the ceremony at two the following day.

In a little over twenty-four hours, Jenny would become Mrs. Cole Randall. He liked the sound of that. He went upstairs to give her the news.

Wayne was never so glad to get home.

"Mira!" he shouted as he ran into the house.

"What's wrong?" Mira demanded as she came out of the back of the house to find her brother standing wild-eyed in the middle of the hall.

"I'll tell you what's wrong! Jenny Sullivan is up and about, and—"

"She is?" Mira stared at him in furious disbelief.

"Yes! You only grazed her. You're just damned lucky she didn't see you when you were taking your shots at her."

She swore loudly. "Damn that bitch! I hate her! God, how I hate that slut!"

"But that's not all I found out." he went on, cutting off her rantings. "Cole was there, and so was Marshal Trent and Frank Goodwin. The ranchers are planning to band together to catch the rustlers. They're planning a trap for us. We gotta get out of here while we still can! We gotta leave now!"

She'd always known her brother wasn't the smartest man around, but she'd never thought he was this stupid.

"Wayne, if they don't know we're doing the rustling, why do we have to run?"

"Because they're going to figure it out! I know it! They'll be coming after us, and when they do—"

"You are so stupid, Wayne," she told him in disgust. "If they don't have any idea that it's us, and if we stop rustling and don't fall into their trap, how will they ever prove it? I don't see what the problem is."

"They're going to catch us! I know it!"

"They are not going to catch us. Not unless we do something *stupid*—like *run!*" she snapped at him.

Wayne was furious and frightened. "I'm sick of you telling me how stupid I am! You're the one who thought you were so damned smart. You're the one who thought you knew what you were doing."

"I do know what I'm doing."

"What the hell are you two shoutin' about?" Russell Jameson demanded, staggering into the hall. He'd been sleeping in a drunken stupor in the parlor when their arguing had roused him. His mood was foul and his temper raging.

"We gotta get out of here, Pa!" Wayne blurted out. "Mira tried to shoot Jenny Sullivan, but she only wounded her. Jenny's still alive, and now they're looking for the ones who did it. I know they're going to find out it was us and come after us. I know it!"

"You don't know anything!" Mira shouted back at him. "They don't know I did the shooting, and they don't know we've been rustling either. There's no reason for us to run scared, you coward."

"Yeah, well, the least you could have done was kill her!"

"Believe me I wanted to, but if you hadn't killed her father in the first place, none of this would be happening."

Russell was staring at Mira. "I thought you were marrying Cole Randall. I thought that rustling was only to tide us over for a while until you'd got him to the altar."

"Things haven't worked out," she hedged, seeing her father's fury and hating the prospect of dealing with him. He was nothing but a useless, nasty drunk, and she had put up with him for about as long as she could stand.

"Why the hell not?" he roared. "You spent the night with him! He should be marrying you after you spread your legs for him that way!"

"Cole didn't bed me!" she threw back at him. "He

slept in the bunkhouse the night I spent over there."

"Sure he did," Russell said, leering at her. "I always knew Cole was a smart one." He laughed drunkenly. "Of course he ain't buying the cow! He done got the milk for free! You're a stupid bitch. I can't believe you're my daughter."

"Neither can I!" Mira sneered. "Why don't you go on back to bed, you old drunk. Get out of my sight! Go sleep it off. I'll handle things around here."

"It don't sound like you're handlin' much at all. You sure as hell ain't handlin' Cole Randall!" Russell glared at her, then looked at Wayne. "And just what good are you? If you had any sense at all, you would have been man enough to figure out a way to save this place without your sister havin' to whore herself!"

"Old man, you better shut up while you're still breathing!" Wayne threatened. He had suffered through endless beatings as a child that hadn't stopped until he'd been big enough to fight back. Since then, his pa had stopped hitting him, but he'd never stopped telling him how stupid he was.

Mira looked from her father to her brother. "While you two continue your discussion, I'm going to ride out to the canyon and tell the boys our rustling days are over. We've got to make sure they lay low and don't try anything else until we give them the go-ahead."

"Then what do you plan to do? Since you're so

smart, how are you going to save the place? We've been just hanging on as it is."

Mira glared at Wayne, the look in her eyes savage. "I'm going to marry Cole."

With that, she turned her back on them both and stalked out of the house. She had a lot to do before she went to find Cole again. It wasn't going to be easy after seeing how attracted he still was to Jenny, but she had to find a way.

As Mira saddled up and rode for the canyon to speak with her men, she grew even angrier and more full of hate for Jenny. She despised the woman with every fiber of her being. Jenny had had Cole at the altar and had thrown him away—and now she decides she wanted him again? There was no way Mira could stand by and let that bitch have him. Cole was hers. She'd been patient, waiting for him to get over Jenny, biding her time as she tried to seduce him. She'd thought she'd been making progress with him. After what had happened at the dance, though, she knew she had to act and act fast. Her bullet might have missed killing Jenny, but she had no intention of missing when it came to making Cole her own.

Chapter Twenty-nine

"You look lovely," Evelyn told Jenny, smiling serenely at the sight of her niece clad in a pretty pale blue gown. She looked beautiful. No longer was she pale and wan. High color stained her cheeks, and her eyes glowed with inner joy. The only reminder of her trauma was a small bandage on her forehead.

"Do you really think so?" Jenny asked as she lifted her worried gaze to her aunt's. She remembered how she'd looked in her full-skirted bridal gown and wondered if Cole would think she looked pretty today so simply dressed. "Last time—"

"Last time you didn't go through with the ceremony," Evelyn told her with a grin. "Believe me, Cole would much rather marry you in this dress than see you in that bridal gown again."

"Bad memories?"

"I'm sure."

"Well, today I intend to erase those bad memories once and for all. Today I'm going to become Mrs. Cole Randall, and I can hardly wait."

"It's almost two o'clock, and Reverend Ford is downstairs with Cole waiting for you. Whenever you're ready, we can go down." Evelyn went to her and hugged her close. "Are you happy, darling? Are you really happy?"

"Oh, yes, Aunt Evelyn," she said, returning her embrace. "I love Cole with all my heart."

"Then let's go get you married."

"I'm ready."

They left the bedroom and made their way down the hall. Evelyn told to wait at the top of the steps while she went downstairs to make sure everything was set. In a minute she was back.

"It's time, Jenny."

They shared one last, loving hug; then Jenny started down the steps. When they reached the hall, Jenny saw the ranch hands gathered on the porch. She looked questioningly at her aunt. Evelyn smiled at her.

"They figured out what was happening when they saw Reverend Ford show up. They wanted to celebrate with you," Evelyn explained. "We couldn't fit everybody in the parlor, so they're going to watch from the parlor windows."

Jenny smiled at her men before turning toward the parlor, ready to go to Cole.

It was time.

Evelyn walked with her to the parlor door before slipping away to join those who were waiting with Cole and the minister. As Evelyn entered the room, everyone turned to see Jenny in the doorway.

Jenny was positively glowing, and she had eyes only for Cole, who was standing apart from the others with Reverend Ford. Her gaze went over him, visually caressing him. She realized he must have sent one of the hands to his ranch to get a suit for him to wear for the ceremony, and he was ruggedly, compellingly handsome. His presence was commanding, and she was drawn to him like a moth to a flame. She could not resist him, and she did not want to—not ever again.

Cole saw Jenny and immediately went to her to take her arm. He still remembered how lovely she'd looked in her bridal gown two years ago. She had been stunningly lovely then, but today he thought her even more radiant, even wearing the simple gown she'd chosen. She had pinned her hair up away from her face, and he could hardly wait to pull the pins from her hair and free the heavy mass to his touch. His thoughts threatened to race ahead to the night to come, and he had to force himself to concentrate on the moment at hand.

This was their wedding day.

At long last, Jenny would be his bride.

"You're beautiful," he said in a low, soft voice meant just for her to hear.

She smiled up at him. "Thank you. I wanted to be—for you."

They shared a secret smile as Cole guided her to stand before the minister.

"Are we ready to begin?" Reverend Ford asked quietly.

Jenny remembered another time when he'd said the exact same words to her. She noticed, too, that the minister seemed a bit nervous as he spoke. It was at this moment that she'd stopped him the last time, but today she only smiled.

"Hurry," she said in a loud whisper. "I've already waited too long to marry Cole."

The minister smiled back at her and began the ceremony. "Dearly beloved . . ."

As Reverend Ford spoke, Jenny glanced up at Cole. All the love she felt for him was shining in her eyes. She found Cole watching her, too. At first when their gazes met, his expression seemed suddenly guarded, almost cautious, as if he feared she would once again run from him. But Jenny stood her ground. She loved Cole and wanted only to spend the rest of her life with him. She gave him a serene, blissful smile, and he knew this time it was right. This time she really would be his. They both turned back to the minister then, eagerly anticipating the vows to come.

They would be man and wife.

Rose sat with Tillie and Melanie watching as Cole and Jenny were bound together in holy matrimony.

She sighed with happiness for them, thrilled that Jenny had won Cole's love, delighted that they were going to live happily ever after together, and overwhelmed with joy that they had found each other before it was too late.

As Rose listened to them taking their vows to love, honor, cherish, and obey each other, tears burned in her eyes. She found Dan slipping, unbidden, into her thoughts, and she wondered why. She'd missed him ever since he'd left with Dr. Murray. She'd hoped that he would come back to the ranch unexpectedly and surprise her, but the hours and days had passed, and she had not heard from him.

Rose couldn't imagine what had happened to make Dan change so drastically. What she'd felt for him had been special and real. What they'd shared had been wonderful and different from anything she'd ever known. It troubled and saddened her to lose Dan so soon after she'd found him.

With an effort, Rose put the sadness from her. This was Jenny's wedding day. She would be happy for her friend. She would celebrate her joy.

Rose vowed to herself, though, that before she left for Philadelphia in two days, she would make the time to seek out Dan. She was determined do it, even if she had to go into the High Time Saloon again to find him. She planned to tell him good-bye and give him and Fernada copies of their pictures.

If nothing else, once she'd gone, Dan would have the picture to remember the time they had together.

"With this ring I thee wed," Cole repeated what the minister had instructed as he slipped the plain gold band on Jenny's finger.

"By the power vested in me, I now pronounce you man and wife," Reverend Ford intoned solemnly over them. "Cole, you may kiss your bride."

Cole needed no further urging. He turned to Jenny and drew her to him, kissing her. It was a cherishing exchange that only hinted at the passion to come. Jenny enjoyed his kiss, but couldn't wait to be alone with him to more fully explore that passion. They'd already agreed to travel to the Branding Iron for their wedding night. They knew they would have more privacy there.

When Cole ended the kiss, everyone in the parlor rushed forward to congratulate them, and the men on the porch let out a cheer.

Frances had planned a party and had set up tables outside. Everyone headed that way, wanting to celebrate.

"I get you first," Rose insisted as Cole and Jenny started outside. "Come on over here. We've got everything all set up."

Cole and Jenny were surprised to find that she'd set up her camera in a sunny area and was ready to take their photograph.

"Thank you, Rose! What a wonderful idea!" Jenny hugged her impulsively.

Jenny and Cole stood still patiently for Rose as she

worked her magic, and then they went to join the others who were already celebrating.

It was a joyous time, a loving time.

"I never thought I would see this day, although I always knew a marriage between them would be perfect," Frances said to Louie and Evelyn, her voice strained with heartfelt emotion.

"They'll do well together," Louie said.

"Yes, they will," Evelyn agreed. She watched as her niece gazed adoringly up at Cole. Evelyn was delighted that they had found true happiness at last.

Jenny saw Rose standing by herself and slipped away from Cole for a moment. She sought out her friend, wanting to thank her for all her moral support and help.

"Rose—I would have given up hope without you," she told her, kissing her cheek.

Rose grinned. "I'm just glad you two are together the way you were always meant to be."

"So am I." Jenny looked over toward Cole. "So what are you going to do about Dan?"

Rose was shocked. She hadn't thought anyone had noticed her distress. "There's not much I can do. I don't know what happened. We had a wonderful time together, and then suddenly he couldn't wait to get away."

"Are you planning to give up without a fight?" Jenny asked.

"No. I was thinking I'd go see him at the High Time once more before I go home."

"Good. Do you love him?" Jenny asked bluntly.

Rose looked deeply thoughtful. "I'm not sure. I've never been in love. How do you know?"

"You know you're in love when that person means more to you than anything in the whole world and you want his happiness more than your own. I can't imagine a life without Cole now. I want to be with him always."

"I know what I shared with Dan was special. But we're so different. What do we have in common?"

"Love? It does conquer all. Do you care about him enough to change for him? To give up something for him?"

"I don't know . . ." She was hesitant, trying to sort out the truth of her feelings.

"That's the question you have to answer. No one can answer it for you. Look in your heart. You'll know."

Cole came to claim her then. "It's about time to go if we're going to make it to the ranch before dark."

Jenny looked up at him and said breathlessly, "I'm ready."

Cole certainly knew he was more than ready to leave. The sooner he was alone with Jenny, the we'd better.

"Good-bye, Rose," Cole said as he escorted his bride to the waiting carriage.

"Think about what I said," Jenny called back as Cole lifted her into the vehicle.

Everyone waved and cheered again as they headed out.

Cole reined in at the cemetery and helped Jenny down. Together they paid a quiet visit to her parents' graves and to Gene's. He'd been buried there late the day before. After a long moment, they started on their way again, their moods brightening in the glow of their love.

When as they were out of sight, of the ranch, Cole reined the horses in and turned to Jenny. Without a word, she knew what he wanted. They came together in a blazing embrace, hungry for each other, no longer wanting to be denied. Cole pulled her against him as his mouth claimed hers again and again. Jenny was as eager as Cole, and she met him in each ardent kiss. She wanted him desperately and could hardly wait to experience the true beauty of his love.

"If this was a bigger carriage, you'd be in trouble right now," he growled as he controlled his raging passion.

"I think I'd like to be in trouble with you," she told him.

He urged the team on again, at an even faster pace. He'd waited his whole life for this night. He could hardly wait to get to the Branding Iron and carry her over the threshold.

Jenny sat close beside him and daringly rested her hand on his thigh as he drove the carriage. She felt him tense beneath her hand and smiled to herself at his reaction. It pleased her to know that she could excite him with just a simple touch. She had never fully understood the power of a woman, but she was learning.

The sun was just setting as they reached Cole's ranch. When Cole had sent for his suit to wear today, he'd let Fred know about the wedding and his plans for their wedding night. He could see Fred now, waiting on the porch for him as he stopped at the hitching rail.

"Evening, Mr. and Mrs. Randall," Fred said, grinning from ear to ear at the sight of them.

"Good evening, Fred," Jenny greeted him as Cole started to lift her down from the carriage.

"I told the boys about the wedding, and we're all real happy for you," Fred went on. "We'll make sure you're not interrupted tonight."

"Good," Cole said firmly.

"You can put me down," Jenny said.

"Not yet," he answered, swinging her up into his arms.

Fred hastily got out of Cole's way as he strode for the front door.

"I have to carry my bride over the threshold," Cole insisted. He opened the door and stepped through. He didn't put her down until after he'd claimed a warm kiss.

"Good night, Cole," Fred called from out on the porch.

He wasn't the least bit surprised when Cole didn't

answer but simply kicked the door shut behind them.

"Lucky man," he said to himself as he started out to the bunkhouse to give the men the news that the boss was home—with his bride.

Chapter Thirty

Jenny gave a throaty laugh as the door slammed shut behind them. "Don't you think you should lock it?" she asked.

"They wouldn't dare interrupt me tonight," Cole replied, heading straight for his bedroom with her in his arms.

"I can walk, you know."

"I don't want to risk you running away from me," he told her, a teasing glint in his eyes.

"The only place I'd run would be right back to you," Jenny told him, then tugged him down to her for a quick kiss as he kept walking.

Cole reached his bedroom and finally had to put her down so he could light a lamp. Jenny stared about the room, taking in the dark, heavy furniture that gave it a very masculine feeling. The bed was wide and looked comfortable. She was going to enjoy finding out just how comfortable that very night.

As she stared at the bed, though, a memory she had long denied returned with a vengeance. All too clearly she remembered Mira talking about how she'd been in Cole's bed. A shudder of disgust racked her, and her joyous expression faded.

"What is it?" Cole asked. He had looked back at her and seen the sudden change in her.

"Nothing—" she lied, wanting to just forget it.

Cole was too attuned to her, though, and he knew something was troubling her deeply. "Jenny—we're married now. We're man and wife. If something's bothering you, you need to tell me. I can't make things better if I don't know what's wrong."

He'd expected to turn away from lighting the lamp, sweep her up in his arms, and lay her on the bed. He'd wanted to make love to her right then—quickly, urgently. But this was more important—something that had to be resolved first. They had to learn to always be honest with each other.

Jenny saw the earnestness in Cole's expression. She knew she would never find the joy she'd hoped for in his arms tonight if she didn't tell him about her conversation with Mira.

"Jenny," he said more softly. "Tell me what's troubling you."

"It's—It's Mira." She watched his expression carefully as she spoke, wanting to see if he was going to try to lie to her or hide anything from her.

"What about Mira?" Cole was confused. He frowned. He had no idea why Jenny would be worrying about the other woman on this, their wedding night.

"She told me," Jenny answered simply.

"Told you what?"

She swallowed tightly. She looked at the bed again and then back at Cole. "She told me about you."

Suddenly he began to understand what had happened. He knew Mira far too well and could just imagine what she'd done. "And just what did Mira tell you about 'us'?"

"She told me she knew how comfortable your bed was and—"

Cole gave a shake of his head and swore under his breath. "When did she tell you this?"

"At the social."

"I don't doubt it. She was probably jealous," he said tightly.

"But is it true?" She had to know.

"Jenny, if we're going to have a happy marriage, it's going to start right now with you trusting me. Mira and I have never meant anything to each other. I was her escort to several social functions, but any relationship between us never went further than a kiss. I've never been serious about her or any other woman. I've only been serious about you."

"How could she have been in your bed?"

"One night right after you came back to Durango, I came home to the ranch to find her here waiting for me. I had no intention of getting involved with anyone, and she knew it. It was late, though, and a storm came up. Mira said the weather was too bad and it was too late for her to ride back home, so I invited her to spend the night."

"Oh."

As aggressive as Mira was, Jenny could only imagine what had happened between them.

Cole could see where Jenny's thoughts were going, and he spoke up sharply. "Don't even think it, Jenny. Mira has always been far more interested in me than I've been in her—especially since you've been back in town. I fixed the guest room for her and then I went and spent the night with the boys in the bunkhouse. Fred and the others are my witnesses. You can go ask them right now, but I swear what I'm telling you is the truth."

"Really?"

"Really. I wasn't about to set myself up for trouble that night, and I had a feeling Mira was going to be trouble. If she told you she was in my bed, she might have come in here during the night, but I wasn't here. If she was in my bed, she was in it alone." Cole met Jenny's gaze and held it with his own as he solemnly told her, "I give you my word on that."

Jenny gazed at the man she loved and knew he was telling the truth. She went to him and looped her arms around his neck, drawing him down to her for a passionate kiss.

"I love you, Cole Randall."

"And I love you."

"Let's make new memories for me in your bed," Jenny said with a throaty laugh.

"I like the way you think, woman."

They moved together to the bed.

"I want to see you tonight, Jenny—all of you," he murmured as he pressed heated kisses to her throat, then moved up to reclaim her lips.

Cole began to unfasten the buttons at the back of her gown as he continued to kiss her.

Jenny did not stand idly before him. She, too, was eager to know the full joy of loving him. She helped him shed his jacket and then worked feverishly to unbutton his shirt. She finished her task before Cole and slipped her hands inside to caress the hard-muscled width of his chest. He was hot and sleek, and she loved the way he felt beneath her touch. Jenny pressed her lips to his chest, and she couldn't help smiling a bit when Cole groaned. She had never been so brazen with him before, and she was loving the freedom of being able to touch him and hold him and caress him.

He was hers.

Cole was growing ever more frustrated with the buttons on her gown. He was close to ripping the offending garment from her. When at long last he finally freed the last button, he reached up to slip the gown from her shoulders.

Jenny drew back and looked up at him. Her eyes were dark with desire. With slow deliberation, she stepped out of her shoes, and then lowered the gown from her shoulders and let it fall to the floor. She stood before him clad only in her chemise and petticoats. She could see the fire burning in Cole's gaze and reached up to loosen the ribbons that held the chemise. Oh so slowly she stripped herself of the last barrier between them.

Cole threw off his jacket and shirt without taking his eyes off Jenny. His gaze raked over her in a heated, visual caress. She was perfect—beautiful.

Cole reached out for her, wanting her, needing her, and Jenny went to him, ready to know the fullness of his lovemaking. He lifted her in his arms, and together they lay upon the bed. Each caress, each kiss was an expression of their love for one another.

Their passion grew unbounded until Cole could no longer wait to be one with her. He had to make her his own in all ways. He left her only long enough to shed the rest of his clothing, then returned to the bed, moving over her. His body was a searing brand upon her, and Jenny gasped at the contact, so intimate.

"I love you, Cole," she told him, looking up at him, her eyes luminous with wonder.

Cole slowly, carefully pressed home the proof of his love for her, breaching her innocence and making her his. With infinite care and tender caresses, he gentled her. His need was great, but he struggled to go slowly, wanting to make this moment special for her. He began to move, glorying in the beauty of their union.

Jenny was an innocent, but her passion for her husband was untamed. She eagerly matched him in each kiss as her desire blossomed. She held on to Cole, thrilling at the power of his love, accepting and giving.

They were one.

Cole sought only to show her the depth of his love for her. He worshiped at the altar of her body. With each caress, he brought her closer and closer to the perfection of their lovemaking. When at last, ecstasy claimed her and she cried out his name, he held her to him, thrilling to know that he had pleased her. He sought his own release then, and lost himself in the mindless joy that was loving her. They collapsed together, their bodies still joined, their hearts beating as one.

They loved.

The night was long and dark, but Jenny and Cole never slept. They were too caught up in the fever of their excitement. Again and again, Cole reached out to Jenny, stoking the embers of her desire, setting her on fire with her need to be one with him. Over and over, the inferno of their passion flamed white-hot as they sought love's ultimate release. Together, they reached the peaks of rapture.

"I never knew loving you could be so wonderful," Jenny told Cole as she rested in his arms. She had been an innocent and had known little of what truly went on between a man and a woman, but this night her husband had tutored her well and she had loved every minute of her lessons.

Cole rose up over Jenny and smiled down at her. "I'm glad I pleased you."

"You more than pleased me," she replied, her voice taking on a husky note. She gave him an inviting smile as she lifted one hand to caress his cheek. "I love you, Cole, with all my heart. I'm sorry I hurt you."

"Nothing matters now except the fact that we're together," he told her, leaning down to give her a gentle kiss. "And I'm never going to let you go."

"Promise?"

"Promise," he repeated, and then he went on to show her how he intended to keep her.

Much later, Jenny sighed happily, "I find I quite enjoy being your wife."

Dawn was brightening the eastern sky when they finally sought rest. Spent from their night of passion, they lay in each other's arms, filled with the peace and joy only true love can bring.

Chapter Thirty-one

Mira had had time to come up with a new plan to seduce Cole as she'd ridden out to talk to the ranch hands the day before. It wasn't going to be easy. She'd already discovered that; she knew she had to act and act fast.

Damn, but she hated that woman!

And she was almost beginning to hate Cole for being so stupid where Jenny was concerned. She couldn't understand why the man wanted anything to do with Jenny after the way she'd treated him. That was why she thought she was perfect for Cole. She would never do him wrong. She would never leave him. She loved him and wanted only to make him happy. One way or another, she planned to prove that to him today.

She would ride straight to the Branding Iron and

find some way to seduce Cole. She ignored the desperation she was really feeling. She refused to acknowledge the nagging thought in the back of her mind that she might fail—that he really might not want her. She wanted Cole and she was going to get him.

She was tired of watching him hover over Jenny all the time. Just because they had to work together to run the Lazy S didn't mean he couldn't marry Mira. Once she had him in her bed, she was certain he wouldn't want to even look at another woman. She intended to keep him so satisfied that the thought of bedding another woman would never occur to him. The trouble was, she had to get him in bed to prove it to him, and so far he wasn't cooperating.

Mira denied the possibility of failure. She wanted Cole more than she'd ever wanted anything in her life. She would not be denied.

She rose before dawn and headed for the Branding Iron, ready to win the man she loved, one way or another. Since her brother had told her that Jenny was going to recover, she figured that Cole would have returned to his own home. She would catch him home alone this morning before he rode out to go to work, and she was going to do everything in her power to get him in bed. Nothing was going to stop her today. Her future, her very well-being, depended on her success.

When the ranch house came into view, Mira was more than ready. The thought of kissing Cole and finally being in his arms drove her on. She wanted him badly, had wanted him for what seemed like forever, and today was the day when she was going to get what she wanted.

Mira didn't see any ranch hands as she rode in quietly, and she was glad. What was going to happen between her and Cole was private—very private. She tied up before the house and went to knock on the door.

Mira licked her lips as she waited for Cole to answer. When she didn't hear footsteps coming toward the door right away, she knocked again a little harder.

Cole was there.

He had to be there!

She was ready for him.

She wanted him.

She couldn't wait any longer to make him hers.

When Mira still didn't hear anyone coming, she reached for the doorknob and tried it. The door was unlocked, and she let herself inside. If it turned out Cole wasn't home, she could wait for a while. And if he still didn't show up, she would let his hired hands know that she'd been there and leave a note for him.

Mira hoped he was just in the back of the house and hadn't heard her knock. She shut the door behind her and went to look for him.

"Cole?" Jenny murmured in a sleep-drugged voice. "Did you hear something?"

She was curled against him, her head on his shoulder, her hand splayed on his chest.

"What?" he asked, still half asleep. His senses were immediately alert to Jenny's nearness, though, and his hand swept over her in a warm caress as he assured himself that the night just passed had been real. A sleepy smile curved his mouth at the memories.

"I heard something. It sounded like someone knocking on the door," she said, all but purring under his touch.

"I told the men to leave us alone. Whoever it is will go away," he told her as he rolled over her and pinned her warm, willing body beneath him, wanting to make love to her again. "If he doesn't, he'd better be ready to find himself another job."

He was just about to return to the sensual Eden they'd created overnight when he heard the front door open. He stopped, frowning, and got up, quickly pulling on his pants.

"Whoever this is had better be ready, because there's going to be hell to pay," he growled. He leaned down to kiss Jenny one last time before he went to see who'd dared to invade their privacy. "Wait here. I'll be right back. Remember where I was—"

"I won't forget," she told him throatily, giving him a heavy-lidded, knowing look.

The look she gave him almost made him forget their unwelcome visitor. He was tempted to take her right then and there, and damn the consequences.

Cole only managed to control the urge with a herculean effort.

"I will be right back."

He hurried from the bedroom, not bothering to pull on a shirt. All he wanted to do was fire whoever had dared to walk in and then get back to his waiting wife. He stalked down the hallway, irritated and impatient. Jenny was waiting for him. This had better be important.

And then he heard Mira call out.

"Cole? Are you here?" Mira was searching the house for him.

"Mira?" Cole snapped as he confronted her in the parlor.

"Hello, Cole." Mira faced him, her gaze going hungrily over him. She'd never seen him bare-chested before, and all she wanted to do was throw herself into his arms and kiss him. She wanted to run her hands over him, to strip away the last of his clothing and—

"What are you doing here?" he demanded. "I thought you were one of my men and there was some kind of trouble—"

"No trouble—at least, not the kind you were thinking of," she said with heavy double meaning as she took a step toward him. It was all she could do to keep from reaching out and caressing that bare expanse of chest.

"What do you want, Mira?" Cole was very aware of Jenny just down the hallway and he wanted to get rid of Mira as quickly as he could so he could get back to his wife.

"I'll tell you what I want, Cole," she began, ready to throw all caution to the wind. "I want—"

She never got the chance to say "you" for she saw Jenny appear in the hallway behind him, wearing only a silken robe.

"Cole? Is something wrong?" Jenny asked, then stopped short as she came face to face with Mira.

"Jenny!" Mira shrieked glaring at her. She couldn't believe it. This was a hellish nightmare. What was that bitch doing here today of all days? And wearing only a robe. Looking as if she'd just made love to Cole all night. "What are you doing here?"

Jenny saw fury light Mira's eyes and took a step closer to Cole.

"Jenny and I were married yesterday," he answered Mira as he slipped a protective arm around Jenny and drew her closer to his side.

That display of affection was the end for Mira.

"You married her! How could you, Cole? She dumped you at the altar! She made you a laughing-stock in front of the entire town, and now you've married her?" Her voice was high-pitched and full of rage as she vented all the hatred she'd kept in her heart for Jenny. Only now, that hatred included Cole. "You should have been counting your lucky stars that I loved you and wanted you!"

Cole stood his ground, not showing any concern as

he talked to Mira in a calm voice. "I love Jenny, Mira. I always have and I always will."

"You're a fool, Cole Randall. You're stupid. She hurt you, and you went back for more." Mira took a threatening step forward, glaring at Jenny with murderous intent, seeing the bandage on her forehead and wishing she'd been a better shot. "Oh, how I wish that first shot hadn't missed!"

At her statement, Cole and Jenny both looked shocked.

"It was you!" Jenny exclaimed, startled by the revelation.

"You're damned right it was me, and I've cursed the fact that I missed killing you every day since!" Mira snarled savagely at her. She realized she'd given herself away, and knew she had to get out of there fast—but not before she wreaked some revenge. She hadn't worn her own sidearm, but she spied Cole's gunbelt on a table near the front door and made a move to grab it.

Cole released Jenny and tried to stop Mira, but she was too quick for him. She evaded him and grabbed up the gun. She spun around, the weapon in hand, aiming straight at Cole and Jenny.

"Mira, give me the gun. This isn't going to solve anything," Cole said, trying to reason with her.

She only smiled evilly, loving the power the gun gave her. She was imagining what it would be like to shoot Jenny first and laugh while Cole watched her die. She wanted to hurt him—to make him pay for his rejection of her.

"If you're both dead, it will solve everything," she told him coldly.

"You can't get away with this," Jenny said.

"Of course I can." Mira was arrogant as she looked at Jenny. "Wayne got away with killing your father, and I got away with killing your hand and shooting you! No one will ever know who killed you today."

Tears burned in Jenny's eyes as the truth was revealed to her. "Your brother killed my father? Why?" she asked in torment.

Mira smiled at her, pleased at her rival's distress.

"Because your father was stupid enough to show up when Wayne and the boys were trying to run off some of your herd," she said simply. "He didn't know what was going on, and he and Wayne started to talk. They'd dismounted, and Wayne managed to hit him from behind when he wasn't looking. It was simple—just like killing you is going to be!"

Cole spoke up quickly, moving to stand before Jenny. "My men will hear the shots and catch you before you can get to your horse, Mira. Give it up."

"Why should I listen to you? You've never cared for me! Why would you care what happens to me now?"

"Turn yourself in, Mira. It's the only way—"

"Turn myself in?" she shrieked again. "So I can

end up hanging or in prison? No! If I can't have you, neither can she. Step out here where I can see you Jenny. Now!"

In that instant, Cole knew there was no reasoning with her. He reacted instinctively, knowing she wanted to hurt Jenny. He shouted to Jenny, "Get down!" as he dove at Mira.

Cole hit her with the full force of his body weight and knocked her gun arm aside just as she pulled the trigger. The shot went wild, and the gun went flying from her fist as Cole slammed her to the floor. Jenny ran to grab the weapon while Cole subdued the still struggling Mira.

"I hate you!" Mira screamed at Jenny.

Cole dragged Mira to her feet and held her pinned against him. He could hear the shouts from his men as they came running up from the stable. Fred and Shorty burst through the front door, their guns drawn, ready for trouble.

"What happened, boss?" Fred demanded as he stared in confusion at the wild-eyed Mira.

Cole quickly recounted the morning's events.

"Paul was murdered?" Fred repeated, shocked by the news.

"And the Jamesons are the ones who've been doing the rustling?" Shorty said in disbelief.

"That's right. Take Mira out to the stable and lock her in the tack room. Have someone guard her until one of you can get back here with Marshal Trent."

Fred looked at Jenny. "I'm sorry about your pa."

Jenny could only nod at him.

"I hate you! I hate you both!" Mira was screaming as Cole handed her over to Fred so he could lock her up.

When they'd gone, Cole closed the door and looked at Jenny. She was standing, pale and shaken, his gun still in her hand.

"I don't think you'll need the gun anymore," he told her, taking it from her and setting it aside.

He took her in his arms and held her to his heart. She was trembling, and he wanted to calm her, to reassure her, to absorb her pain and erase the horror that had just been revealed to her. Neither spoke for a long moment as they treasured the closeness of their embrace.

"You saved me again," Jenny told Cole softly, looking up at him and managing a small smile in spite of her tears. "You're my hero."

Cole bent to her and kissed her gently, tenderly.

"I'm sorry about your father." His words were heartfelt.

"So am I," she whispered. "Papa never got to know that we loved each other. He never got to see his stubborn daughter finally realize just how truly wise he was."

"Oh, I don't know," Cole said to soothe her. "I think Paul probably knows we're married right now."

"I hope so."

"I love you, Jenny."

"Show me how much, Cole," she whispered.

And he did.

Epilogue

Four Months Later
Philadelphia

"I am so excited for Rose! Her dream has come true—she has her own gallery," Jenny said as Cole helped her descend from the carriage in front of the impressive three-story brick building that now housed the Stanford Photographic Gallery.

They had made the trip to Philadelphia to celebrate the moment with Rose. Her help in publicizing the Lazy S had brought a steady stream of visitors to the ranch, and Rose was featuring her photographs of Durango and the ranch at this, her premiere exhibition.

"Shall we join the festivities?" Cole offered her his arm and Jenny took it happily.

Rose had been watching for them and hurried forward to greet them. The gallery was a high-ceilinged room with large, arched windows that afforded good lighting. There were alcoves off to the sides providing special sites for selected photographs.

"Cole! Jenny! I am so glad you could come!" she told them happily.

"Congratulations." Jenny went to her and gave her a warm hug. "I've missed you, but it looks like you've been keeping busy these last few months."

"I have, but everything has turned out wonderfully. We've already got quite a crowd here."

"I can see," Jenny said, noting the large number of people milling about inside studying Rose's work.

"Shall I give you the grand tour?"

"Absolutely. We can hardly wait."

Rose led them through the exhibits. They already knew how talented she was, but seeing all of her collected photographs emphasized her unique ability.

"And I've saved the best for last," Rose said as she stopped before the alcove that held her Western photographs.

They moved into the area, studying the pictures she'd taken of the mountains and the townspeople. She even had their wedding picture on display.

"I can't believe you included us," Jenny told her.

"Of course I included your picture! You're the perfect example of the spirit of the Wild West. Jenny had to save the ranch, so she took charge and did what she had to do, and Cole, you were her hero. I've known you were wonderful since the night of the dance when you saved her from Clint," Rose said with a laugh.

They laughed, too, at the memory of the dance that had ultimately brought them back together.

"That isn't all he saved me from," Jenny said adoringly as she looked up at her handsome husband. "Do you know what else he was doing all that time?"

"This sounds intriguing." Rose looked at Cole with open interest.

"He was paying all my bills—out of his own money to help me. He never told me. I didn't even find out until long after we were married and I accidentally found a few of my bills on his desk at the Branding Iron."

"You were right, Jenny. Cole is definitely a wonderful man. No wonder you love him so much."

They moved on, and Jenny noticed the photograph of the High Time Saloon with Dan and Fernada standing out front. She frowned, remembering how Rose and Dan's relationship had ended so suddenly and with no real explanation.

"Did you ever hear from Dan again?" Jenny asked.

"No, not after that day out at the Lazy S." Rose's expression faltered a little as she thought of Dan. "I went back to the saloon to see him and drop off copies of the photographs the day I was leaving Durango, but Dan wasn't there. I asked Fernada if she could tell me where I could find him, but she wasn't sure. I had to leave without seeing him again."

"You really cared about him, didn't you?"

"It took me a while to realize it, but I did. I know we were very different, but what we had together was special. I never got the chance to tell him, though. I don't know what happened. I don't know why he changed, and I guess I never will." Rose looked at the photograph of Dan standing by himself, and her heart ached for what could have been.

"Maybe it's time you considered another excursion to the Wild West," Jenny suggested.

"You know, I've deliberately kept myself busy getting the studio ready so I wouldn't think about him."

"And now?"

Rose lifted one hand to carefully touch Dan's picture. "Now I know I need to talk with him again. I need to find out if what we felt for each other was real or—"

"It was real, Rose."

At the sound of Dan's voice so close behind her, Rose gasped and spun around.

"Dan! You're here!" She was astonished to find him standing before her, looking quite the gentleman. He was devastatingly handsome in his expensive suit, and her heartbeat quickened at the sight of him.

In spite of all those looking on, Dan gathered Rose close and kissed her.

"I've missed you, Rose."

"And I've missed you, too," she replied breathlessly.

"Will you marry me?" Dan had waited long enough for this moment; he wasn't waiting any longer.

"You want to marry me?" She stared at him in wide-eyed wonder, thrilled that her fantasy was coming true. Ever since she left Durango, she'd been dreaming about Dan and trying to figure out what had gone wrong.

"Yes, and I know how you feel about living out West, so . . ."

"What do you mean?" She frowned, not understanding what he was talking about.

"I heard you that day at the Lazy S when you said you wanted to come home to Philadelphia. I'm ready to do whatever you want so we can be together."

"So that's what happened that day—"

"I want you to be happy, Rose. And I want us to be happy together."

"You would move here for me?" With that realization she fell even more in love with him.

"Yes, and there are a few other things you need to know about me that I never had time to tell you."

"I don't need to know anything except that you love me." She looked up at him. "I love you, Dan, and, yes, I will marry you—and I'll move to Durango, if that's what you want."

"Can we compromise and settle in St. Louis?"

"Isn't that where your family is?"

"Yes, and it's time I took my responsibilities to my

family more seriously. It's time for me to go back home and help run the family business."

"Anyplace you want to live is fine with me as long as we're together. But what business is your family in?"

"We're in the carriage business," he answered. "And, Rose?"

"Yes?"

"I'm not poor." He wanted to tell her how successful the business was and how he'd left home because he'd wanted to prove to himself that he could make his own way in the world without relying on his family's name or fortune.

She lifted a hand to touch his cheek, stopping him from saying any more. She smiled up at him. "It doesn't matter to me if you're rich or poor, Dan. I love you."

Rose kissed him again as everyone looked on.

"It looks like the grand opening of Rose's gallery is quite a success," Cole said quietly to Jenny.

She looked up at him with a conspiratorial smile. "I'm glad you had that talk with Dan the night you went drinking at the High Time a few weeks ago."

"So am I."

"It looks like you've helped to make Rose's dream come true. Her handsome prince did find her and sweep her off her feet." Unable to help herself, Jenny rose up on tiptoe to kiss him. "Thank you, darling."

"It was my pleasure," he responded.

"Do you think they'll be as happy as we are?"

"I hope so."

Jenny smiled up at Cole, certain that they all were going to live happily ever after.

Author's Note

Dear Readers,

I knew I wanted to be a writer by the time I was nine years old, and, in fact, had already started writing and publishing my own "books" by then. My publisher was Bobby House and I pounded out my three page "novel" on a portable manual typewriter. Even now re-reading my first book "Flood!" written in 1959, I have to smile.

Leisure Books is being kind enough to publish "Flood!" in its original unedited form for me here in *Brides of Durango:Jenny*, my 29th novel. I wanted to show you what to look for in young writers, so you can encourage your son or daughter to aspire to a writing career. Who knows?

They may grow up and sell to a real New York publisher just like me!

Best always,
Bobbi Smith

“Flood!”

Written by Roberta Frances Smith

Published by Bobby House

“Flood!”

It was raining, raining so hard not even a dog could get across the back-yard safely. The apple orchard was already under two inches of water. the water was already up to the first step on the screened-in-back porch.

Jeff, Ken, Karen, and Darla slept soundly in their rooms. Suddenly Jeff awoke, 8 years but scared, he popped out of bed to check on the twins. They two were awake, but as calm as two kids could be. He gathered them up in his arms and said, “You stay here while I get Darla.” Out of the room, down the hall, and into her room. “How dare you” she said in surprise. “Come on,” he yelled so to not awaken their parents. So down the hall they all trotted, Darla, Ken, Karen, and Jeff. Mother and Father were drinking coffee when they called them to come down. Later when the twins had fallen asleep,Mother said, "It's a flood and the moving van will be here in a moment." The next day all you could see was the top of the house. Insects, snakes, dead animals, broken of limps of trees, people swimming for their lives, roofs, furniture, and turned over boats. Rain stilled poured down in buckets and soon the water would reach the height of the dam and the whole valey would be washed away.

Thenn all of a sudden Ken shouted "Jeff youv'e got to save him Jeff, you've just got too." So he dove into the rushing river and resued the half dead sheep. The rain stopped and the dam didn't brake. A month later the house was ready to be lived in.